FLYAWAY VACATION SWEEPSTAKES!

This month's destination:

Exciting ORLANDO, FLORIDA!

Are you the lucky person who will win a free trip to Orlando? Imagine how much fun it would be to visit Walt Disney World**, Universal Studios**, Cape Canaveral and the other sights and attractions in this area! The Next page contains tow Official Entry Coupons, as does each of the other books you received this shipment. Complete and return *all* the entry coupons—**the more times you enter, the better your chances of winning!**

Then keep your fingers crossed, because you'll find out by October 15, 1995 if you're the winner! If you are, here's what you'll get:

- Round-trip airfare for two to Orlando!
- 4 days/3 nights at a first-class resort hotel!
- $500.00 pocket money for meals and sightseeing!

Remember: The more times you enter, the better your chances of winning!*

*NO PURCHASE OR OBLIGATION TO CONTINUE BEING A SUBSCRIBER NECESSARY TO ENTER. SEE BACK PAGE FOR ALTERNATIVE MEANS OF ENTRY AND RULES.

**THE PROPRIETOR~~~~~~~~~~~~TED WITH THIS PROMOTION.

VOR KAL

D1005568

FLYAWAY VACATION
SWEEPSTAKES
OFFICIAL ENTRY COUPON

This entry must be received by: SEPTEMBER 30, 1995
This month's winner will be notified by: OCTOBER 15, 1995
Trip must be taken between: NOVEMBER 30, 1995-NOVEMBER 30, 1996

YES, I want to win the vacation for two to Orlando, Florida. I understand the prize includes round-trip airfare, first-class hotel and $500.00 spending money. Please let me know if I'm the winner!

Name_____

Address _____ Apt. _____

City   State/Prov.   Zip/Postal Code

Account #_____

Return entry with invoice in reply envelope.

© 1995 HARLEQUIN ENTERPRISES LTD.   COR KAL

FLYAWAY VACATION
SWEEPSTAKES
OFFICIAL ENTRY COUPON

This entry must be received by: SEPTEMBER 30, 1995
This month's winner will be notified by: OCTOBER 15, 1995
Trip must be taken between: NOVEMBER 30, 1995-NOVEMBER 30, 1996

YES, I want to win the vacation for two to Orlando, Florida. I understand the prize includes round-trip airfare, first-class hotel and $500.00 spending money. Please let me know if I'm the winner!

Name_____

Address _____ Apt. _____

City   State/Prov.   Zip/Postal Code

Account #_____

Return entry with invoice in reply envelope.

© 1995 HARLEQUIN ENTERPRISES LTD.   COR KAL

Words were not enough to comfort a man whose son was missing.

Heather laid her hand ever so gently on the side of Lucas's face.

And it came to her: she had never touched this man before in all the years she'd known him.

The idea astonished her. This dark, intimate stranger was family, her brother-in-law. She had known him since she was a child. Yet at this moment, touching him, she was absolutely certain she had never touched him before.

Had it been on purpose? Had she avoided physical contact with him? Had he avoided touching her?

It seemed, at that moment, as she cupped his warm cheek in the palm of her hand, that there had been some secret, silent agreement between them always. Never to touch.

And now...

Now she had broken that agreement....

Dear Reader,

September is an extra-special month for Special Edition! This month brings you some of your favorite veteran authors, three dynamite series and a celebration of special events! So don't miss a minute of the fall festivities under way.

Reader favorite Christine Rimmer returns to North Magdalene for the latest JONES GANG tale! THAT SPECIAL WOMAN! Heather Conway meets her match—and the future father of her baby—in *Sunshine and the Shadowmaster*. Gina Ferris Wilkins's new series, THE FAMILY WAY, continues in September with *A Home for Adam*, a touching and poignant story from this award-winning author. Diana Whitney's THE BLACKTHORN BROTHERHOOD continues with a story of the redeeming power of love in *The Avenger*.

And this month, Special Edition features special occasions in three books in our CONGRATULATIONS! promotion. In each story, a character experiences something that will change his or her life forever. Don't miss a moment of any of these wonderful titles: *Kisses and Kids* by Andrea Edwards, *Joyride* by Patricia Coughlin, and from a new author to Silhouette, *A Date With Dr. Frankenstein* by Leanne Banks.

But that's not all—there's lots in store for the rest of 1995 and Silhouette Special Edition! Not to give away our secrets yet, but safe to say that the rest of the year promises to bring your favorite authors in very special books! I hope you enjoy each and every story to come!

Sincerely,

Tara Gavin
Senior Editor

Please address questions and book requests to:
Silhouette Reader Service
U.S.: 3010 Walden Ave., P.O. Box 1325, Buffalo, NY 14269
Canadian: P.O. Box 609, Fort Erie, Ont. L2A 5X3

CHRISTINE RIMMER

SUNSHINE AND THE SHADOWMASTER

Published by Silhouette Books
America's Publisher of Contemporary Romance

For Diana "Whitney" Hinz, because I can tell her anything and because she never met a stray cat she didn't adopt.

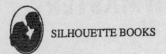 SILHOUETTE BOOKS

ISBN 0-373-09979-7

SUNSHINE AND THE SHADOWMASTER

Copyright © 1995 by Christine Rimmer

This edition published by arrangement with Harlequin Books S.A.

® and TM are trademarks of Harlequin Books S.A., used under license. Trademarks indicated with ® are registered in the United States Patent and Trademark Office, the Canadian Trade Marks Office and in other countries.

Printed in U.S.A.

Books by Christine Rimmer

Silhouette Special Edition

Double Dare #646
Slow Larkin's Revenge #698
Earth Angel #719
*Wagered Woman #794
Born Innocent #833
*Man of the Mountain #886
*Sweetbriar Summit #896
*A Home for the Hunter #908
For the Baby's Sake #925
*Sunshine and the Shadowmaster #979

*The Jones Gang

Silhouette Desire

No Turning Back #418
Call It Fate #458
Temporary Temptress #602
Hard Luck Lady #640
Midsummer Madness #729
Counterfeit Bride #812
Cat's Cradle #940

CHRISTINE RIMMER

is a third-generation Californian who came to her profession the long way around. Before settling down to write about the magic of romance, she'd been an actress, a sales clerk, a janitor, a model, a phone sales representative, a teacher, a waitress, a playwright and an office manager. Now that she's finally found work that suits her perfectly, she insists she never had a problem keeping a job—she was merely gaining "life experience" for her future as a novelist. Those who know her best withhold comment when she makes such claims; they are grateful that she's at last found steady work. Christine is grateful, too—not only for the joy she finds in writing, but for what waits when the day's work is through: a man she loves who loves her right back and the privilege of watching their children grow and change day to day.

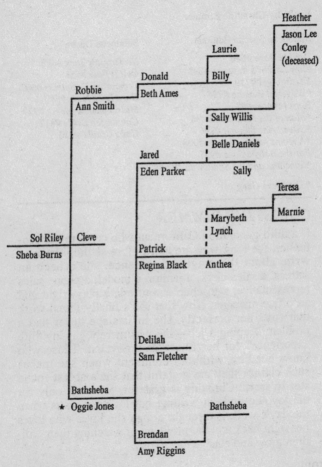

Note: Broken lines indicate previous
marriage(s).
★ One illegitimate son: Jack Roper

Chapter One

Heather Conley hadn't been expecting company. She flipped on the porch light and pulled open the front door to find her nephew standing there on the welcome mat in the balmy June darkness.

He smiled. "'Lo, Aunt Heather."

"Mark." In spite of the late hour, Heather felt an answering smile lift the corners of her mouth. "What a great surprise."

Mark looked her up and down, noting her robe and pajamas. "You were already sleeping, huh?"

"No, actually, I was in bed, but not asleep yet." Assuming that his father, Lucas, would be with him, Heather clutched the facings of her robe together and cast an apprehensive glance beyond Mark's shoulder toward the front gate.

Mark caught the direction of her gaze. "I, um, came alone."

Heather looked at Mark again. She knew he saw the questions in her eyes, but he didn't answer them, only asked, "Well? Are you gonna let me in? I'm really hungry, Aunt Heather. All I ate today was a couple of candy bars."

Heather was silent for a moment, studying Mark in the glow of the porch light. His T-shirt looked wrinkled and his sneakers were coated with dust. "What is this, Mark? Are you telling me you came all the way from Monterey alone?"

Mark lowered his head and stared hard at his grimy sneakers. "Yeah, I came alone."

Heather could hardly believe her ears. "But that's so dangerous." Mark said nothing, so Heather asked, "Who said you could do such a thing?"

"No one."

"You're saying you...ran away?"

Mark was silent again. Heather stared at his bent head in disbelief. Mark was a very well behaved boy. Running away was just not his style.

"Has something happened at home, Mark?"

Mark shook his head and continued looking at his sneakers. "Nothing special," he mumbled. "Nothing that hasn't been happening for a while now."

"What does that mean?"

"Nothing. I told you. Nothing."

"Well, then, why would you—?"

Before Heather finished the question, Mark's head shot up. He yanked his thin shoulders back and glared at her—hard.

Heather suppressed a gasp. He was the image of his father right then, his lip curling in aloof disdain, his eyes icy with impatience.

"Look. Can I come in or not?" His voice was as hard as his expression. Heather had no doubt right then that if she told Mark he couldn't come in, he would turn and disappear into the night without a backward glance.

But then, she had no intention of doing any such thing. She stepped back. "Of course you can. Please. Come on in."

Mark watched her face for a moment more, as if gauging her sincerity. Then he muttered, "Okay," and stepped inside.

Heather shut the door and flicked off the porch light. "Did you bring anything?"

"You mean clothes and stuff?"

"Yes."

He shook his head. "Naw. I've got nothin'. Just myself."

She thought how vulnerable he looked right then, all boy—and very lost. A hank of black hair had fallen into his eyes. She reached out and smoothed it back.

"And you're hungry, you said?" The tenderness she felt for him was there in her voice.

He met her eyes and slowly smiled. "Starved."

"Why don't you go clean up a little? I'll see what I can do about food."

"Sounds great."

He went ahead of her, through the living room and the dining room, to the downstairs bath off the kitchen. Heather washed her own hands at the kitchen sink and then set to work slicing ham and cheese and assembling two nice, fat sandwiches.

"This looks great, just great," Mark said when he emerged from the bathroom.

Heather gestured at the table. "Eat. Then we'll talk."

Mark ate both of the sandwiches, along with two tall glasses of milk. Then he finished off half a bag of chocolate chip cookies, washing them down with more milk. At last, he sat back in his chair and grinned at his aunt. "That was just what I needed. Thanks."

Heather, who'd hovered nearby keeping her own counsel while he eased his hunger, leaned against the kitchen counter and folded her arms across her chest. "So what's going on?"

Mark's dark eyes grew wary again. "What do you mean?"

Heather looked at him patiently. "Mark."

"What?"

"You ran away. Why?"

Mark suddenly found his empty milk glass of great interest. He wrapped his fingers around it and turned it in slow, hard circles, as if he could screw it into the kitchen table.

"Come on, Mark," Heather prompted. "Talk to me."

Mark groaned, looked at the ceiling, and then at the milk-filmed glass again. "All right," he said, and then said nothing more.

"All right, what?"

Mark shot her a surly look.

Heather scowled right back. "I'm listening."

He went on turning the glass. "All right. My father's not home. He's never home. I got tired of it is all. So I hitched a few rides and here I am."

"Oh, Mark."

Mark released the glass. "Don't look at me like that, Aunt Heather. I'm fine. Nothing happened to me. I know what I'm doing."

"Mark, you are ten years old."

"Going on eleven. And I was careful, honest. I only hitched with truckers. You can almost always trust a trucker. You know that."

Heather suppressed a shudder at the things that might have happened to him in the two hundred and seventy-five miles between Monterey and the small Sierra foothill town of North Magdalene. "What you did was very dangerous. And wrong. Does anyone know where you went?"

Mark was turning the glass again. "Rudy Fitch, Buddy Tester and Christos Knockopopoulis."

"Who are they?"

"The truckers who picked me up."

Heather only looked at him.

Mark was mature for his age and had the IQ of a budding Einstein. He was also a sensitive boy. He felt the weight of his aunt's disapproving silence. He shot her a glance, then slumped in his chair a little. "Okay. Not funny. I'm sorry."

"When did you leave home?"

"This morning. Before daylight."

"And you didn't tell anybody that you were going?"

"Right. I didn't." He was defiant again.

"Your father will be worried sick."

"Like I said, he's not there. He's gone on another book tour." Now Mark was sneering. "He probably doesn't even know I left."

Heather turned for the drawer where she kept her personal phone book. She pulled out the book—and Mark leapt from his chair and grabbed her arm.

"Please, Aunt Heather..." The veneer of cynicism had vanished. Mark was suddenly his true self: a ten-year-old boy pulling out all the stops to get what he wanted. He tugged on her arm and looked up at her with pleading, puppy-dog eyes. "Don't send me back. Please. I just want to stay here for a while. With you."

Heather gently shrugged off his grasp. "The most important thing right now is to call your father and let him know where you are."

"I told you. He's not even there."

"Mark. I'm sure whoever was taking care of you—"

"The housekeeper. Hilda."

"All right. I'm sure Hilda has figured out you're missing after all this time. And I'm sure your father has been contacted. And I'm also dead positive he's going nuts about now wondering where you are and if you're safe."

"Okay, okay." Mark held up a hand. The puppy dog look had vanished. His eyes gleamed with excitement. "But just wait a second. Just listen."

"Mark—"

"No. Listen. I got it. I got what you could do. You could just call my father's housekeeper and say it's all right. Say that I'm here with you and you want me to stay here. That you... invited me. Yeah. That would be good. You invited me and I came and now it's okay with you if I stay. That would work, Aunt Heather. I know it would. I know my father would let me stay here if you said it was all right. He let me stay here before."

The open entreaty in the young face squeezed Heather's heart. She stared at him, softening.

Mark pressed his advantage. "It was so great, wasn't it? When I stayed here. Remember what you said? You said that you loved having me here and I could come anytime. Remember? You said that. And I know that you meant it."

"Yes, Mark. I did." Heather couldn't hold back a fond smile. She *had* loved taking care of Mark last winter. He had come, with his father, for the funeral of Heather's husband, Jason Lee. After the funeral, Lucas had allowed Mark to stay on with Heather until school started up again after New Years. Having someone to look after for those awful first days had kept Heather from completely surrendering to the grief that had threatened to swallow her alive.

Mark watched her with fierce concentration. His face was flushed with frantic hope. She knew he saw the way she hesitated, that he sensed the direction of her thoughts. "So let me stay now. Please?"

"Oh, Mark."

"Please?"

Heather longed to give him the answer he wanted. But that was impossible. He had run away from home. That was the issue here. And she was going soft when Mark needed firmness.

She quietly insisted, "Stop this, Mark. You can't just run away from home and expect me to cover for you."

Mark refused to give up. "You liked having me here, I know it."

"Of course I did."

"I wrote you ten letters since then. You answered every one."

"That's true. I treasure your letters. But that isn't the point. You have run away from home, Mark. That is a very serious thing."

Mark saw that all his plans and pleading were getting him nowhere. "I don't have a home." He spun away from Heather and dropped heavily into his chair once more. "I live in a big house with a bunch of people who get paid to take care of me. I visit my mom in Arizona twice a year and she always looks at me like she's not sure who I am. And my Dad's never around either. He's always locked up in his study—or else he's away on a book tour."

Heather watched him for a moment, not sure what she should say to him. Then she reminded him gently, "Come on, Mark. I'm sure both your father and mother love you very much."

He snorted in disgust. "You sound just like a grown-up."

There was no sense in denying it. "I am a grown-up."

Mark snorted again. "I thought you were on my side."

"I am on your side."

"Then call my father's housekeeper and tell her I can stay with you."

"I can't do that."

"Great. Fine." Mark folded his hands over his chest and focused his angry gaze on the far wall.

Heather looked at him, feeling weary. She wanted to say more. But talking was getting them nowhere. He'd said he'd left Monterey before dawn that morning. It was now past eleven at night. His father should be called immediately.

Heather looked down at the phone book in her hand—and realized she was dreading making the call.

The truth was, Lucas Drury intimidated her. He was too intense, too intelligent, too *everything,* as far as Heather was concerned. Her beloved Jason Lee had been Lucas's half brother. Yet no two men were less alike. Jason Lee had had the knack of putting people at ease. Lucas, on the other hand, made them sit up and take notice; he put people on guard.

Heather shook herself. The call had to be made. And Lucas probably wouldn't be there anyway. Mark had said he was away on a book tour.

Heather moved to the end of the counter, where the phone hung on the wall. She opened her little book to the *D*'s and punched up Lucas's number. It was answered on the first ring.

"Yeah?"

Heather recognized the deep, resonant voice immediately. So much for that book tour. She swallowed, because her throat had gone bone-dry.

"Hello, Lucas? It's Heather. Heather Conley. In North Magdalene?"

"Heather." Lucas repeated her name as if hearing from her was a big shock. And it probably was. The last time Heather and Lucas had spoken had been when he had picked up Mark after Mark's visit last winter. She and Lucas rarely saw each other.

"What's going on?" Lucas demanded now, wasting no time on friendly chitchat.

"I, uh, didn't expect you to be there," Heather said, and realized how stupid the words sounded almost before they were out of her mouth.

"Well, I'm not supposed to be here. I'm supposed to be on a publicity tour. But Mark disappeared some time this morning. I got in from New York just an hour and a half ago. We're all going nuts here, trying to figure out where he went."

Heather dragged in a big breath. She wanted to say this calmly. Lucas was such a volatile man. "Well, Lucas. That's why I—"

Lucas got the picture before she finished her sentence. "Is he there? In North Magdalene? Have you got Mark?"

He was jumping ahead of her, just as she'd feared he might. "Lucas, I—"

"Just answer my question. Is Mark with you?"

"Yes. Yes, he's here."

"I'll kill him. Is he all right?"

"He's fine, Lucas. Perfectly safe."

"Let me talk to him."

Heather glanced at Mark, who was still glaring daggers at the wall.

In her ear, Lucas demanded, "Heather? Are you still there?"

Heather turned away from Mark and spoke quietly into the phone. "Lucas, maybe you should go a little easy here. Something is really upsetting Mark. And I don't think yelling at him will help matters any."

"Don't tell me how to deal with my own son. Put him on the line. Now."

Heather took another long, slow breath and reminded herself that she never should have expected Lucas Drury to listen to advice from her. "Hold on," she said, then put her hand over the mouthpiece and turned to Mark again. "Your father wants to talk to you."

Mark slowly shifted his glance from the wall to his aunt. "He's home now? In Monterey?"

"Yes. Obviously, when he heard you were missing, he went right back there."

For that remark, Heather received a sullen look, one that clearly said, *Yeah, right. Go ahead and defend him.* But then Mark did hold out his hand. The phone cord was long enough to stretch to the table, so Heather passed over the receiver.

Mark cradled the phone between his chin and his shoulder and folded his arms over his chest once more. "Yeah."

Heather suppressed a sad smile. Mark sounded just like his father—only a couple of octaves higher.

"I'm fine," Mark mumbled. A moment later he insisted crossly, "I *said* I'm okay." Then he admitted, "I hitched."

After that, Lucas did all the talking. Mark listened to the voice on the other end of the line, his young face growing more unhappy by the second. Once or twice, Mark tried to speak, but his father ran right over him. Finally the boy muttered, "All right, I will," and held out the phone to Heather.

Heather took it. "Yes?" The single word was caution personified. Lucas really did make her nervous.

"Put him to bed," Lucas commanded. "I'll be there in the morning to take him home." Then the line went dead.

Heather held the phone away from her ear and grimaced at it, thinking that Lucas Drury was running true to form. He never wasted time on being polite when he could bark an order at a person and then hang up on them. She turned and hooked the receiver back in its cradle on the wall. When she faced Mark again he was watching her.

"He's coming to get me," he said.

"I know." Heather cast about for something encouraging to say to him. All that came to mind were platitudes. She went ahead and said one. "Things will look better in the morning."

Mark wasn't buying any platitudes. "No, they won't. Things will never look better. Not until he listens to me. And he won't do that. He won't listen to anybody. He's too busy. He's got too much to do."

Looking at Mark's glum face then, Heather felt about two inches tall. She knew that she'd let him down. Out of all the places or people he might have run to, he'd chosen her. The message was clear. He'd hoped she might help him. But she hadn't helped him. When it came to the moment of truth, Lucas had run over her as easily as he'd dominated Mark.

"Oh, Mark..." she began, and then didn't know how to continue.

The boy shook his head. "Look, Aunt Heather. It's not your fault. I know that. And I'm tired now, okay? I think I should get ready for bed."

Heather put Mark in the small downstairs bedroom off the dining room. It was the same room he'd slept in when he stayed with her over Christmas vacation the previous winter. She gave the boy one of Jason Lee's old T-shirts to sleep in and offered a shower, to which the fastidious Mark readily agreed.

After Mark was through in the bathroom and had been in the bedroom for several minutes, Heather went in to say good-night. She found him already in bed, his dusty jeans and wrinkled shirt laid neatly across a straight-backed chair in the corner, his sneakers lined up nearby, dirt-stained white socks stuck inside them.

"You left the light on," she said. "You can't sleep with the light on."

"I knew you'd be in. You always came in to say good-night when I stayed here before."

Heather approached the bed and perched on the edge of it. "I'll take your clothes now and put them in the washer before I go to bed."

He objected almost before she'd finished speaking. "No, never mind about doing that."

"Why not?"

"Because." He looked up at the ceiling and then at her once more. "My dad said he'd be here real early. And he'll want to get going. He won't want to wait for my clothes to get dry."

Heather considered Mark's reasoning, then conceded, "You may be right, but it only takes a half an hour to run the wash cycle. I'll just wait up and switch them to the dryer before I go to bed."

"Please don't do that, Aunt Heather. Just get some sleep, okay? I made enough trouble for you already to-night."

"It's no trouble, Mark."

"It's late. And I know you have to work tomorrow. It won't hurt me to wear dirty clothes. So just go to bed, okay?"

Heather was touched. He really was a very sensitive boy. And he was right. It was late and she was due in at work at six-thirty the next morning.

She agreed, "Fair enough. I'll leave your dirty clothes right where they are."

He smiled at her then, a wise, sad smile. She smiled back, thinking that his hair looked very black against the pillow. It was still wet from his shower. She wanted to reach out and smooth it a little, in a gesture that would have been a reassurance both to herself and to him. But she didn't do it. Though he seemed resigned to his fate of being collected and returned to Monterey by his father, she sensed he would turn his head away at her touch.

Since she felt he didn't want her to touch him, she tried to reassure him with words. "Your father *does* love you."

"I know." It was a reluctant admission.

"He's just...um..." Heather had no idea how to continue. She'd been raised in a family of complex and difficult men. But Lucas Drury was beyond even her experience. When he was seven years old, he'd stabbed his own father with a carving knife. And as a young man, he'd barely escaped doing hard time for assault and battery. Now, he was an international celebrity who wrote the kind of books that keep people from sleeping at night. The newspapers and entertainment magazines called him the Shadowmaster, a name that referred both to the spookiness of his stories and the fact that each one had the word "shadow" in the title.

Heather had read all of those stories. She'd read the first one out of family loyalty, because Jason Lee's brother had written it. But after that, she read them because, even though they often had her sleeping with the light on, they were absolutely impossible to put down.

However, having read all of his books didn't make her an authority on Lucas Drury himself. No, she hadn't the faintest idea what made the man tick. So how in the world was she going to explain him to his ten-year-old son?

Mark came to her rescue with a groan. "Oh, Aunt Heather. You don't have to say anything. Like I said before, it's not your fault, anyway. I know that."

Heather smiled. She'd come in here to comfort Mark, and ended up with *him* reassuring *her*.

Mark added, "It's just something I gotta work out my-self, I guess."

"And I know you will—you and your father together."

He made a face at that. Lucas was still very much the bad guy in Mark's mind.

Heather dared to point out gently, "Maybe your father is a little hard to talk to, but what *you* did today—running away—was wrong and dangerous."

Mark pressed his lips together. "I told you. I can handle myself."

"That's not the point. And I'm not finished."

"Okay, what?"

"What you did was wrong and dangerous."

"Yeah. Okay."

"However..."

"*What?*"

"*You* are a great kid. An incredible kid. A smart, funny, wonderful, terrific kid."

His tan skin pinkened a little. She knew she had pleased him. "Sure," he said, skeptical.

"That's how I know your dad's an all-right guy."

"How?"

"He's raising you, isn't he? And you're turning out just wonderfully.

"Oh, right. Gag. Puke."

"You're much too modest."

"You're blinded by my brains and good looks."

Heather laughed at that, and her glance fell on the night table by the bed. Mark had emptied his pockets there: a few crumpled bills, some change, a Milky Way wrapper, and a Swiss army knife.

At the sight of the knife, Heather stopped laughing. The knife had been Jason Lee's and he had prized it.

She thought of her dead husband, holding the knife, remarking that the "damn thing's got more attachments than a hound dog has ticks.'' There were two metal files and a little pair of scissors, a corkscrew, a toothpick and tweezers—not to mention four different knife blades. On one end, at the place where the tweezers were stored, the surface had been chipped. Jason Lee used to rub his thumb on that chipped place, "For good luck," he said. Then his light eyes would go misty and he'd tell her how someday he'd pass on that fine knife to their first son.

But, of course, now there would be no son. So Heather had given the knife to Mark.

Mark saw where she was looking. "I always take it. Wherever I go."

"Jason Lee would be glad." Heather's throat felt tight. It had gotten so she could think of Jason Lee most times now without that heavy surge of loss all through her body. But wrapping her mouth around his name could still be a challenge. Often when she did that, her throat would close up for a minute and the metallic taste of grief would slide along her tongue.

"If you want to kiss me good-night, I guess you can," Mark said, and she knew he sensed her sadness and sought to ease it by allowing her to touch him now.

Heather put on a bright face. "Gee, thanks." She bent and brushed her lips against his forehead. His skin was smooth and smelled of soap and a little leftover road dust. She stood. "Get some sleep now."

"Okay."

She went to the door and switched off the light.

"Aunt Heather?" Mark said from the shadows across the room.

"Hmm?"

"If I lived here with you, I never would have run away."

His words made a lightness inside her. How lovely if that could really happen. The house was much too big for her now. And sometimes her loneliness was like a vast, empty space inside her. Having Mark in the house would fill up that emptiness.

But of course, such a thing was impossible. Mark would never live with her. And Heather knew she had to say so.

"Your place is with your father, Mark."

He said nothing to that. Only turned his face to the wall.

Heather sighed and tiptoed out, closing the door quietly behind her.

The doorbell rang at five-thirty the next morning. Heather was still in bed, but awake. She was due at Lily's Café in an hour. However, she had no intention of leaving the house until Lucas had come to collect Mark. So she was lying there staring at the clock, trying to decide whether to call her boss, Lily Tibbits, at home, or wait until Lily got to work herself to give her the news that her head waitress was going to be late.

But now the problem was solved. Mark's father was here and Heather wouldn't be missing any work after all.

The doorbell rang again. Lucas Drury was an impatient man. Heather jumped from the bed and shoved her feet into her slippers. Then she yanked on her robe and ran to let him in.

When she pulled back the front door, dawn was just breaking on the horizon. Her brother-in-law stood on her porch, hands in his pockets, feet braced slightly apart.

Heather blinked at the odd, momentary trick of the light, which made him seem slightly unreal, as if his body itself had been cut out of pure darkness. It appeared as if he had no face. Still, Heather had no trouble recognizing him. She knew him by his stance, by his height and leanness—and by the commanding set of his shoulders.

"I got here as quickly as I could."

That voice of his, at once sophisticated and rough-edged, sent a little shiver skittering along the surface of Heather's skin. The dawn light behind him grew a tiny bit brighter, enough that it seemed to wrap around him a little. Now she could begin to make out the shape of his mouth, his nose, the darker shadows where his eyes were.

Lucas turned his head to the side. She saw his strong profile. Then he faced her again. His features retreated into darkness.

"Well, may I come in?" The words were low, and almost teasing.

Heather thought of one of his books, for some crazy reason. *Shadowfall,* it was called. In it there was a lonely vampire who lived in darkness, preying only on the hopelessly ill and the evil. And then one night, while stalking a murderer, he saved a woman of innocence and light. He found out where she lived by looking into her mind. He took her home. And after that, he tried to stay away from her, to protect her from himself.

But her attraction was too strong. At last, he came to the window of her room in the deepest part of the night. And he asked her, "May I come in...?"

"Heather?" Lucas said.

She blinked. "Oh. Yes. Come on in."

Heather pulled back the door and moved out of his way. He stepped over the threshold, filling the room with his intensity and a faint, tempting scent, like sandalwood and something else—something indefinable, both spicy and exotic.

The shades were still drawn and the room seemed very dark. So Heather went over and turned on the floor lamp beside the couch. The quick wash of light banished the shadows to the corners of the room.

"There," Heather said, rather unnecessarily, smiling nervously and squinting a little as her eyes adjusted to the brightness.

Her brother-in-law remained standing near the door. Now, with the light, he was clear to her.

He was all in black—soft pleated black slacks, a black sport shirt, black belt and black shoes. The lean, hard muscles of his arms looked very stark, somehow, against all that dark fabric.

"You were still sleeping," he said. He was looking at her tangled hair and the robe that she'd pulled so hastily over her summer pajamas.

"No. No, I was awake. I was just lying there."

"I thought you had to be at work early. Is that right?"

"Yes." It was so strange. He seemed rather shy. She'd never in her life thought of Lucas Drury as shy. "At six-thirty. I work at six-thirty."

"Right."

"I was going to call my boss to say I'd have to be late. So I could wait for you to come get Mark, I mean. I was just lying there thinking about that."

"Calling your boss?"

"Yes. Exactly. But now you're here."

He looked amused, but in a nice way—a gentle, *shy* way. "Yes. Now I'm here."

"So I won't have to call."

"Right." He was silent, still smiling. And then something occurred to him. "Listen. About the way I acted on the phone. I'm sorry. I was pretty frantic about Mark and I took it out on you."

"Oh." His apology warmed her. "Well, it's all right. It's Mark that matters."

"Yes."

She felt so strange, standing here talking to him. She hardly knew him, really. He had moved away when she was very young.

And yet, this morning, he did seem different, *nicer* than usual, somehow. And since he seemed nicer, she dared to suggest, "Something really is bothering Mark, Lucas. He said he feels that you don't *listen* to him."

She watched his face change, watched the gentle humor and shyness vanish. "Oh, really?" The words were cold.

Heather remembered the way she had let Mark down last night. She didn't want to do that again. She made herself go on, "Yes, he really *misses* you, I think, because you're so busy all the time. He feels that you neglect him and—"

"Is this the beginning of a lecture on parenting, Heather?" His silky-rough voice chilled her. His smile was as icy as an Arctic wind.

Heather wanted to hunch her shoulders and slink away. But she didn't. It didn't matter if he disliked hearing this, or if she shook in her slippers when he gave her that freezing look. She had to say these things, for the sake of a wonderful kid who'd been so unhappy he was willing to hitchhike alone from Monterey in search of someone to listen to him.

"This isn't a lecture," Heather said. "It's just what Mark told me. That you don't listen to him. That you're too busy for him. You might think about that when you . . . do whatever you're going to do, about his running away."

"All right, Heather. I'll think about it."

She matched his condescending tone. "Thank you."

He regarded her for a moment. She had absolutely no idea what might be in his mind, but she refused to drop her eyes.

She thought about Jason Lee again. How very different this man was from Jason Lee. Lucas was dark, tall and lean-muscled, where Jason Lee had been blond and husky. Lucas's eyes were hooded, unreadable, his face all hard planes and angles. In Jason Lee's face, there had still been the softness of youth. He'd smiled so easily, been in love with life and everything about it . . .

"Now where is Mark?" Lucas spoke harshly.

Heather put away her thoughts of her dead husband. "Still in bed. Come on. We'll wake him up."

She turned and went through the arch to the dining room, not stopping to see if Lucas followed. She didn't need to look, really. Though he moved as quietly as a stalking panther, she could *feel* the reality of him, filling the space right behind her.

At the door to the bedroom, she knocked, then waited, poignantly aware of Lucas beside her.

"Mark?" She knocked again.

When he didn't answer that time, Heather gently turned the handle and swung the door inward.

It took her several seconds to register what she saw. The bed was neatly made, the T-shirt she'd given Mark to sleep in had been folded and laid on the chair in the corner. Mark himself was nowhere to be seen.

Chapter Two

"Where is he?" Lucas turned on her. "What the hell is going on?"

Heather just stared at him, her mind still unwilling to believe the evidence of her eyes.

"Where is my son?" Lucas demanded.

Heather gulped. "I . . . I don't know. This is where I left him. In that bed. Last night."

"Well, he damn sure isn't there now." Lucas strode into the room and threw back the closet door. Inside, there were spare blankets on a shelf, some winter jackets and four empty plastic hangers—but no Mark.

Heather cast about frantically for some other place he might be. "The bathroom?"

The house had once belonged to Lucas's stepfather and Lucas had lived there himself for several years. He knew where the downstairs bathroom was and wasted no time in getting there, with Heather close on his heels.

It was empty.

Lucas took charge then. "Go upstairs," he commanded. "Check all the rooms, the closets, everything. I'll look around outside."

Heather didn't argue. Before he'd finished giving the orders, she was headed for the stairs in the dining room. She searched the rooms upstairs thoroughly, calling Mark's name as she looked, but she got no answer. With dread weighting each step, she returned to the first floor. She found Lucas in the bedroom where Mark had slept.

"Nothing?" he asked flatly, when he saw the look on her face.

She shook her head and tried to swallow down the lump that had lodged in her throat. "How about outside?"

"The same." Lucas ran a hand through his black hair. "I was just looking around. Seeing if he left anything that would tell us what's happening here."

"And?"

He shook his head. "Nothing." He stared down at the neatly made bed. "I guess we can rule out kidnapping as a possibility, though."

Heather hadn't even considered such a thing. "You thought maybe he was *kidnapped?*"

"Not really, no. But it does happen."

"But not here. Not in North Magdalene."

He gave her a very patient look. "It happens everywhere. But the fact that the bed is made seems to indicate otherwise."

Heather tried her best to keep up with him. "Why?"

"Mark's a very neat boy. And making the bed before he ran away again is something he would do. On the other hand, if someone had taken him out of here by force, it's highly doubtful they'd have stopped to straighten up the room first."

That made sense to Heather. And something else came to mind. "His clothes."

"What?"

"Last night. I wanted to wash his clothes for him. But he wouldn't let me. Now that I think about it, it was like he didn't want me to take those clothes out of the room."

"Because he was planning to put them on again as soon as he thought you were asleep?"

"Yes, I'll bet that was it."

"So it's pretty damn likely that he did run away again."

Heather had thought exactly that from the first. But Lucas was fighting it. And she supposed she could understand why. He'd driven all night, probably furious with Mark, but certain that he had the situation under control.

But now Mark was gone again. The situation was not under control. Not in the least.

"He *has* run away again, hasn't he?" Lucas demanded.

"Yes, I think so," Heather answered gently.

Lucas sank to the edge of the bed, leaned his elbows on his knees and looked at his black shoes. "Where would he have gone next?"

Heather thought about that. "Maybe to my uncle Patrick's."

Lucas looked up. "Why there?"

"I have a cousin, Marnie, who's Mark's age. She and Mark made friends last winter."

"Marnie," he said. "Yes. I remember Mark mentioning her. Anywhere else?"

"He might go to Kenny Riggins's, Marnie's friend. The three of them hung out together most of the time. And maybe to my Grandpa Oggie."

"*Oggie Jones?*" Lucas uttered the name as if it tasted bad. "Why would my son go to Oggie Jones?"

Though Heather adored her grandfather, she didn't waste time defending him. Grandpa Oggie was a very outspoken old fellow. He often rubbed people the wrong way.

She explained, "Mark and my grandfather seemed to hit it off. Mark was always stopping by my aunt Delilah's, where Grandpa lives now, to visit with him."

"Who else?"

"That's all I can think of offhand."

"Call them, then. Now. Your uncle's house first."

Heather went to the kitchen where, with Lucas looking impatiently on, she called her uncle Patrick's house. Her aunt Regina answered. Heather quickly explained the problem and Regina said that she hadn't seen Mark since last January. She left the phone to ask Marnie, but Marnie said she hadn't seen Mark, either. Before she hung up, Regina promised to call Heather right away if Mark showed up at her house.

"Well?" Lucas said when Heather hung up.

"They haven't seen him."

"Call your grandfather."

Heather dialed her aunt Delilah's house and spoke with her grandfather.

"What did he say?" Lucas demanded almost before Heather could disconnect the line.

"He says he hasn't seen Mark, and he'll call if he does see him."

"Fine. Call the Riggins kid."

The results of that call were the same as the previous two.

"They haven't seen him?" Lucas asked when Heather had hung up.

Heather shook her head.

"Think. There must be somewhere else he might go."

Heather pulled out a chair for herself and sank into it. "I'm sorry. Mark only stayed with me once—and then only for a couple of weeks. As far as I know, when he wasn't with me, he was with Marnie and Kenny—or my grandfather. No one else comes to mind."

Lucas seemed to be studying her. "Let me ask you this. If Mark acted so strangely last night, why didn't you keep a closer watch on him?"

Heather sat very still. She knew exactly what was happening here. Lucas wasn't ready to deal with his own responsibility in this. So he was setting her up to take the blame for Mark's second disappearance.

"Did you hear my question, Heather?" he asked, prodding her.

She looked him straight in the eye. "Yes. I did."

"Well?"

Very slowly and deliberately she explained, "The way he acted didn't seem so strange while it was happening. It was only looking back on it, after I saw that he was gone this morning, that it seemed odd to me."

"So what you're saying then, is that he behaved strangely, but you ignored it—until now, when it's too late to do anything."

Heather decided she'd had enough of his sideways remarks. She cut to the point. "Are you accusing me of not watching out for Mark?"

He lifted a black eyebrow at her and looked at her as if he wanted to burn a hole in her with his eyes. "*Did* you watch out for Mark?"

Though the power and intensity of the man intimidated her, Heather steadfastly refused to cower before him. She remembered the first rule of dealing with an overbearing male: never let him see you sweat. She'd learned that rule

early on, having grown up in the rowdy family known lo-
cally as the Jones Gang.

She told Lucas, "Yes, I did watch out for Mark. And I'll
do everything I can now to find out where he went. In fact,
I think I'm doing pretty well here, all things considered. If
anyone's guilty of ignoring Mark, it certainly isn't me."
She paused, just a moment, to let that sink in.

Then she continued, "Besides, as far as I can see it, our
job right now is to find out where Mark went, not sit
around discussing who's to blame that he's run away
again." Heather put both hands on the table and pushed
herself to her feet. "And now what I'd like is a cup of
coffee. I'll make some for you, too, if you'll stop acting
like a jerk."

Lucas looked up at her for a moment, his gaze watchful
and measuring. Then he said, very gently, "I'd like that."

She nodded. "Good, then." She carefully pushed her
chair beneath the table and went to the counter. She was
scooping coffee grinds into a filter when Lucas spoke from
behind her.

"I apologize. You're right. You're not the one to blame
here."

Heather kept scooping coffee. Otherwise she surely
would have cried. If she'd ever wondered how much Lucas Drury really cared for his son, she never would again.
The raw truth had been there in his voice just now.

"Apology accepted," Heather said without turning,
because she sensed he didn't want her to see him right then.
She poured cold water into the reservoir, slipped the filter
basket in place and switched on the coffeemaker before she
faced Lucas again. By then, he looked as composed and
aloof as ever.

"Though it's a slim bet, I should call my housekeeper in Monterey, see if maybe Mark has been in touch with them there."

"Yes, of course. Go right ahead."

Heather waited while he made the call, then looked at him questioningly after he hung up.

"Nothing," he answered bleakly. "Any ideas about what to do now?"

"Yes, I think so."

"I'm listening."

Heather hesitated. What she had in mind was the next logical step, but it wasn't an easy one to take. "I think we're going to have to call the sheriff's station."

Lucas rubbed his temples, then he turned and walked over to the window that opened onto the backyard. He stuck his hands into his pockets, planted his legs slightly apart and stared out at the new day.

Heather tried to soften the seriousness of it all a little. "Actually I can just call my uncle Jack at home. He's a deputy at the station now."

Lucas didn't turn. "Who the hell's your uncle Jack?"

"He's my father's half brother. Grandpa Oggie is his dad. Didn't you meet him last winter?"

"If I did, I don't remember him. And I never heard of Oggie Jones having a son named Jack."

"Neither did we. Until last fall. It's a long story, but now Uncle Jack lives here in town. He's head of our local volunteer search and rescue team and he's a sheriff's deputy, too."

"I see," Lucas said. And then he was silent. He went on staring out the back window.

Behind Heather, the coffeemaker gurgled and sputtered as it finished filling the pot. Heather waited—for the coffee to be ready and for Lucas to give her the go-ahead to make the call.

But apparently, Lucas wasn't quite ready yet to accept what had to be done. When he spoke, it wasn't about Mark at all.

"The walnut tree looks the same," he said of the old tree in the middle of the back lawn. He turned his hooded gaze on her. "Did you know I built a fort in that tree, years ago?"

Heather nodded. "Don't you remember? It was still there when Jason Lee and I came along. We played in it, too."

"You and Jason Lee." He gave a low chuckle. She could hear affection in that chuckle—and she could hear pain. "Joined at the hip from the first day of kindergarten, right?"

She smiled a little herself, feeling close to this strange man at that moment, connected to him through their mutual love for another man who was with them no more. "We were best friends. Always."

"My brother was a happy kid."

"Yes."

"And a happy man."

Heather tasted tears at the back of her throat. She swallowed them, then carefully said, "I need to call my boss and tell her I'll be late this morning. And then after that, we really should report Mark missing."

Lucas just looked at her.

She held up her hands, palms out. "I don't know who else to call, Lucas."

Lucas's shoulders lifted in a shrug. He turned back to the window and his contemplation of the old walnut tree. "Yeah. I know. Call your boss. And then your uncle. Go ahead."

Chapter Three

Lily Tibbits yelled for a few minutes when she learned her head waitress was going to be late. But Heather wasn't bothered. She worked hard for Lily—and Lily always yelled when things didn't go her way. Heather waited until Lily had to stop for a breath and then promised to be in as soon as she could.

Heather hung up and called her uncle Jack. He said he'd be right over.

While they waited for Jack, Heather offered Lucas some breakfast. He said he wasn't hungry. And she realized she didn't have much of an appetite, either. So she excused herself to go to her room, where she swiftly changed into the jeans, white shirt and tennis shoes she always wore to work.

The doorbell rang just as Heather finished tying her shoes.

"Hey, Sunshine," Uncle Jack said when she let him in. Uncle Jack always called her Sunshine. It was the name people had started calling her when she began working part-time at Lily's seven years before, when she was only sixteen. Now she responded to it as readily as she did to Heather.

"Uncle Jack." She gave him a quick, fond hug. Then she stood back and grabbed his arm. "Come on. Mark's father is in the kitchen."

They found Lucas sitting at the table staring into his empty coffee cup. He glanced up when Heather led Jack in. The two men exchanged a long look.

Then Jack stuck out his hand. "Lucas, right?"

"Yeah."

"I'm Jack Roper."

Lucas stood and the two men shook hands.

"Our biggest problem," Jack said when Heather and Lucas had described the events leading up to Mark's disappearance, "is that if Mark doesn't want to be found, he's going to be working against us all the way. It's one thing to bring out the search and rescue crew when the missing person is lost on a mountain somewhere, praying for rescue—and it's another thing altogether to hunt down a runaway. Also, since Mark has hitchhiked on his own before, it's fully possible that he's taken to the road again. He could be in another state by now."

Still, Jack promised that everything that could be done would be done. He questioned Lucas and Heather in depth and even read the letters that Mark had sent Heather, though in them he found no clues as to where Mark might be now.

"Someone should be here to answer the phone at all times," Jack said, "just in case Mark decides to get in touch."

Since Heather had to work, she called around until she found someone willing to sit by the phone all day. Tawny, who was Heather's Aunt Amy's teenaged sister, arrived ten minutes after Heather called her. Meanwhile, Lucas contacted his house in Monterey and gave instructions that the phone there was never to be left unattended.

Next, Jack took Lucas down to the sheriff's station, where Lucas filled out a missing person's report. Within an hour from the time Jack Roper had arrived at Heather's house, there was an all-points bulletin out on the missing boy.

Jack mobilized the local search and rescue unit and they set to work in teams, looking for signs of Mark in the woods surrounding North Magdalene. Meanwhile, the sheriff's deputies had the job of knocking on doors all over town, branching out from Heather's house, asking anyone and everyone if they had seen Lucas Drury's ten-year-old son.

Heather produced a recent school picture that Mark had sent her. They managed to make a fairly good photocopy of it on the copy machine over at the North Magdalene School, so they could put together a flyer about Mark. The deputies carried copies of the flyer with them, passing them out to everyone they interviewed. And before Heather went in to work, she walked up one side of Main Street and down the other, tacking up a flyer on every available surface.

Sheriff Pangborn assigned Jack the job of personally interviewing Marnie Jones, Kenny Riggins and Oggie Jones, the three people in town most likely to have more

information about Mark. Lucas wanted to be there for
those interviews.

Jack reluctantly agreed. "All right. But you'll be an
observer and that's all."

Lucas swore that he'd keep his mouth shut.

They went to see Marnie Jones first.

From a chair in the corner of Regina Jones's big, old-
fashioned living room, Lucas studied the girl. She had
short-cropped brown hair, blue eyes, a pugnacious nose
and a dirt smudge on her cheek. A quick, ruthless intelli-
gence shone in her eyes. And "pint-size hell-raiser"
seemed to be written all over her. Lucas's guess was that
this girl would be fiercely protective of anyone to whom
she'd given her friendship.

He wondered at his quiet, well-behaved son. How
strange that he'd have chosen this feisty Jones kid as a pal.
But then it struck Lucas: Marnie Jones was exactly the
kind of friend he himself would have chosen when he was
a boy—had anyone in this gossip-ridden, inbred town been
willing to *be* his friend.

Guilt pierced Lucas, twisting deep. Heather had said
Marnie and Mark were real buddies. But until today, he'd
only been vaguely aware of Mark's friendship with the girl.
His sister-in-law, who'd spent two weeks with Mark last
winter, seemed to know more about his son than *he* did.

"Marnie, I want you to tell us where Mark is," Jack
Roper instructed.

"I don't *know,*" Marnie replied tightly. "I told you, I
haven't seen him since last January."

Regina Jones, Marnie's stepmother, stood behind the
girl. She put her hands on Marnie's shoulders. "You must
tell them whatever you know, Marnie. It's very important."

"It's the God's truth, Gina. Last winter's the last time I saw him. And I don't know where he is or where he went. Cross my heart and hope to die."

Regina looked at Jack. "She's telling the truth. I'm sure of it."

Lucas, silent in his corner chair, thought so, too. He wrote fiction for a living, after all. And to be good at that, you had to have a handle on body language. Marnie sat with one ankle hooked across the other knee and both hands wrapped around her raised leg. Her chin was stuck out. She looked ready for a fight, if it came to that. But she didn't have that pulled-in, cagey look that would have said she was hiding something. And she didn't look the least bit nervous, either.

No, the signs weren't there. Not a one.

Jack said, "All right, Marnie. Then do you have any idea of where Mark might have gone? Can you think of someone he might have asked to help him?"

The little chin protruded further. "Yeah. Me. He could have asked me. But he didn't."

"What about where he might have gone?"

"Far away, prob'bly." The words had escaped her lips before Marnie realized they would only bring on more questions. She ducked her head a little, like a turtle pulling into its shell.

But Jack Roper didn't allow her to retreat. "Why do you think he would go far away?"

"Don't know," Marnie mumbled, as if by answering out of the side of her mouth, she could make the questions go away.

"Marnie," Regina Jones said softly.

Marnie glanced up at her stepmother. "Aw, Gina."

"Tell them all you know, honey."

Now Marnie shifted uncomfortably, lowering one sneakered foot to the floor and crossing the other one on her knee. She glanced back at her stepmother again. Regina nodded in encouragement.

"It's just . . . what he said in his letters."

"What letters?" Lucas demanded. "You have letters from my son?"

"Lucas." Jack gave a quick shake of his head.

"Sorry," Lucas muttered.

"Answer the question," Jack said to Marnie. "Do you have letters from Mark Drury?"

Marnie looked rebellious, but she did nod.

"We need to see them," Jack said.

Marnie stuck her thumbnail in her mouth and chewed on the cuticle for a moment.

"Marnie." Regina made the name into a reprimand.

"Oh, all right. I'll get them." Marnie bounced to her feet and disappeared down a hallway.

She returned a few minutes later carrying a stack of envelopes tied together with fishing line. Jack held out his hand.

Marnie clutched the letters to her chest for a moment, then stuck them out. "I want 'em back."

Jack smiled as he took them. "You'll get them."

"When?"

"Marnie." Regina was shaking her head.

"I got a right to know. They belong to me."

"Soon," Jack promised. "I want a chance to read them carefully, and then I'll return them."

Nothing was going to stop Lucas from reading those letters, too. He decided the best way to see to that was to ask Marnie if he could look at them. "I'd like to read them, too," he said quietly.

Marnie turned her blue gaze on him. "They're mine."

"I know. And I'm asking. Will you let me read them?"

Marnie took her time answering. She looked at Lucas through narrowed eyes, clearly doubtful that he could be trusted. Lucas suppressed a sigh of relief when she ruled in his favor. "All right. You can read them. But I want them back as soon as you're done."

In another room, a baby began to cry. Regina started to excuse herself. Jack said there was no problem. They could see themselves out.

They interviewed Oggie Jones next. Lucas had never much cared for the crafty old troublemaker.

It was a local legend that Oggie Jones had stolen his now-deceased wife, Bathsheba, from Lucas's father, Rory, decades ago. Rory had later married Lucas's mother and Lucas had come along. Indirectly, he supposed, Lucas owed his existence to old Oggie Jones.

But Lucas had never managed to muster up any gratitude. For one thing, it was hard to be grateful for the hell on earth that his early childhood had been. And beyond that, Lucas just plain didn't like Oggie's attitude.

The old loudmouth thought he knew it all and had no qualms about telling any and everyone exactly what he knew. And then, when the fool finally shut up, he'd do it with a gleam in his eye that seemed to say he was hoarding secrets too important to share. It irritated Lucas no end to think that his son had befriended this particular old man.

They found Oggie sitting in his easy chair at his daughter's house where he lived now.

"Come in, come in!" The old coot laid it on thick. "What can I do for you, son?" he asked Jack, who evidently really was his son. Jack had that Jones look about him; there was no mistaking it.

"We want to ask you some questions about Mark Drury," Jack said.

"'Course you do. Fire away."

Jack asked the same questions he'd asked Marnie: if Oggie had seen or heard from the boy since the previous winter.

"No, son. Can't say as I have. Can't say as I have. But this here situation is no surprise to me, I gotta say."

"Why not?" Jack asked.

Oggie didn't hesitate to elaborate. "Simple. That boy can't *communicate* with his father. He needs Attention. Capital *A*. So he's finally gone and done something that will get him what he needs." He snorted and turned his beady eyes on Lucas. "You caught on yet that you ain't doin' a father's job too well, Lucas Drury?"

Jack frowned at his father. "Back off, Dad."

"It's all right, Jack," Lucas said. He looked at Oggie. "Quit running us in circles, old man. Tell me. Where is my son?"

"Lucas, I'll ask the questions," Jack said, then turned to Oggie. "Where is Mark, Dad?"

"Can't rightly say as I know."

"What's that mean, Dad? You don't know—or you can't say what you know?"

Oggie snorted and muttered for a minute, then confessed, "All right. I *don't* know. But if I did, I'm not so sure I'd tell you."

"Are you telling us the truth, Dad?"

"Hell, yes. I ain't no liar."

"Dad."

"Okay, okay. Gimme a bible to swear on or somethin'. My answer ain't gonna change."

"Has Mark written to you or spoken to you since last winter?"

"Didn't I already say no to that?"

"If he contacts you, Dad, I expect you to tell us right away."

"Sure you do," the old geezer chortled.

Lucas found he respected Jack Roper more by the moment as the deputy calmly asked, "*Will* you let us know right away, Dad?"

"Aw, hell. Sure. You know I will. Now you two want a beer or somethin'? I think there's a couple a lights in the fridge. You know my gal, Delilah. She won't stock nothin' but lights."

Jack said thank-you anyway, but they had to go.

They talked to Kenny Riggins next. It was more of the same. Kenny swore he hadn't seen or heard from Mark. Kenny, at least, was respectful of both Deputy Jack Roper and Lucas. But then, Kenny wasn't a Jones.

"I'd like to look at the letters you got from Marnie," Lucas said after they'd left the Riggins house.

Jack said he'd go over them by that afternoon. And then Lucas could have them—as long as he made sure to return them to Marnie after he'd read them.

Lucas promised he would, then asked, "What next?" He knew he'd go insane if he couldn't be doing something about finding Mark.

Jack gave him an understanding look. "Come on over to my place. We'll find you some other clothes. Then you can join one of the search teams."

Chapter Four

By the time Heather tied on her apron that day, there was only one thing on everyone's mind at Lily's Café: the disappearance of the Shadowmaster's son.

And in a tiny town like North Magdalene, if a subject was on everyone's mind, then what everyone did was gossip about it—in depth and in public. Few stopped to consider that Mark was Heather's nephew and that thoughtless words about the boy might distress her. Mark was public property now. And besides, Heather had been born into the Jones Gang, the most notorious and talked-about family for miles around. So no one felt too guilty about discussing Mark in front of her. They reasoned that she certainly ought to be accustomed to hearing gossip about her loved ones by this time.

And they were right. Heather *was* accustomed to hearing endless tales about the people she loved. Too bad being used to it didn't make it any easier to take.

Still, she did what she had to do. She kept her mind on her work and did her best to ignore all the talk. She succeeded pretty well, too.

But then, in midafternoon, Nellie Anderson and Linda Lou Beardsly, two of the town's most respected citizens, slid into a booth at the back.

Nellie and Linda Lou put in identical orders: turkey salad sandwiches and ice tea. Nellie pointed out, as she always did, "Not too much ice, Sunshine, dear. I like a good, strong glass of tea."

"Of course, Mrs. Anderson," Heather said, just as *she* always did. She turned to put the order up on the wheel.

And behind her, it began.

Nellie announced in a whisper loud enough to be heard two counties away, "I keep thinking about it. It's so awful. And it's all a complete mystery, evidently. No one has a clue where that boy has gone."

Heather turned from hooking the order in the window to see Linda Lou's head start bobbing up and down. "I heard that the volunteer fire crew is out in force already. And they've brought in the helicopters. I declare. One of them flew over my place so close I could count the fillings in the pilot's teeth. Took five years off my life. Paisley Parker says they're even going to be calling in some dog teams from the California Rescue Dog Association."

"Yes," Nellie confirmed sagely. "It's all terribly overwhelming. All of it." She leaned closer to Linda Lou. "Did you meet that boy last winter?"

"I did. And he seemed such a nice, polite boy, too—even if he did associate with that miniature hooligan, Marnie Jones."

"I know," Nellie said. "That boy is a puzzle any way you look at him. As you said, he *is* a nice boy. And I can't help asking myself, how is that possible—considering his father and all?"

Heather, who had their teas ready, marched up to the booth and plunked them down. "Two ice teas," she said, trying to inject enough disapproval into the words that the two ladies would lower their voices, at least.

"Thank you, dear," Nellie said, then turned right back to Linda Lou and intoned, "Blood, in most cases, will tell."

Heather knew there wasn't much else she could do, short of coming right out and asking the ladies to pipe down. And doing such a thing, in the end, would probably cause more trouble than it would cure. So Heather returned to the counter and left them to their scandalmongering.

In the booth, Linda Lou was still nodding. Heather thought it was surprising that her head didn't break off. "Yes, and I swear, when you think about it, is it *really* so astonishing that the boy's run away? I mean, as you just said, considering his father. Oh, I do declare, anyone who writes stories like that can't be normal, now can he?"

"Oh, well, now," Nellie said. "I hate to make judgments on those books of Lucas Drury's. After all, I've never read one."

Heather couldn't believe her ears. The day Nellie Anderson hesitated to make a judgment was a red-letter day indeed.

But if Nellie was hesitating to pass judgment here, Linda Lou wasn't. She jumped right in. "Those books are bad." She was whispering now, too. Like Nellie's whisper, Linda Lou's could be heard through steel walls. "I tell you. Bad. And I'm one who knows. I have read them all."

Nellie was appalled. "No."

Linda Lou hung her head. "Yes."

"Oh, Linda Lou. I can't believe my own ears. I remember you told me you read the first one he wrote, and I understood that. You've always been a reader, and it's only fair to give even the most questionable forms of literature one chance. But I assumed that after one book, you'd have had quite enough."

"Yes. So did I. But they're like drugs, those stories of his. You read one, and you know it's bad for you. But can you make yourself stop reading? No, you cannot."

"Oh, Linda Lou."

"I know, I know. There's no excuse. I did what I did."

"Well, it's not your fault if you can't help yourself."

"Oh, Nellie. You are so sensitive..."

"Well, I like to think I understand the human heart."

"And you do understand," Linda Lou concurred. "You understand utterly.... But back to that poor Drury child."

"Yes." Nellie rubbed her pointed chin, ruminating. "As we've both said, the signs were all there. His father writes those horrible books. And then, of course, there was Lucas Drury's childhood."

Linda Lou shook her head instead of bobbing it. "Exactly. A horror story in itself."

Nellie was ready with all the gory details that everyone in town had heard a million times. "Stabbing his *own* father like that when he was only seven years old. Though, the good Lord knows, Rory Drury had it coming. Not only a drunk and a womanizer, but a wife beater, too. Bless that poor woman's heart."

For once, Linda Lou was a little lost. "What woman?"

"Norma. Remember? Lucas Drury's mother, Norma. Passed away herself just a few years back."

Linda Lou took a sip of her tea. "Oh, yes, of course."

"And at least that poor woman got her chance for a bit of happiness in the end, after Rory finally died of liver failure."

"And though it may sound shocking," Linda Lou declared, "I have to say I agree with you that no one could fault Lucas Drury for stabbing his own father—under the circumstances, I mean."

"Yes, he was only trying to protect his dear mother, after all," Nellie said. "And yet, something like that's got to *damage* a person."

"Absolutely. And it did, we know it did. One only has to read those awful books."

And don't forget that assault and battery scandal."

"Yes, yes. Of course."

"Lucas Drury was a grown man by then. Fully responsible for his own actions."

"Too true, too true. The way I heard it, his ex-wife, the boy's mother, got him out of that one."

"She certainly did. Some fancy lady lawyer from Arizona. Notice the *ex* before the word *wife*. They're divorced, of course. I'm sure Lucas Drury isn't the kind to stick in there and make a marriage work."

"No, of course not, not with his past."

"And now he's rich as sin."

"Money made from writing those awful books."

"Exactly."

"What is the world coming to?"

"I don't know. I simply do not know...." Nellie looked up, smiling. "Ah, here's Sunshine with our sandwiches. A little mayo on the side, please?"

It was like that all day.

Heather kept working, kept doing her best to tune out the gossip, but by the time she finally went home at six, she was ready to throw the next tale-teller into Lily's deep-fat fryer. And worse than all the awful rumor-spreading and the in-depth dissection of Lucas's life, there was no real news about Mark.

Periodically, someone from one of the search crews or the sheriff's office would come in for a sandwich or a cold drink and Heather would pump them for any information they could give her. But there simply wasn't a clue. By the end of the day, the sheriff's deputies had turned the town upside-down, interviewed everyone who lived there and looked through every unoccupied structure. They'd beat the bushes as far as the river on the west and Harleyville Diggins to the east, with three Forest Service helicopters circling out in a radius of twenty miles from the center of town. All to no avail.

And the only responses to the all-points bulletin were from the news media, wanting to know more. By the end of the day, a half-dozen reporters from all over the state had come into Lily's to ask questions about Lucas Drury's missing son.

So Heather went home tired, discouraged and sick at heart. Tawny stayed by the phone while Heather drew a bath. She soaked in it for a long time. The water helped ease her tiredness, but the heartsickness she felt was something that only Mark's safe reappearance could wash away.

After the bath, Heather tied up her hair in a ponytail, pulled on a big T-shirt and an old pair of shorts and went down to press a few dollars into Tawny's hand and send her on home. She'd just opened the refrigerator and was staring at the brightness inside, trying to decide if she felt up to barbecuing some chicken, when the doorbell rang.

She knew it would be Lucas. She ran into the front room and pulled back the door to find him standing there in the fading light of day.

His clothes were different. He now wore faded jeans and a dark T-shirt, as well as sturdy lace-up hiking boots, the kind of clothing suitable for scouring the woods and fields in search of a missing ten-year-old boy.

"It's getting dark," he said. "So they suspended the search. We start in again tomorrow, at daybreak."

"Any news?"

He shook his head. "Listen. I won't keep you. I just came to ask if I could take those letters Mark wrote you. I'd like to read them, if you don't mind."

Heather stared at him. He was acting so careful, so polite. It wasn't his style at all. And it hurt, to see him this way. It deepened her feeling of heartsickness.

She knew what this new behavior meant. He *was* careful. His son was missing. The world had spun out of his control. He had to tread carefully now.

Heather forced a smile for him and tried her best to sound offhand and casual. "Don't just stand there. Come on in." She stepped back from the doorway.

He didn't move. "No. I have to get over to the motel. I want to see about getting a room."

In her mind, Heather pictured the lumpy beds and depressing decor of North Magdalene's one motel. It seemed a very grim place to have to stay at an already difficult time.

"So if you could just get the letters..." Lucas went on.

"No way," she said quietly.

He looked at her, his jaw tightening. But he was a desperate man, desperate enough to ask in a rough whisper, "Please. I...haven't handled any of this right with Mark. I'm beginning to see that now. And I need to read the letters he wrote. I need to understand what was in his mind and what he was feeling."

She realized he'd misunderstood her. "Oh, Lucas," she said, her voice as torn as his. "I didn't mean the letters. Of course you can read the letters."

"Then what?"

"I meant no way are you staying at the motel."

"Why?"

She couldn't believe he didn't know. "You are *family,* Lucas. You grew up in this house. Do you honestly think I would let you stay anywhere else?"

He looked at her very strangely, she thought. She wondered what in the world he might be thinking. But then all he said was what people always say when they're trying to be polite. "I . . . really don't want to put you out."

"You're staying with me," she said. "I don't want to hear any more about it. Now get whatever you need from your car and come inside."

Heather gave Lucas the same room Mark had slept in. He asked for a shower and she told him where she kept the fresh towels in the downstairs bathroom. While he cleaned up, Heather put the chicken on the gas grill outside, stuck two potatoes in the microwave and prepared a green salad.

Lucas called Mark's mother, Candace Levertov, in Phoenix as soon as he was finished in the bathroom. Heather was setting the table as he spoke to his ex-wife.

When he hung up, Heather turned to him and asked, "Is she okay?"

He nodded. "Candace is a very tough lady."

"I have another extra bedroom, you know. So when she gets here, she can come right to the house and get comfortable."

Lucas actually smiled at that. "Slow down. She's not on a plane yet."

"When will she be here?"

"I don't know."

"Oh," Heather said, as if she understood. But she didn't understand. Not at all. If she had been in Candace Levertov's position—

Heather cut off the thought. She *wasn't* in the other woman's position. And she had no right to make judgments on the way Mark's mother had decided to deal with this situation.

"She's on a major case right now," Lucas said from behind Heather. "And it's going to take her a little while to clear her calendar."

"I understand," Heather said. She carefully folded two paper napkins into triangles and tucked them under the lips of the plates, then set the forks on the napkins, and put the knives and spoons where they belonged.

"Listen, Heather..."

She turned to look over her shoulder at him. "Hmm?"

"You don't have an answering machine. If I'm going to stay here, I'd like to get one by tomorrow, if that's all right."

"Of course. That would be a good idea."

"In fact, I think I'll call my housekeeper. Have her bring me the answering machine, some clothes and a few other things, including fresh clothes for Mark, too. That way, when we find him, he'll have clean things to wear."

She didn't miss the subtle stress he'd put on the word *when*, as if he were secretly thinking *if*, and had stopped himself from saying it at the last minute.

"Is that okay with you?" he asked.

"That's fine. Whatever you think."

"Good. Do you think Tawny would be willing to baby-sit the phone during the day until this is over?"

"I'm sure she would."

"Of course, I'll pay her. And I know this is going to result in a mammoth phone bill. So before I leave, I'll be sure to—"

"Lucas. Please. We'll work it all out. Now come on, sit down. Eat your dinner."

He did as she told him. The meal was silent and quick.

When it was over, Heather called Tawny, who agreed to take care of the phone for as long as they needed her. Then Lucas made a few more calls, including the one to his housekeeper, who promised to be there by the next afternoon with everything Lucas required. As Heather was putting the last dish into the dishwasher, Lucas asked for the letters again.

"Of course. I'll get them."

Heather went upstairs and came down with the small stack of correspondence. She found Lucas at the kitchen table, wearing a pair of black-framed glasses, reading what appeared to be another letter like the ones she held in her hands. A stack of similar letters sat at his elbow. Heather set her letters down beside the others.

Lucas glanced up. "These are Marnie's. She gave me permission to read them after Jack looked them over." He sounded polite and careful again, the way he'd sounded most of the evening.

"Mark wrote to her, too?"

"Yeah. He's had a computer ever since he was five. He likes to play games on it. And do his homework. And write letters, too."

Heather smiled. "Well. He comes by it honestly, doesn't he?"

"What?"

"Writing."

That seemed to please Lucas. He actually smiled. "I suppose you could say that." He readjusted his glasses.

"Listen to this. This is from last February, about a month after he stayed here."

Lucas began to read.

"Marnie, do you know that all of the time that there is is happening all at the same time? I don't really understand that, but I read it and it made sense to me just for a moment, while I was reading, you know? And that there are particles smaller than atoms called quarks.

"I miss you. And Kenny. I never had a normal life, you know? I'm real rich, I guess, because my dad's rich and he says that whatever he's got is mine, too. But it doesn't matter. That was the thing, about last Christmas. I felt like I was normal. Just another kid. What I did was I pretended in my mind that I lived with Aunt Heather, that I would never have to leave there. Because being in North Magdalene was like I always thought it could be. To have friends. And just to be one of the kids. To go home at night and have Aunt Heather make me eat my squash.

"I'll be back in the summer. No matter what. One for all and all for one. Signed in blood.

Your friend, Mark"

The paper crackled a little as Lucas set it on the table. He took off his glasses and set them on the letter, then rubbed his eyes.

Heather volunteered softly, "He wrote something similar to me, about coming back in the summer."

Lucas sighed. "I told him we'd try to come here as soon as school got out, when I finished the book I was working on last spring and before I started my next book tour."

"But that didn't happen."

"No." He looked up at her. "The book I was working on took a little longer than I thought it would. And then my publicist came up with five extra cities for the tour and the 'Today' show, too. It seemed too great an opportunity to pass up."

"So you canceled the trip here."

"Right. Mark was upset when I told him. He begged me to call you and arrange for him to come alone. But I . . ." Lucas looked away, took in a deep breath, then finished at last, " . . . just didn't get around to it."

Lucas picked up his glasses again, turned them over in his hands. "I could say I had a million things to do, getting ready for the book tour, and that that's the reason I couldn't pick up the phone and ask you if Mark could come for a visit. But you wouldn't buy a lame excuse like that, would you?"

Heather, still standing at his side, said nothing. He was right. She wouldn't buy it—even if it was the truth.

Lucas stared at the glasses in his hands, but Heather knew he wasn't really seeing them. He was seeing Mark, picturing him, as Heather kept doing, all alone out there somewhere in the dark.

"He's always been such a good kid," Lucas said. "No trouble. Ever. It's been too easy to do just what your grandfather accused me of today."

"You talked with my grandpa?"

He nodded. "Jack let me sit in on the interviews with Oggie and Kenny and Marnie."

"And what did my grandpa . . . accuse you of?"

"Of pushing Mark to the side of my life." A low groan escaped Lucas. "Sweet God, let him be all right." He threw the glasses to the tabletop with more force than was good for them.

Heather stared down at the dark crown of Lucas's head. The urge to offer comfort was strong.

She thought to herself, *If he was Jason Lee*... and knew that if he were, she would wrap her arms around him, hold him close, soothe him with her cherishing touch and the warmth of her body.

But he wasn't Jason Lee.

Lucas looked up. His eyes, which as a rule regarded the world so coldly, now burned with raw agony.

He dared to say it. "What if we don't find him?"

Heather couldn't bear to hear that. "Oh, Lucas. It will be all right," she heard herself promising. "He hitchhiked all the way from Monterey. Almost three hundred miles by himself. He's a very resourceful kid. He's okay. And we'll find him. You'll see."

Lucas longed to believe her, she could see it in his eyes. He would give anything to believe her.

She could think of nothing more to say. And words, anyway, were not enough. She lifted her hand and laid it ever so gently on the side of his face.

And it came to her: she had never touched this man before in all the years she'd known him.

The idea astonished her.

He was family, so it shouldn't have been possible.

She had known him since she was only a child. Yet at this moment, touching him, she was absolutely certain she had never touched him before, even in passing. He'd left town when she was hardly in grade school. And after that, he'd returned only for brief visits, to witness the weddings or funerals that marked the changes in the family down the years. And never, during those visits, had she even once lifted her face to his for a fond, salutary peck of a kiss. Never had she moved close to him for a quick hug of greeting or farewell.

Had it been a purposeful thing? Had she *avoided* physical contact with him? Had *he* avoided touching her?

It seemed, at that moment, as she cupped his warm cheek in the palm of her hand, that there had been some secret, silent agreement between them always. Never to touch.

And now she had broken that agreement.

Her hand remained against his cheek. He held her gaze as he lifted his own hand to cover hers.

Heat shot up her arm and straight down into her most private place.

Heather drew in a long, shuddering breath. Beneath her fingertips, his skin was warm and smooth, freshly shaven in the shower he had taken not too long before. And the scent of him was suddenly everywhere. Sandalwood and spice. Exotic. Dangerous.

"Lucas." The voice was another woman's voice, not her own at all. Her own voice had never been so husky, so wayward, so full of desire.

"Yes," he said, the word so soft she hardly heard it.

And Heather knew what she wanted to do: she wanted to bend down and press her lips to his. She wanted to feel his breath inside her mouth, to know the questing stroke of his tongue. Never in her young life had she wanted anything so much. That she even dared to imagine such a thing stunned her.

It was so wrong, so totally forbidden, that she gave a small, sharp gasp and yanked her hand free.

Lucas said nothing. He sat very still.

After a moment, Heather managed to speak in a bland, hollow voice. "It's getting late."

He nodded. "Yes. And tomorrow will be a long day."

"Good night, then."

"Good night."

She turned and left him there, careful to walk slowly so they could both pretend she wasn't fleeing to the safety of her room.

The next morning, Heather had breakfast ready at five. Lucas ate quickly and thanked her politely for the meal.

"You're welcome. Take the key." She pointed to the key she had laid out on the counter earlier so that she wouldn't forget to give it to him. "You're going to need to be able to get in and out of the house if I'm not here."

He thanked her again, grabbed up the key and left to join the search and rescue crew.

Once he was gone, Heather relaxed a little. She thought about how distant and courteous he'd been over breakfast.

And she found it reasonably easy to tell herself that nothing had really happened between them the night before. Mark's disappearance had her on edge, that was all. And she'd read way too much into what was actually only a tender touch and a shared glance.

Lucas's child was missing. She had offered him words of comfort. She'd caressed his cheek; he'd clasped her hand. It was nothing to lie awake all night over—though that was exactly what she had done.

It was a rough time, that was all. Her reactions to things couldn't be trusted right now. The wisest course of action would be to forget that those few strange moments had ever happened.

Which was precisely what she intended to do.

Tawny appeared at Heather's door at five-thirty, so Heather arrived at the café before Lily that morning. She did all her own prep work, and then did most of her boss's, too.

"I could get used to this," Lily told her, when she arrived at six.

They opened the doors at seven.

It was a busy morning. The café was packed with locals, as well as the usual summer contingent of tourists. And today there were other strangers—reporters mostly, Heather found out soon enough, each trying to elbow the other to get the real scoop on the Shadowmaster's son. The reporters made awful nuisances of themselves, quizzing all the customers. And then Tyler Conley, a cousin of Jason Lee's, spilled the beans to one of them that their waitress was Mark Drury's aunt. After that, Heather could hardly take an order without being asked what Lucas Drury was *really* like.

In spite of the brisk business, to Heather the day seemed interminable. And her nerves were shot. It was nothing short of an emotional roller coaster, waiting for news that they'd found some sign of Mark, experiencing fierce hope and then crushing disappointment every time the phone rang and it was only someone wanting a tuna on rye.

Around noon, Heather was taking an order from a party of five when Tamara Wilbur, Lily's other waitress, called out to her.

"Hey, Sunshine! Phone!"

There were three more orders left to take, so Heather instructed over her shoulder, "Get a number. I'll call back."

"Uh-uh. He says only you can take this order. And it can't wait."

Heather gave her customers a rueful smile. "Sorry. Be right back."

She went to the end of the counter by the cash register and took the phone from Tamara, who lifted her eyebrows significantly and then whispered, "Your uncle Jack. About you-know-who."

Heather's heart bounced up and seemed to lodge in her throat. Her hands felt clammy. Heather dried them on her apron and put the phone to her ear. "Hello, this is Heather."

"Listen, Sunshine," her uncle Jack said. "I know half of the reporters in town are hanging around there. So pretend to take an order or something, all right?"

"Sure." Heather swallowed and grabbed the take-out pad near her elbow. "Okay. I'm ready. Go ahead."

"Can you get out of there?"

"For how long?" She scribbled two hearts with arrows through them onto the pad.

"This won't take more than half an hour, tops. Put something in a bag and pretend you're doing a special take-out order."

Heather glanced up. She felt that everyone was watching her, which of course wasn't really true. She wanted to ask for some specifics—like why he wanted to see her. And what in the world was going on?

She gulped again. Was it bad news? Or good? Her heart pounded like a bass drum in her chest.

"Er, could you tell me . . ." The sentence died uncompleted. She couldn't think how to go on without giving away that the call concerned Mark.

Uncle Jack took pity on her. "Listen. We've found a Swiss army knife. You know, one of those knives with enough attachments to do everything but balance your bank statement for you?"

"Yes," Heather said, though how she got the word out was a mystery to her.

I take it with me. Wherever I go, Mark had said.

Jack went on. "Lucas says you gave Mark a knife like it."

"Yes."

"If it was the one you gave Mark, could you identify it?"

"Yes, I could."

"Come down to the station then, all right? And try not to let anyone follow you."

"Right," she said. "I'll get that order to you as quick as I can."

Chapter Five

Heather studied the knife Jack had handed her. It was sealed inside a plastic bag. She looked for the tiny chipped place and found it.

"It's the knife I gave Mark."

"Are you sure?" Jack asked.

She nodded. "There's a tiny chip missing right here, see?" She held up the bag and pointed. "Right where the little tweezers fit in. Jason Lee had that knife for years, and that little chip was always broken off." Heather glanced from Jack to Lucas, who was sitting, very silent, in a corner of the small interviewing room. "Where did you find it?"

"In a big drainpipe," Jack said. "At the base of Sweetbriar Summit. Over in Sweetbriar Park."

"*When* did you find it?"

"About an hour ago."

"Did you find anything else?"

Jack shrugged. "A few footprints and not much else. It's been a dry year, so we couldn't follow his trail much more than a few hundred yards from the pipe. Our guess is he slept there."

"In the pipe?"

"Right. For that first night after he left your place—or maybe even last night. Maybe both. We can't say. We'll keep a close watch on the area now, though, in case he returns to it."

Heather cast about for any small thread of hope to hang on to. "So that means he didn't take off hitchhiking. That he's somewhere reasonably nearby, at least."

"Not necessarily," Jack said. "You say he owned that knife. And we believe the footprints we found were his. They're the right size and the right sole pattern—we *think*. So the chances are he was in that pipe at some point. And that's all we can say right now."

Heather stared at the knife in her hands. "It isn't much, Uncle Jack."

"I know, Sunshine." Jack's voice was gentler. "Believe me. I know."

She looked up. "Which way did his footprints lead?"

"Around the base of Sweetbriar Summit in a southerly direction, more or less parallel with the river. We're following up on them. But so far..."

"It's okay. I get the picture." Heather held up the bag that contained the knife. "I take it you want to keep this?"

"For a while," Jack said.

In the corner, Lucas shifted in his chair. It seemed to Heather that she could feel the frustration and despair radiating off him.

"Okay." Heather handed the knife to Jack and got up from the plastic chair her uncle had offered her when she first came in. "Is that all, then?"

"Yeah. Thanks, Sunshine," Jack said.

"Anytime. You know that." She turned for the door that lead to the reception area of the small sheriff's station. But before she went out, she stopped.

She sought Lucas's eyes. "Walk out with me."

Without a word he rose to his feet and moved to her side, reaching around in front of her to open the door. She went out ahead of him. When they passed through the reception area, she waved a friendly greeting at Don Brown, who was manning the front desk.

She didn't turn to Lucas until they were out the door and standing on the station's steps. And when she did stop to face him, she had to stifle a gasp. In the bright light of day, he looked terrible, his skin gray, his eyes lined and haunted.

"What do you want, Heather?"

Her heart went out to him. She wanted to help him, to alleviate his suffering somehow. But all she could think of to offer was the mundane solace of a good meal. It was better than nothing, she supposed.

"Come back to the house with me. I'll make you some lunch."

"Aren't you supposed to be working?"

"I'll call Lily. She'll shout a lot, but she'll survive."

Lucas studied her for a moment, then shook his head. "Thanks. I'm not hungry."

She glanced around. The station was a few miles outside of town and the small parking lot was deserted. "Lucas, please..."

"Please what?"

"Don't... give up hope."

His lips flattened into a thin line. "I'm not."

She scanned his face again. "You look awful. I'm worried about you."

"Listen. Across the river, they're still searching. I want to get back to them."

"I know. I just—"

"It's all right," he said. But of course, she knew it wasn't. "Just go back to work, why don't you? Just let it be."

"Lucas, if you need me—" She lifted a hand.

He ducked away. "Don't."

She let her hand drop, thinking of the night before and feeling her face flame. She had almost done it again.

"I'm sorry," she said, and then felt more a fool than before.

"Don't be. Just go. Go back to work."

There seemed nothing else to say. So she turned and fled down the steps to where her car waited. She slid in behind the wheel, shoved the key into the ignition and got out of there as fast as she could.

There were reporters by the gate when Heather got home that afternoon. She told them to stay off her property and that she had no comment to make about the missing Mark Drury or his famous father. But through the rest of the afternoon into the evening, every time she glanced outside, they were there, standing idly by the gate, or sitting in parked cars, biding their time.

Lucas came in after eight.

She turned from the counter where she was peeling potatoes to give him a welcoming smile. "Did you have to kill any reporters to get past the gate?"

He tried to joke about it with her. "Only two. The rest turned and ran."

"Good. That oughtta teach 'em."

"Let's hope so."

There was a moment of uncomfortable silence. Heather turned back to the sink. She'd found it painful to look at him. He looked even worse than he had earlier at the sheriff's station. She couldn't help feeling that she was witnessing a man being slowly destroyed, from inside, by fear for his son.

"Your housekeeper was here a few hours ago." Heather scraped at the potato she was peeling as she talked. "I asked her to stay but she was anxious to get back. The things she brought are in your room. Except for the answering machine. That I hooked up myself, so we can be sure we never miss a call, even when we're outside or something." She glanced over her shoulder at him. "I hope that's okay."

He forced a grim smile. "It's great. Thanks." Then he excused himself to take a shower, as he had the night before.

After he finished his shower, dinner was ready. The two of them sat down to eat. They hardly spoke through the meal. And Lucas had to jump up to answer every time the phone rang, which was often.

Once, after he sat down from taking a call, Lucas looked up and told her, "I'm going to offer a reward. A million dollars. For information leading to Mark's safe return."

"Can you afford that?"

He nodded. "You think it's enough?"

"Yes. I think it's plenty."

When dinner was out of the way, Lucas called his publicist at home to break the news that he still had no idea when or if he could continue with the book tour. Next, he contacted his agent—also at home—and repeated the same thing. After that, he made other calls. He arranged for a notice to go out on the national wire services about the million-dollar reward.

Between calls, the phone rang. It seemed to Heather that every time Lucas hung up, the phone shrilled out again. Most of the calls were from reporters who'd managed to obtain Heather's number from someone in town. Lucas spoke to them all, because he wanted the news of the reward to get out. After a while, Heather left him alone with the phone and went about taking care of a few household chores.

She was down in the basement, putting a load of clothes in the dryer, when Lucas called to her from the top of the stairs. She started the dry cycle and ran up the steps to the kitchen.

Lucas gestured at the phone receiver, which he'd laid on the counter. "Eden, I think she said."

Heather reached for the phone eagerly. Eden was her stepmother, and Heather adored her.

"How are you holding up over there?" The warm, vibrant voice lifted Heather's sagging spirits a little. Eden was a wonderful woman. She'd taken Heather's bitter, reclusive father and made him into a happy man.

"Things have been better."

"Your father's lurking by my elbow. He says to say we're here if you need us."

"I know. And I'm glad."

"How is Lucas doing?"

Heather glanced at the man in question. *Lucas is a wreck,* she thought, but opted for saying, "Could be better," so he wouldn't guess they were talking about him and she could avoid getting one of his disdainful frowns.

"Why don't you bring him over?" Eden suggested.

"Now?"

"You bet. We'll have coffee. Or something stronger, if you'd like. And we'll talk. It helps to talk, at a time like this."

"You know your stepmother." Heather heard her father's teasing voice near the mouthpiece. "She thinks talking solves everything. That's why she never stops."

"Oh, you..." Eden chided. "Go away. I'm doing the talking here."

"Exactly," Jared Jones growled.

"Don't listen to him," Eden said to Heather. "Listen to me. And bring Lucas over here. Now."

Heather looked at Lucas. He regarded her through those hooded, unreadable eyes. She put her hand over the mouthpiece. "It's my stepmother. She's invited us to come over there."

"Now?"

"Yes."

"No. But tell her thanks." He turned and went out through the dining room.

Heather spoke to her stepmother. "I don't think so, Eden. But thanks."

"Are you sure?"

"Positive."

"Then promise me..."

"Yes?"

"If Mark isn't found tomorrow, you and Lucas will come here for dinner."

Heather thought about that. The idea was appealing to her. It would be so comforting, to hold her baby half sister, Sally, in her lap and bask in the glow of the happiness that Eden and her father shared. But she was pretty sure Lucas would never go for it. And she knew she was not going to want to leave him alone if another day had gone by with no sign of Mark.

"Oh, Eden," Heather started making her excuses. "I don't think it's a good idea. It would be very late. After eight."

"It doesn't matter. You get him here. And yourself, too. You need family around you now. This is a hard time."

"But I don't see how—"

"Find a way. Promise me."

"I—"

"I'm not taking no."

Heather surrendered. Right then, tomorrow night seemed a million years away. She'd worry about getting Lucas to go with her when the time came. "All right. We'll be there, *if* they don't find Mark."

"All right, honey. And don't forget. We love you."

Heather told Eden that she loved her, too.

Of course, the phone started ringing again the moment the receiver met the cradle.

"I'll take it," Lucas said from behind her. He was carrying what looked like a small gray suitcase. "It's probably for me anyway."

"All right." She moved out of his way.

He set the little suitcase on the table. Heather realized it was a laptop computer when he flipped it open and she saw the screen. Then he went and answered the ringing phone.

The call was from Mark's mother. Lucas launched into a detailed explanation of the day's events.

Heather left him alone and went into the living room, where she tried her best to watch a situation comedy while she waited for her clothes to dry. When the show was over, she went down to the basement, folded the clothes and took them upstairs to put away.

Then she stuck her head in the kitchen, where Lucas was sitting at the table typing at the laptop. The phone rang again just as she entered the room. He got up to answer it. She mouthed a good-night at him and he waved in response as he muttered "Hello?" into the mouthpiece.

Heather went upstairs, brushed her teeth and changed into her pajamas. She climbed between the sheets and switched off the light, thinking she was tired enough that she'd be asleep in minutes.

But sleep was fickle after all. The phone kept ringing. And since she had an extension by her bed, she was jarred from a doze twice before she reached over and unplugged the darn thing. But then she could still hear it, down in the kitchen, distant but disturbing. And after a while, she found herself waiting for the low drone of Lucas's voice as he dealt with the people who called.

Finally, very late, the house fell silent. Either Lucas had turned off the ringer and let his answering machine handle things, or they were giving him a break for the night.

Heather lay, wide-eyed, listening to the silence, wondering what was the matter with her. It was perfectly quiet now. She shouldn't be lying there staring at the ceiling waiting for... what, exactly?

She realized what it was. She was waiting for sounds of Lucas moving around down there, for the noises that would mean he was getting ready for bed. She was having trouble relaxing because she hadn't heard the water running in the bathroom, or the creaking of floorboards that would tell her he was settling down in the room below hers. As soon as she heard those sounds, she could relax.

So she waited some more.

But the sounds didn't come.

After a while, she just couldn't stand it. She slid from her bed, pulled on her robe and tiptoed barefoot out to the small landing at the top of the stairs. She leaned over the rail and looked down the stairwell into thick, unrelieved darkness. As far as she could make out, all the lights were off down there.

Treading carefully, Heather went down the stairs. When she reached the dining room, she paused, her hand on the newel post. The door to Lucas's room was opposite where she stood. It was closed. No light gleamed under it. Apparently Lucas had gone to bed without her hearing him.

Heather dropped to the bottom stair and leaned her head against the newel post. She wanted to go to Lucas's door and knock on it, to ask him if he was all right. But then again, it seemed inappropriate to go knocking on his door in the middle of the night.

So she did nothing. She sat there in the dark at the base of the stairs, tired enough that she fell to musing.

Across the hardwood floor, between herself and the door to Lucas's room, loomed the big, polished mahogany dining table. The rich wood gleamed in the spill of moonlight from outside.

That table had once belonged to Lucas's grandmother, Cecilia Drury, back all those years ago, when the Drury Ranch claimed most of the land for miles around.

Rory, Lucas's father, had been Cecilia's only child. People said Rory had loved only one woman: Bathsheba Riley, whom he'd lost forever when Oggie Jones came to town. After Bathsheba married Oggie, Rory became a wastrel—because of thwarted love, most folks said.

Over the years, the massive tracts of Drury land had been sold off, parcel by parcel. When Rory died, Lucas and his mother, Norma, had been the only Drurys left. The land was gone, and so was all the money.

Norma had married Jason Conley, bringing with her to Jason's house the few fine pieces of furniture she had managed to keep. And now Cecilia Drury's table held the place of honor in the Conley dining room—while the Conley house and everything in it belonged to Heather, who was a Jones by birth.

What would cruel old Rory Drury have thought had he known that one day all that was left of his family's belongings would be owned by the granddaughter of his archenemy, Oggie Jones?

Heather shook herself. This was ridiculous. She couldn't sit here on the stairs all night, ruminating on the origins of her furniture. Either she had to get up and knock on that door or go back to bed.

She put her hand on top of the newel post and pulled herself to her feet.

And then, from the dark living room to her left, she heard the smallest sound. She held utterly still, not sure really what she had heard.

No more sounds were forthcoming. But it didn't matter. She was suddenly sure of where Lucas could be found.

Her feet whispered across the bare floor as she approached the arch that led into the living room. She saw Lucas sitting in the easy chair in the corner. He'd opened the curtains and run up the shades—so he could look out at the night, she supposed.

Though he said nothing, she knew he watched her as she went to the end of the couch nearest his chair and sat down, gathering her feet up to the side and wrapping her bare toes in the softness of her robe.

After she was still, he seemed to watch her for a moment more, then he asked in a voice that sounded vaguely amused, "Worried about me?"

She sat a little straighter in her corner of the couch. "Yes, I was. A little."

"Only a little?"

"All right. More than a little." She looked at him levelly—or at least at the shadowed shape of him. She couldn't see his features very clearly in the dark.

"I'll survive," he told her. "I always do. Worry about Mark. He's the one who needs it."

"I am. I do."

Lucas looked away, toward the front windows. "Candace needs one more day, to get things squared away. And then she'll be flying into Sacramento. She'll rent a car from there."

"All right." Heather shifted a little, leaning on the armrest—and wondering why she didn't say good-night and retreat to her room where she belonged. She'd checked on him and he was all right—or as all right as a man whose only child is missing can be.

His head swiveled toward her again. "Candace is one hell of a lawyer, you know?"

She nodded. "I've heard that, yes."

"If it weren't for her, I might still be locked up tight in an Arizona penitentiary."

"Yes."

"What does that mean, *yes?*"

"It means I've heard about...how she defended you."

"I'll bet you did. This is North Magdalene, after all, right? And people will talk."

She saw no reason to argue with that. "Yes, people will talk."

But he wouldn't let it go. "Small minds in small places." Now his voice was bitter. "How the hell can you live here?"

She answered gently and firmly. "I love it here. I would never live anywhere else."

He said nothing for a moment. Then he softly sighed, "I'm sorry. I'm being an ass."

She smiled. "It's okay. You're entitled. Up to a point."

He rested his head on the back of the chair. Silence filled the darkness.

Heather looked out the window across the room, at the stars and a tiny sliver of moon gleaming between the leaves of the locust tree beyond the gate.

"Did you know that Mark changed my life?"

She started at the sound of his voice and looked at him. He seemed to be watching her again. His head was lifted and facing toward her.

"No," she said. "Not really. Though now I think about it, it doesn't surprise me. Kids have a tendency to do that." She suggested, carefully, "Why don't you tell me about it?"

"About how Mark changed my life?"

"Yes."

"It's not important."

Heather peered at him through the darkness. She wished she could see his face more clearly, but she knew that if she switched on a light everything would be ruined. In spite of what he said, she was reasonably sure that the tone of his voice meant he was willing to talk a little about himself and his son—here, under cover of darkness in the middle of the night. She thought that would be a good thing, lights or no lights.

"I'd like to hear it," she said, "if you'll tell me."

"What you should do is go to bed. It's late."

"I know."

"Well?"

"Talk. Tell me about how it was for you, after you left home. And about Candace. And Mark."

"Heather?"

"Yes?"

"You're too good."

"It's true. I'm wonderful. Now please. Tell me."

He moved around in the chair, settling in as she had done on the couch. And then he began, "I left home the day after I graduated high school."

"Yes. I remember that."

"And after I left, I wandered around a lot, taking odd jobs, kind of living on the road, really."

"Wasn't that lonely?"

He gave a dry chuckle. "What's lonely? Everyone's lonely."

"Not everyone. Not always."

"Tell me you're not lonely now, Heather."

She smoothed her robe a little. "This isn't my story. It's yours."

"Right. My story."

"Go on."

He looked out the window again. "You've heard about the assault and battery charge?"

"Yes. But only in bits and pieces. Tell me about it."

He let out a breath. "Well, when it happened, I was living in Phoenix, working as a roofer, making fairly good money, or so it seemed to me then. At least, I had enough money to get an apartment. One of those courtyard type of places, where you look across a walkway lined with century plants into your neighbor's living room.

"The apartment across from mine was rented by a woman who had two little boys. And lots of boyfriends that came and went. But then after a while, she seemed to settle down with one guy."

"And?"

"Unfortunately her steady boyfriend had a bad habit."

"What?"

"He liked to beat up her kids. Twice, I heard one or the other of those kids yelling and I'd go over there and make him stop. Finally, that bastard went too far. I heard one of the boys screaming and I went over there. When I broke in the door, the kid was bleeding. And he wasn't screaming anymore.''

Lucas made a low, disgusted sound. "I don't know. I just lost it. I'm sure it's all wrapped up in my father, and the way he used to beat on me and my mother. But whatever it was, I saw red. I jumped on that worthless piece of garbage. And when I was done with him, he couldn't *crawl* out of there.''

"What happened then?''

"I drove him and the kid to the hospital.''

"And then?''

"The cops came after me at work the next day. It turned out I'd beat up the son of a very important person. They threw the book at me. Since I didn't have more than a few hundred dollars to my name, they gave me a public defender.''

"Candace?''

"Right. No one believed I had a chance, because that guy I'd beat up was in bad shape. I had done major, permanent damage to him. But Candace was good, you can't believe how good. She got me off.''

Lucas shook his head and gave a low chuckle. "I idolized that woman. And she deserved it. She was—*is* the best. I was twenty-four. She was thirty. She came from a good family and she radiated class. The kind of woman who would never look twice at a loser like I was. But she shocked me. She *did* look. We became lovers.''

"And she got pregnant?''

"Yes. But by the time that happened, it was pretty much over between us. It had been 'lust' at first sight, I guess you could say. But it wasn't something that lasted that long.''

"So...she came to you, and told you about the baby?''

"Yeah. She was straight with me. And when she told me, I don't know, something happened inside me." Lucas leaned forward in his chair, as if seeking a clearer view of Heather than the darkness would allow him. "Do you understand? Can you believe what that meant to me? I had nothing. I *was* nothing. And yet she and I had made this baby. And the baby was everything I never was. Hope. A possible future. A chance to start over and make a different kind of life."

"Yes," Heather answered softly. "I do. I understand."

Lucas sat back again, as if her answer had satisfied him. "It seemed so important. That the baby have a chance. I got down on my knees to Candace. I begged her to keep the baby. I promised her, if she'd just have the baby, I'd make something of myself and take full responsibility for the kid within five years."

"And she agreed?"

"Yes. She even married me, so the baby could have my name with no questions asked. But the marriage wasn't much more than a formality. And we went ahead and got a divorce a few years later. Neither of us was the marrying kind, anyway."

He fell silent.

Heather prompted, "And then what happened?"

He shifted in the chair again, then went on. "At first, Candace kept Mark with her. But then gradually, she admitted she just didn't have the time to be a round-the-clock mother. Mark came to live with me. And by that time I'd discovered I had a talent for writing horror."

He actually chuckled then. "Hell. I've always scared people. I figured I might as well get paid for it."

"So what you're saying is, you did it."

"What?"

"Kept your promise. To make something of yourself."

"Yeah. I kept my promise. But the point is, it was all supposed to be for Mark. If it wasn't for Mark, for me swearing I'd get my life together to give my kid a chance, I'd still be living on the road, picking up odd jobs and knowing I'd turned out just like my mean old daddy said I would, nobody with nothing. Mark is the reason for everything I am. Everything I have. I've worked like a dog for ten years to make a secure life for him. And somehow, in the process, I've managed to drop Mark himself completely out of the equation. Which is why I'm sitting here in my stepfather's dark parlor after midnight, hearing my own damn voice over and over in my head, 'Not now, Mark. Later, Mark. Soon, Mark...'"

Heather had that urge again to reach out to him, to touch him. But she controlled it.

And he continued in a hollow voice. "I can't stop thinking the worst. I can't stop thinking that there may never be a *soon*. There may never be a *later*...."

Lucas lapsed into silence, then he told her, "In a day or two, if there are no new leads, they'll start talking about calling off the search. When a kid runs away, there's only so much they can do. Because he could be anywhere. He could be in L.A. In Colorado. New Mexico. Or dead in a ditch somewhere, with his head bashed in."

It was too much. Heather spoke up. "Don't..."

"I thought you wanted me to talk." His tone was mocking now, cold.

"Not like that. It's not good. You can't afford to talk like that. You can't even let yourself *think* like that." Heather stood. "You have to clear your mind, get some sleep."

A harsh sound came from Lucas. "Get some sleep for what?"

''So that when morning comes you'll have the strength to get up and start looking for Mark all over again.''

Lucas rose, then. He came toward her, out of the darkness. When he was close enough to touch her, he stopped. She could feel his gaze moving over her, as he studied her in the pale moonlight from outside.

''How old are you, exactly?''

''Twenty-three.''

''Hell,'' he scoffed. ''Only a kid.''

Heather stiffened as if she'd been slapped. He had just revealed something of himself to her. And he'd gone too far. Now he wanted to withdraw. So he was taunting her, putting her in her place by calling her a child.

But Heather wouldn't be put in her place. She said, ''I was a straight-*A* student in high school, did you know that?''

He made a low, noncommittal sound, as if her history didn't interest him.

She went on anyway, ''I could have had scholarships to some pretty good colleges. But I didn't go after a scholarship. Maybe you could say I had no ambition. Or maybe my idea of success is just different than most people's. Because I always knew what I wanted from life. I wanted to marry Jason Lee and have a family with him, to raise kids here, in this town that I know like I know my own heart.

''And I got what I wanted. The way I looked at it, I had everything. A man I loved. And finally, last fall...'' She hesitated, not really believing what she was about to tell him. And then she heard herself say it, '' ...I had a baby on the way.'' She took in a deep breath. ''But I lost the baby.'' She swallowed, convulsively. ''And you know what happened to the man I loved. He died in an operating room after being trapped in a landslide working on a county road."

The dark room seemed terribly quiet after that. From outside, Heather could suddenly hear the crickets singing and the night birds calling to one another through the trees.

"I'm sorry," Lucas said.

Heather waved a hand, already regretting what she'd just done, wondering what in the world had possessed her to tell him about the baby. So few people knew. She'd only been two months along when she'd miscarried. It had happened just a week before Jason Lee died.

"Heather?" Lucas's voice was gentle. "I really am sorry. I didn't know about the baby."

She swallowed and drew herself up tall. If she had said more than she should have, then the least she could do was make certain he got her point.

"Your apology is accepted. But from now on, respect the fact that I have lived through a rough time, too. And if I was more a girl than a woman before I lost my baby and my husband, you can bet I was totally grown up by the time I watched Jason Lee being lowered into the ground. Don't call me a kid."

"I won't." It was a vow. "Ever again."

"Good, then. I'm satisfied."

He was quiet, looking at her. Then he asked, very softly, "Are you really satisfied?"

She blinked. Even in the darkness, she was close enough to see his eyes. They had changed. They shone soft and deep. All at once, it was last night all over again.

"I don't—"

"Heather. Yes, you do."

She stared at him. Not understanding. Yet knowing all too well.

He said her name again, on an exhalation of breath. And then, slowly and deliberately, he raised his hand.

She smiled at him, then disappeared down the hallway as well.

"He said her name might be an endearment of sorts.

Laughing, she played with her cup, looked down at him.

Chapter Six

Heather let out a small gasp and stepped back before Lucas succeeded in touching her cheek.

"You're afraid," he accused in a rough whisper. "Afraid to let me touch you."

"I . . ." Her mind went blank. She had no idea what to say.

He said pointedly, "*You* touched *me* last night."

She backed up another step, toward the end of the couch.

"Or was that only my imagination?" His voice was heavy with irony.

Heather bit her lip and shook her head.

"Well, then . . ." He waited.

She made herself say something. "I shouldn't have done that. Touched you. Last night."

"Why not?"

"You know why. It's not right."

"Because I'm Jason Lee's brother?"

Her heart was beating deep and fast. She forced herself to answer him. "Yes. Because of Jason Lee. Because of everything."

"Jason Lee is dead."

She only stared at him. What was there to say to that?

He wouldn't let it go. "You still love him, don't you?"

"Yes."

"You're one of those women who thinks she has to be *in* love to *make* love, right?"

He was mocking her again. But she wasn't going to let that sway her. She had her beliefs and she lived by them. "Yes, I am."

"There are other reasons for two people to touch." Now his voice was silky. Soft and tempting. Dangerous.

"What reasons?" she asked in a dazed voice before she could stop herself.

And he told her. "Pleasure. Forgetfulness. Comfort. Making love can soothe pain, help you forget your loneliness for a while."

Heather tried not to think that what he said made a scary kind of sense. "None of those reasons are enough for me."

"They're not?" He sounded sad, then.

She clung to her principles, though she couldn't stop thinking that he was right. She knew loneliness so intimately, since her husband had died. And principles were cold consolation in the deepest part of a solitary night.

"I told you," she said, surprised at how firm her voice sounded. "I had everything. When I let another man close to me, it won't be to settle for less than what I had before."

Lucas let out a long breath. His eyes were so strange, so haunting, so keen. They seemed to see right inside her mind, to know that she wasn't really as steadfast in her conviction as she wanted to be.

In fact, if he were to try to touch her again, she wasn't absolutely certain she would stop him....

But he didn't try.

He only murmured a rueful, "You're right, of course." Then he whispered a gentle good-night and left her standing there.

The next morning was like the morning before. Neither of them mentioned what had occurred in the night.

But the air was thick with tension. Too much had been said to pretend anymore that nothing was going on between them. So they tread cautiously with each other. They avoided eye contact. They spoke only when they had to.

Lucas ate his breakfast quickly and left before dawn. Heather was relieved to see him go. She poured herself a second cup of coffee and sat down at the table again, thinking she'd relax a little before Tawny came and it was time to head over to Lily's and another day of fielding reporters and praying every time the phone rang that it would be good news about Mark.

But she just couldn't sit still. She dumped her coffee down the drain and went upstairs to finish getting ready for work.

The day was a waking nightmare. It crawled by without a single bit of news about Mark. At Lily's there was talk of mountain lions. And how easy it would be for a boy to tumble down an abandoned mine shaft, or fall into the river and drown.

Heather spent her time trying not to listen to the grim chatter, messing up her orders and doing her best not to think about Lucas and the night before. Her shift was over at three. When she walked out onto the street and closed the door of the café behind her, she realized she'd never in her life been so glad to see a workday come to an end. She marched over to the post office and picked up three day's worth of mail, then stopped by the grocery store for some butter and eggs.

But when she reached her house, she almost wished she were back at work. She had to run the gauntlet of news-hungry reporters to get to her own front door. Inside she was greeted by Tawny, who had a list of messages a mile long.

Again, Tawny stayed until Heather had indulged in a nice, long bath and opened all her mail. Then, with Tawny relieved of duty, Heather went over the list of messages to see if there was anything she could handle for Lucas. There wasn't.

As the evening approached, Heather found herself both anticipating and dreading the moment Lucas would walk in the door. She felt pulled in a hundred different directions at once. She was scared to death for Mark. She prayed continuously, a silent litany to God. *Let him be well. Please, God. Return him to us. Let him come back safe....*

She just couldn't relax. She was too keyed up. The phone calls were driving her crazy. But when the phone didn't ring, her memories wouldn't leave her alone.

She relived that awful, shattering moment when they had told her about Jason Lee. She hadn't made it to the hospital in time to be with him. They came out and told her that he had died while they were operating on him.

She kept seeing herself. Standing in that waiting room, feeling utterly alone, though her father and Eden and Grandpa Oggie had all been there.

The doctor had said, "I'm sorry, Mrs. Conley. He didn't make it."

And she had made this strange, low, moaning sound and clutched her middle, where there was no baby. Nothing left. Of her lifelong love....

And now, not even a year later, there was this. Mark vanished. And Lucas, hurting, reaching out to her, needing any comfort she could give him.

And tempting her with so much more.

Lucas returned at twilight, as he had the two previous nights. Heather was waiting for him in the living room.

At the sight of him, she had to school her expression to hide her dismay. He looked like a man who'd already seen his son in the grave.

"Anything?" she asked.

"Nothing. And tomorrow they'll be going to half the number of search teams. They're all starting to believe he must have left the area. No one seems to know where else to look."

Heather had risen from her chair when he came in. Now she sank back into it. "I see."

He looked away. "I want to get cleaned up."

"Of course."

She waited to hand him the endless list of phone messages until he'd washed off the day's dust and changed his clothes.

He quickly scanned the pages. "Nothing urgent here."

"I thought the same thing when I looked them over to see if there were any I could take care of for you."

He looked up from the tablet, a weary approximation of a smile on his haggard face. "You're terrific, you know?"

Her hand itched to reach out, to reassure him with a touch. She clenched it at her side. "I only wish I could do more."

"You've done a lot. More than I deserve, that's for damn sure."

"No..."

"Yes." He raked a hand back through his still-damp hair. "And I'm sorry. About last night. I hope you'll forgive me. I was out of hand—and out of control."

"It's okay," she said, and realized she meant it. Now that he was here, and they were talking honestly, she found she felt better than she had all through the endless, awful day that just passed.

"Thanks," he said, then added low, "You're keeping me sane, you know. Single-handedly. I'm going to owe you for the rest of my miserable life."

His words made a warm glow all through her. But she had to take issue with them. "No. You won't owe me anything. We're family, Lucas. You'd do the same for me. I know you would. This is a terrible time, that's all. And we're getting through it the best we know how."

He made a noise in his throat. "I suppose."

She ordered her mouth to form a bright smile. "But I'll tell you what."

"What?"

"If you really do think you owe me, you can pay me back right now."

He regarded her warily. "How?"

"My stepmother invited us to dinner. Let's go."

He grunted. *"Now?"*

"That's what I said."

"Heather, I don't really feel like—"

"I know you don't. But that's not the point. You said you owed me. Now I'm telling you how to pay me back."

"Heather..."

"You want to see a grown woman beg?"

"Damn it."

"Just say you'll come. It'll be good for you. Please?"

"I just—"

"Say yes."

He sighed. "All right. But I want to take Marnie's letters back to her. I should have done it yesterday, but somehow I didn't get around to it."

"We can stop on the way over to my dad's house."

"And I've got to call Candace."

"It's no problem. Make the call. I'll get someone over here to handle the phone. And then we'll get out of here."

Candace wasn't there, so Lucas left a message that he'd try again in a couple of hours. As soon as Tawny returned, they went out the front door together, muttered "no comment" a few times to the reporters waiting out by the gate, and climbed with some relief into the quiet cocoon of Lucas's big, expensive car.

Marnie came to the door when Regina called her and looked at Heather and Lucas rather warily.

"Thanks," Lucas said and held out the stack of letters. Marnie took them. "It's all right."

There was an awkward moment, where they all just stared at each other, thinking about Mark, not knowing what to say. Then Heather reminded Lucas that they had to be on their way.

Marnie seemed relieved then. "Yeah. See ya."

Heather glanced back over her shoulder as they went up the front walk to the car. The girl was standing in the doorway, watching after them, her stack of letters in her hand.

Jared Jones's rustic cabin lay on the outskirts of North Magdalene, more in the woods than in the town. Jared himself came out to greet them.

"Glad you could make it." He held out his hand to Lucas. "Good to see you, Lucas."

Lucas took the proffered hand. "Jared."

Heather hugged her father, heartened as she always was whenever she saw him. To Heather, Jared Jones represented strength and security. Her father was the kind of man who would protect those he loved at any cost.

For years after Heather's mother had died, Jared had been at war with the world. And people had wondered how his only daughter could have grown up to be such a happy soul when her father was the surliest man in town.

What people didn't understand was that Heather's father had never been angry at her, only at the rest of the world. Heather herself had always felt cherished and secure. To her, it made perfect sense that she'd matured into a woman who trusted other people and was eager to love and be loved.

All Heather had ever wanted, when it came to her dad, was for him to find happiness.

And now he had.

"Come on in," Jared said. "Eden's got dinner on."

The house was warm and smelled of good food. Since baby Sally was already in bed, Heather tiptoed in to see her. She was sleeping on her back, her fat fist in her mouth. Heather bent over her, very carefully, and brushed a kiss on her round cheek.

Since it was already near nine, they sat down to eat as soon as Heather rejoined the others. Eden, who was quite a conversationalist, kept a steady stream of chatter going. She spoke of the progress they were making in rebuilding the Hole in the Wall and the Mercantile Grill, the family-owned bar and restaurant that had burned down last October. And she talked about Sally, who could pull herself to her feet now and say a few basic words.

But Heather realized pretty quickly that dragging Lucas here had been a mistake. The few times Eden delicately broached the subject of Mark's disappearance, Lucas either refused to respond or else redirected the talk to some other topic. He made it very clear he didn't want to speak of his missing son.

And since the one subject on all their minds couldn't be discussed, the dinner was a bleak affair. By the time they'd struggled through coffee and dessert, it was past ten and Heather said maybe it was time that they left.

Lucas was ready at the door almost before the suggestion was out of her mouth.

Heather apologized on the way home for insisting they go out when he wasn't up to dealing with company.

"Don't be sorry," he replied. "It was a nice gesture." He glanced at her. "They look happy. Your father and Eden."

She nodded. "They are." And then she smiled. "Who woulda thought it, huh?"

Lucas chuckled. "Yeah. In fact, I'm beginning to suspect that all the Jones men have gone and settled down for good."

"It's true. There's my dad and Eden. And Uncle Brendan's got Amy. Patrick's found Regina. Sometimes I'm amazed when I think of it. Because when I was a little girl, it seemed like none of them would ever find what they were looking for. Even my uncle Jack was a loner, from what I've heard. But now he's happily married to Aunt Olivia."

Lucas turned onto Heather's street. "I have to believe, if all the Jones boys can end up happy, that *anything* is possible."

Their eyes met once more. Heather knew that his thoughts mirrored hers.

If anything's possible, then maybe we'll still find Mark safe and sound....

When Lucas parked the car in front of the gate, the street looked deserted. The reporters appeared to have taken a break for the night. They made it all the way inside without having to say "no comment" once.

Candace had called in their absence. She had finally managed to clear her calendar and would be flying in to Sacramento the following morning. She planned to rent a car and drive straight to North Magdalene.

"Great," Heather said. "I'll make up the other bedroom for her."

Since it was late, Lucas drove Tawny home. Heather climbed the stairs and spent some time changing sheets and straightening the extra room up there. When that was done, she was ready to go to bed.

She'd heard Lucas return a few minutes before, so she went downstairs once more and said good-night to him. He looked up from a phone conversation to mouth "Sleep well," at her.

As she had been for days now, she was tired but keyed up. Still, she put on her pajamas and climbed into bed.

By then, it was nearing midnight. Downstairs, it was quiet. Heather closed her eyes.

But it was no good. She lay in the darkness as she had the night before, seeing Mark's face, picturing Lucas's haunted eyes—and remembering Jason Lee in his Sunday best, lying in his fine, expensive coffin looking like a stranger on the day that they buried him.

The minutes ticked by until they added up to an hour. It was now one in the morning. And she had to be up before five.

Someone had once told her that you couldn't die from lack of sleep. Eventually, when you got tired enough, you'd simply have to drop off. But personally, Heather was beginning to wonder. She'd gone three days now and maybe slept four hours in all that time.

She had to do something to make herself settle down.

Maybe a glass of warm milk would do it.

With a little moan of frustrated weariness, she climbed from the bed, pulled on her robe and made her way down the stairs to the kitchen.

She didn't realize Lucas was sitting there at the table until she put her hand on the light switch and his voice came out of the dark.

"Don't turn it on."

Heather froze. "Are you all right?"

"Just don't turn it on."

She dropped her hand. "Okay."

He moved a little in the chair, then confessed, "I couldn't sleep. I came out here. To work."

She made out the shape of the laptop computer on the table before him. The screen was dark.

Lucas grunted. "Hell, who do I think I'm kidding? There's no hope for work right now. I really came out here because I couldn't stand being alone with myself in the bedroom." He let out an ugly bark of laughter. "But you know what? It doesn't matter where I am. It's just as bad one place as another. There's no rest and there's no peace."

Heather knew exactly what he meant. She left the doorway and went to stand near him. He was watching her, through the darkness.

How she ached for him. And for herself. And for anyone and everyone awake and suffering in the depths of an endless night.

"What?" He sounded wary. "What is it, Heather?"

She felt so terribly drawn to him. And she longed so to touch him. Before she could catch herself, she reached out and pushed her fingers through his dark hair. The strands were silky, as she'd known they would be, silky and warm.

For a moment, he was very still. And then, slowly, he moved his head to the side, away from her caress.

His eyes shone at her, deep and knowing, through the dark. "Go back to bed, Heather."

She knew he was right. That was what she should do: turn around and go back up the stairs to her room. And her lonely bed.

But she didn't move. She just stood there. His words of the night before came into her mind: *Making love can soothe pain, help you forget your loneliness for a while...*

"Listen." His voice was flat. "You don't want to do anything you'll regret later."

"I won't—"

He cut off her denials. "Don't tell me lies."

She dared to reach out once more, this time laying her hand against his cheek. It was wet, as she had known it would be, with tears he hadn't wanted her to see. He stiffened.

"Don't," she murmured urgently. "Don't back away. Please."

He took in a long breath and slowly released it. Then he was still, allowing her to touch him. She brushed at the tears, oh so gently, with her thumb. "Lucas, I..."

"What?"

"I..." Her throat closed off. She tried again and somehow managed to get the words out. "I don't want to go back to bed alone."

He captured her wrist then. "Why?"

"Oh, Lucas."

"Why?"

"Because...I hurt for you."

"Pity." He made a sound of disgust.

"No. Not pity. Understanding. And not only that. Not only for you. But for me, too. For my pain. And my loneliness. And for all the awful, endless nights alone." She closed her eyes, seeking the words, finding them at last. "I guess in a way, I've been dead myself, since last winter. And with Mark gone, the world seems a grim and dangerous place. But when I touch you, I feel alive again...."

He was still holding her wrist. Her heart seemed to stop as he turned her hand over, carefully pried open her fingers and placed a kiss in the center of her palm. A shiver coursed through her at the touch of his lips and her heart started beating again.

"What about tomorrow?" His breath was warm against her palm. "How will you feel then?"

"I... don't know."

He gently closed her fingers once more. "Go back to bed."

"Oh, please..." she whispered, shameless in her need now. "Try to understand. I... only know how I feel right now. That I want what you said last night. A little comfort. And forgetfulness."

He was silent. Her heart sank. But then he asked, "You're sure?"

"Yes."

Another silence. She felt her nerve deserting her. He was right. She would feel differently, come morning.

But then a miracle happened. He whispered to her, the sound as soft as velvet, through the dark.

"All right. If it's what you want. Come closer, Heather. Come here."

Chapter Seven

Like a woman in a dream, Heather stepped between his knees and touched his tear-wet face again.

Lucas remained perfectly still. She let her hand stray, allowing herself the indulgence of tracing his features, all those sharply cut planes and angles. His eyelids felt so thin and delicate beneath her fingertips. They quivered a little. She stroked them, each in turn, very lightly, until they seemed to relax.

He caught her hand again. His eyes came open, seeking hers. "I don't have anything... for contraception."

"It's all right," she heard herself whisper. "It's my safe time."

Holding her gaze, he brought her fingers to his mouth. His tongue came out.

Heather moaned a little as his tongue touched the pad of her middle finger. He took her finger into his mouth. She moaned again. It was like silk in there. Wet silk. His teeth scraped her knuckle. She felt her knees going wobbly.

She swayed a little before him. He reached out the hand that wasn't holding hers and clasped her waist.

She thought he meant to steady her, but then she understood that he was after something else. He pushed her backward just a little, and brought his knees together. His hand slipped in below the sash of her robe. He traced the inside of her thighs, a quick, brushing, upside-down V. Even through the fabric of her pajamas, it was a stunningly intimate caress. With a small, sharp gasp, she took his meaning and parted her legs.

He pushed the robe away a little and clasped her waist again, urging her forward now.

"Oh," she said, as she found herself sitting on his knees, facing him, her legs apart and her bare feet dangling just above the floor.

He smiled, then. She could see his white teeth and the lifted curve of his mouth. He took both of her hands and put them on his shoulders. She returned his smile, tremulously, feeling steadier now that she had his hard, strong shoulders to hold on to.

And then he put a hand on her throat. "Warm," he said. "Soft."

He began to caress her. He touched each of her earlobes in turn, taking them between his thumb and forefinger, rubbing them and setting off sparks that seemed to trail down into the center of her. He cupped her nape, beneath the fall of her hair, then brought his hand forward again to follow the shape of her jawline. He touched her lips, rubbing them lightly. She smelled her own floral scent on his fingertips.

And then his hand strayed downward. His fingers slid inside her robe again.

She shivered.

He withdrew his hand. "Afraid?" he asked.

She nodded, since she couldn't have spoken right then for the life of her.

He put both hands on her waist for a moment, another steadying gesture. And then he went to work, untying the sash of her robe.

The knot gave way. He pulled the sash free and dropped it to the floor. The robe fell open. He pushed at it, until she slipped her arms out of the sleeves and it, too, was gone.

He started on the buttons of her pajama top. They fell open quickly. Too quickly. Her heart was beating painfully against her ribs, a scared rhythm, but a hungry one, too. Heat flared in the center of her and seemed to pulse outward, so that it felt as if ribbons of flame arrowed down to her toes and out to her fingertips.

He parted the top.

And he said a word that was deep and husky and crude as well.

He touched her nipple, and she felt how hard it was, aching with want.

Heather couldn't bear it. She wrapped her hand around his head and pulled him toward her.

His mouth closed over her breast.

She cried aloud, a needful, famished sound. He kissed one breast and then the other, taking the nipples deep into his mouth, where it was so silky and so wet.

Down inside her, the fire went molten, a slow, delicious, burning ache.

And then he was lifting his head, looking in her eyes. "I've never kissed your lips." He whispered the words tenderly, with a touch of humor and no small amount of wonder.

Gently, carefully, he leaned forward until his mouth touched hers. Briefly he brushed her lips. He pulled back, then kissed her, quickly and softly, once more.

And then he wrapped his hard arms around her and pulled her up tight against him. Her eyes widened. She could feel him intimately, even through their clothing.

His mouth found hers.

It was a long, deep, brazenly carnal kiss. In her whole life, Heather had never known its like. It went on and on, as his hands roamed her back in smooth, knowing strokes. She never, ever wanted it to stop.

But at last, he pulled back. "Wrap your legs around me," he said as he stood. Heather did as he bid her. He carried her swiftly through the dining room and into the downstairs bedroom.

Once there, he lowered her to the bed. Then he went to the windows and pulled back both the curtains. Starlight bathed the room in its faint, silvery glow.

He turned to her, a silhouette against the night. Very quickly, he removed all of his clothes and dropped them on the chair in the corner.

When he was naked, he came to her, reached for her and swiftly slid away the pajama top and the bottoms, too.

Then he lay down on the bed with her, in the silvery light. He pressed his hard, lean body against her soft one. And he stroked her—long, arousing caresses that made her whimper in surrender long before he rose above her, parted her legs and settled himself between them.

She moaned as he entered her. He slid in very deep.

The feeling of having him there was so good, so right, that tears filled her eyes and overflowed, running down the sides of her face, into her tangled hair. She moved with him, by instinct it seemed, as if she'd been born to do this act with this man.

And she thought, in a far-off sort of way, of her family, of the deep, dark streak within all of her grandfather's sons. Hell-raisers, all of them. Her uncles and her father. It took each of them so long to make their peace with life.

And she herself, so different, she'd believed, from the rest of them. Born happy. And living happy. Marrying a man of light and goodness, settling down at nineteen, having neatly escaped the dangerous darkness that ran in her blood.

Or so she'd thought. Until recently. Until she lost everything.

And now there was tonight.

She'd stumbled upon fulfillment. In this time of fear and sorrow. Here, in the darkness, as it never should have happened. Yet it *was* happening.

A dark miracle, this night. It was lifting her outside herself, for the first time in so long. So that what her mind kept whispering was wrong, was somehow good and right—and so utterly, unbelievably sweet.

Lucas pushed in deep. Heather moaned.

"Come with me." It was a command. And a challenge. And a sweet, beguiling taunt.

She looked up at him. There was only one answer. "Yes, Lucas. Anything. Anything you want . . ."

And he moved faster, deeper, on and on. She went with him, wrapping her legs around him, holding him to her so that what they shared became a passing back and forth of energy, white-hot—and expanding to encompass all the earth.

She cried out. And so did he. They both stiffened, pressed tight together.

And then, with a long, shared sigh, their straining bodies went limp in tandem.

Lucas didn't withdraw, but held her close, rolling a little so they lay facing each other on the rumpled chenille spread. One of the windows was open partway and a gentle night breeze blew the gauzy undercurtains, cooling the sweat of their passion and making Heather shiver a little.

"Cold?"

"Not very. It'll pass."

His hand strayed up, to smooth her hair off her cheek. She knew he felt the wetness of her tears, though he said nothing about it.

She tucked her head beneath his chin and stroked the sleek muscles over his ribs, wondering idly how his body could be so hard and fine when he sat at a chair for a living, inventing awful tales that Linda Lou Beardsly couldn't make herself stop reading.

He murmured, "Could you sleep now?"

She nodded against his throat. "Yes, I think so."

"So could I," he said. "But I don't want to sleep."

She knew exactly what he meant. This was their time, this night, this moment. The world was a perilous place. Who could say what the morning would bring?

He slipped out of her then. She made a small sound of disappointment at the loss.

But he quickly put his hand there, at her feminine heart. She gasped.

He said, "Yes." And his hand began to move.

Heather responded mindlessly, raising her hips to give him better access.

"Yes," he said again. She moaned. His hand went on doing those shocking, wonderful things.

He whispered to her, "I want to touch all of you. To know every inch of you. I want to turn you inside out, between now and morning. And I will...."

* * *

They did sleep, hours later.

And Heather was the first to wake, not long before dawn. She woke smiling, because right then all she felt was a warm glow of satisfied contentment. She looked over and saw Lucas sleeping beside her.

He lay on his stomach, one hand flung out and the other under his head. The curtains were still open, letting in enough light that she could see him fairly clearly. He was very pleasing to look at, Heather decided. So she stared at him rather shamelessly for a time, admiring his hard buttocks and sculpted back, his lean, beautifully shaped legs and feet. And she blushed a little, thinking of the things he had done to her, the things she had begged him to do.

But soon enough he groaned and stirred and opened an eye. " 'Lo."

"Hello."

"What time is it?"

She glanced over her shoulder at the clock on the nightstand by her side of the bed. "Almost five."

"God." With another groan, he rolled to his back and sat up. "Back to real life." He reached across her and flicked on the lamp.

"Oh!" Heather blinked at the sudden brightness, and put her hand over her eyes.

"What is it?" Lucas asked.

"Nothing. Just the light. It surprised me, that's all."

"Shall I turn it off again?"

"No. No, of course not." She made herself lower her shielding hand.

But it wasn't easy. For now all the soft shadows had hard edges. And the full impact of what she and this man had done in the night seemed to be bearing down on her like a runaway train.

"Heather."

She clutched the sheet close against her breasts and looked at him, a look she tried to make bright and alert. "Hmm?"

"Are you all right?"

She nodded, biting her lip, wondering where her pajamas had ended up. "I want to take a quick shower and then—"

"Heather."

"I . . . what?"

He touched her face then, trapping a stray lock of hair with his finger and guiding it behind her ear. "I smell regret."

He was right, of course. Daylight was coming. Real life, as he had said. She didn't want to regret what they had done. It had been beautiful.

But in the bright light of day, she knew what she would think about it.

Yes, it had been beautiful. It had helped them both survive a night that otherwise would have been close to unbearable.

But it had still been wrong.

His hand fell away. "I'm right, aren't I?" His voice was gruff.

Heather didn't know what to say to him. And there wasn't really time now to talk about it, anyway. "Look. We should get moving, don't you think? The search crews always get started right at dawn."

"We're going to talk about this."

"Not now."

"All right. Tonight."

She gestured with her hand, a futile movement. "Sure. Over dinner. When your ex-wife is here."

"What are you getting at? Candace and I are Mark's parents, but that's all. There's nothing else between us anymore."

"I know that. I understand that."

"Then believe me. She'll leave us alone if we want to be alone."

He was very close to her, virtually backing her against the headboard. The scent of him beguiled her. He looked at her earnestly. And he didn't appear quite so haggard as he had last night. That doomed, dead look was gone from his eyes.

Had what they'd shared done that for him?

"Lucas, I . . ."

"What?"

"This is all just so . . . confusing to me."

"You weren't confused last night."

"I know."

"Then what's the matter now?"

She raked her tangled hair back with her fingers. She kept remembering the things they'd done. The things she had felt. She'd never felt like that before.

Not with her own husband. Not with Jason Lee.

And that seemed a horrible admission to make. A betrayal, in a way, of all that Jason Lee had been to her and of the love that was supposed to have lasted both of them a lifetime.

"Heather?"

She blinked, and came back to herself. "Yes? What is it?"

Lucas pulled away, enough that she no longer felt trapped by his nearness. "Look." His eyes were hooded once again, his tone reserved. "You're right. There's too damn much to worry about now. We'll let it be."

Relief swept through her—followed by a strange, sad wave of regret.

He went on, "And you're right about the search crews, too. We'd better get up and get going."

She nodded, eager to agree with him, eager to put more distance between the two of them. "Yes, yes, we should."

He rolled off the bed on his side and scooped his clothes from the chair. "I'll hit the shower."

She looked away from his slender, sculpted nakedness. "Me, too."

He turned and left for the bathroom.

The minute he was out the door, Heather jumped from the bed and scrambled around on the floor until she found her pajamas. She pulled them on swiftly, ran to the kitchen to collect her robe and then headed for the stairs to her own room.

After she was showered and the smell of their lovemaking no longer clung to her, Heather began to feel marginally better about everything. And once she had her clothes on, she felt better still.

She and Lucas were two single people. No one had been hurt. It had been . . . one of those things that happen. And it had been beautiful. And it would never happen again. That was all.

Heather brushed on blusher and a little mascara and tackled her hair with the curling iron. Then she rushed down the stairs to throw some breakfast together.

Lucas was already in the kitchen when she got there. He had the coffee started and was pulling a carton of eggs from the refrigerator.

He turned when he heard her come in and held out the eggs. "Scrambled easy. Good enough?"

And something happened deep inside her. Something moved and tightened and yearned.

Oh, no, she thought, *this can't be. It was only supposed to be for last night. Now we go back to our real lives, to who we really are....*

But her silent admonitions to herself did no good. All she wanted to do was rush to him and press her body against his. To lift her mouth eagerly for a warm, welcoming good-morning kiss.

"Right?" he was asking her.

She ordered her foolish mind to remember the question. It was about the eggs. About how she liked her eggs.

"Yes, scrambled easy," she managed to croak. "That's just fine."

And right then the phone rang. Lucas was closest to it, so he shut the refrigerator door and turned to pick it up.

"Yes?" he said. "Hey, no problem." Then, after a moment, "Yeah. Come right over." He hung up.

"Well?" Heather asked.

Lucas turned and leaned on the counter. "That was Jack. He says he's been thinking. He's got a theory he wants to run by us."

"About Mark?"

"Yes. About Mark."

Heather's heart lifted. Before he found his family in North Magdalene and settled down with Olivia Larrabee, Heather's uncle Jack had been a crack detective, famous for his tracking skills. If Uncle Jack had a theory about where to look for Mark, then Heather couldn't wait to hear it.

"You said you wanted to be in on whatever I came up with," Jack told Lucas twenty minutes later when he sat at Heather's breakfast table with a cup of coffee steaming in front of him. "So I've come to you with this before doing any follow-up at all."

"I appreciate it," Lucas said.

"It's just a theory," Jack warned.

"So let's have it."

Jack leaned his elbows on the table and wrapped both hands around his coffee cup. "The way I see it, Mark wants to be here, in North Magdalene." Jack shifted and sat back in the chair. "He came all the way here on his own when he first ran away. And then I think it's fair to assume, since we found his knife, that he stayed in the area at least for the first night after that."

"So?"

"So the more I've gone over this thing, the more convinced I am that he didn't take off hitchhiking again. I think he only hit the road in the first place to get here. And now that he *is* here, he hasn't left."

"But if he's hiding, then where?"

"I don't know where. But I do believe we would have found a sign or two of him beyond the Swiss army knife if he was still on his own with this thing."

"Someone's helping him, someone's shown him a good place to hide."

"Exactly."

"But who? We questioned everyone in town and got nowhere."

Jack sipped from his cup. "Think back. That first day, we searched all of North Magdalene. We questioned every family and we went through every vacant building."

"Right. So?"

"We also talked to the three people we thought might possibly help Mark to hide if he went to them—Oggie Jones, Kenny Riggins and Marnie Jones."

"And?"

"Then, the *next* day, we found the knife in the pipe. Which led us to believe that Mark had spent at least one night on his own, with nobody knowing where he had gone.''

Lucas was catching on. "You think he went to Marnie or Kenny or Oggie after we talked to them, is that it?''

"I'll do better than that. I think he went to Marnie. She's quick and tough and loyal as they come.''

Heather, standing by the counter, thought of Marnie's wary look when they'd given her Mark's letters the night before. And the way the child had stood in the doorway, watching after them, as they walked back to the car.

But Lucas had another idea. "Why not Oggie?'' he suggested. "When we talked to him, he seemed to understand exactly why my son had run away. Isn't it possible he would help Mark to hide, if Mark went to him?''

"No," Jack said. "I rule out my dad.''

"Why?''

"Because he takes being a father too seriously. He might lecture you on your mistakes with Mark from now until doomsday, but he'd never let any man go through three days and nights of living hell thinking his son might be gone for good.'' Jack let out a rueful sigh. "Still. I have been wrong once or twice in my life. So, of course, we'll go talk to him again, if we get nothing from Marnie.''

"What about Kenny?''

"Uh-uh. I don't think so. Kenny's not crafty or tough enough to find Mark a safe place to hide and then manage to keep him in food and water without getting caught. Kenny might be in on the secret. He might be helping out, taking orders. I gathered from the letters Mark wrote Marnie that the three of them were all very tight. But the brains behind this operation is Marnie Jones. She's our girl. I'll bet money on it.''

"Marnie," Lucas murmured. "He went to Marnie Jones.''

Jack nodded. "And he did it *after* we'd questioned her and she'd honestly told us she hadn't seen him. I'll bet she'll have more to tell us now, if we put the pressure on. And I'll bet she's helped Mark to hide somewhere very close to town, maybe even right in town, somewhere we'd already eliminated that first day."

Jack had planned to let Lucas come along with him to Marnie's house, with the firm understanding that Lucas would not interrupt Jack's questioning of Marnie in any way. But when Heather begged to come, too, Jack let out a groan.

"This *is* a damned police investigation, you know, Sunshine."

"I know, Uncle Jack. That's why I promise you, I'll sit in a chair and listen and not say a word."

Uncle Jack grunted and grumbled some more, then he gave in just as Tawny arrived to take care of the place. They went to Marnie's house right away, even though it was barely light outside. Jack drove his sheriff's department four-by-four, with Lucas in the front beside him and Heather in the caged-in back seat.

When they got there, Patrick Jones answered the door. "What the hell's going on?" Patrick demanded of his early-morning visitors. His hair was sleep-rumpled and he was still buttoning up his shirt.

Regina, in a high-necked bathrobe, peered over his shoulder. "Don't leave them standing on the porch, my darling. Invite them in. I'll start the coffee."

"Yeah, right," Patrick grumbled. He stepped back, gesturing Heather and Lucas and Jack inside. "Have a seat." He waved at the couch and chairs in the living room.

They all sat down as Teresa, Marnie's older sister, appeared from the hall, tying the sash of a quilted lavender robe around her waist. "Is everything all right?"

Patrick gave her a sleepy smile, "Your guess is as good as mine, Tessy. C'mon. Sit down."

Teresa padded into the room and sat on the stool of the upright piano that stood against a side wall.

Just then, Regina reappeared. "Coffee in a few minutes."

Patrick grinned sleepily at his wife. "Get over here, Gina."

Regina came and perched beside her husband. He tossed a muscular arm across her shoulders and they shared a quick, intimate smile.

Heather, in a chair across the coffee table, watched her aunt and uncle together and felt that same forbidden yearning she had experienced a little earlier that day, when she entered her kitchen and found Lucas at the refrigerator.

She couldn't help herself. She glanced at Lucas, who was sitting in a chair to her left. He caught the glance. His eyes probed hers.

She quickly looked away.

"Okay, what's up?" Patrick asked Jack.

"Nothing for sure," Jack answered. "But we'd really like a few words with Marnie. Is she here?"

"Sure." Patrick spoke to Teresa. "Go get her, Tessy."

Teresa jumped from the stool and headed off down the hall again.

Patrick asked, rather grimly, "Can you give us a hint or two about what's happening here?"

"Of course," Jack said. He launched into the theory he'd shared with Lucas and Heather a half an hour before. But he only got halfway through it, because Teresa appeared, a frown between her smooth, young brows.

"Marnie's not there," Teresa said. "The window's open wide. And the pajamas that she was wearing last night are in a pile on the floor." The girl wrinkled her nose. "It kind of looks to me like she got dressed and got out quick. I guess she didn't want to talk to you guys."

They went immediately to Kenny Riggins's house. And this time they didn't waste a minute sitting in the living room making idle chitchat.

Kenny was roused from sleep and brought to stand before Deputy Jack Roper.

He shuffled his feet and stared at his bare toes and squirmed and shook. But he held up under Jack's relentless questions for fifteen full minutes.

Then, reluctantly, he raised his head. "You gotta understand. I swore never to tell." There was sweat on his upper lip and his freckles looked bleached out.

Jack's voice, which up until then had been firm and uncompromising, now turned gentle. "I know you did, Kenny. But this can't go on forever, now, can it?"

Kenny wiped the sweat off his upper lip while his lower lip quivered. "Marnie will kill me."

"No, she won't," Jack said evenly. "Think about it. I'll bet all three of you have been wondering, just a little, how to bring this mess to an end."

Kenny gave his toes another long, miserable look. Then he dared to raise his head again. "When I took him a sandwich yesterday, I think Mark was crying. He tried not to let me know, but I think he was, right before I came. Even in that spooky, dark old house, I could see his eyes were red."

In the chair beside Heather, Lucas was sitting very still. Too still. Heather knew that he wanted to grab Kenny and shake him until the boy blurted out where Mark was. But he was containing himself. Barely.

Jack prompted, "Come on, son. It's over. Tell us where Mark is."

There was an awful, hanging moment of silence.

And then Kenny blurted out, "Okay. He's at Marnie's Grandpa Oggie's old house. You know, the one he used to live in before he moved in with Marnie's Aunt Delilah?"

Lucas shifted in his chair. Heather glanced his way in time to see him fling Jack an I-told-you-so look.

"Are you saying that Oggie Jones is in on this?" Jack asked, before Lucas could jump in and scare the boy to death.

Kenny gulped and shook his head. "No, sir. He ain't. He's a *grown-up*. This was only us. The three Mountaineers."

"The what?"

"Uh, you know. Mountaineers. Like Musketeers. One for all and all for one. You know."

Jack solemnly nodded. "I see."

"It's just his house we used is all, because it's kinda off by itself. And Marnie said her grandpa never goes near there, now he's set up all nice and comfy at her Aunt Delilah's place."

Lucas could contain himself no longer. "Are you sure my son is there, at Oggie Jones's house?"

Kenny gulped again. "He was there yesterday, when I took him that sandwich. And Marnie told me last night that she snuck out after dinner to take him some things. Maybe he could have left. I don't know." He glanced rather helplessly from one grown-up to another. "Mark's real smart, you know. He could do anything. I think he's there. I don't know...."

Lucas turned to Jack. "Let's go."

Jack took a moment to confer with Kenny's father. Joshua Riggins promised that Kenny wouldn't be going anywhere for a while. If the boy was needed for more questioning, Jack would know where to find him.

Within minutes of leaving the Riggins place, they swung into the overgrown yard in front of the house where Heather's father had grown up. Jack turned off the engine. The place looked deserted. All the tattered old curtains were closed. Two of the windows to the right of the tiny front porch were broken, their sharp, jagged edges catching and reflecting back the light of the morning sun.

Lucas reached for the door handle.

Jack put his hand on Lucas's arm. "Hold on."

"I'm going in."

"Fine. Go up to the door and knock."

"What?" Lucas stared at Heather's uncle in disbelief.

Jack actually smiled. "Just knock. And wait."

"But what if—"

"Look. I'll go around the back, in case he gets cold feet at the last minute and decides to try to run for it. He's in there, don't worry. I saw the curtains move. And from what Kenny told us, he's ready to deal with you. If you can be reasonable... Can you be reasonable, Lucas?"

"Uncle Jack's right, Lucas." Heather spoke from her seat in the cage behind Lucas. "Mark is in there. I can feel it. But you mustn't go at him harshly. You must give him a chance to come to the door and let you in."

Lucas turned and looked at her, a raking look.

She didn't look away. "Please, Lucas."

Lucas dragged in a breath and lowered his gaze. "Hell. I know you're right. I'll do it your way."

She smiled at him. "You won't regret it."

He met her eyes again. "I hope not."

Jack and Lucas got out of the four-by-four at the same time. Jack circled around behind the house as Lucas mounted the rickety steps to the door. Heather followed more slowly behind Lucas, pausing in the middle of the overgrown front lawn.

At the door, Lucas turned to look at her. Though he was in the shadows of the porch roof and she couldn't really see his eyes, Heather nodded anyway, trying with everything in her to telegraph her support—and her certainty that everything was going to work out all right.

Lucas faced the door again, raised his hand and knocked.

The door swung inward at the touch of his knuckles on the rough wood. Lucas didn't hesitate. He stepped over the threshold and disappeared into the shadows within.

Heather longed more than anything to follow him. But she knew this was something he had to do alone.

Chapter Eight

Lucas moved swiftly out of the small entranceway and into the living area to the right of the door. To his left he could see the kitchen, including the corner of an ancient stove and a rusted Formica-and-steel table. Before him lay the living room.

Outside, the sun was fully risen now. Shafts of buttery brightness shone in between the rips and creases of the ancient curtains, making a crazy quilt of light and darkness across the buckled hardwood floor. In the shafts of sunlight, dust motes whirled and danced.

Deep in the room near the wall to the kitchen, beyond the shifting beams of light, a boy and a girl sat on a badly sprung horsehair sofa. Lucas had to squint through the dazzling patterns of glare and shadow to see them. Both of them seemed to be staring at him through solemn, anxious eyes.

"Mark?" Lucas asked witlessly, unsure for a moment if he really saw what he thought he saw.

The children went on looking at him.

It was Marnie who finally spoke up, just as Lucas's eyes began to adjust to the strange play of light in the room. "I came to warn him you'd be coming for him." Mark nudged her with his elbow, a caution not to incriminate herself further. Marnie had no use for caution. She held her stubborn chin high. "But he wouldn't run away again."

Mark shot her a dark look, then faced Lucas. "It's not her fault, Dad. She's my friend. She did what I asked her to do."

Through the arch to his left, Lucas heard a door open and close. Footsteps crackled across peeled-up linoleum.

Jack Roper appeared. He lounged in the arch for a moment, as Marnie and Mark craned their heads around to look at him. Then Jack signaled to Marnie. "Come on with me."

Marnie scratched that stubborn chin of hers. "You arrestin' me, Uncle Jack?"

Jack strolled over to the sofa and stood looking down at the girl. "Not yet. But don't push me."

Marnie turned to Mark. "You want me to go?"

Mark nodded. "Yeah. You've been the greatest. But there's nothing else you can do for me now."

"You sure?"

"Yeah. I'm okay."

Marnie rose with great dignity. "Maybe you want to handcuff me, Uncle Jack."

"Maybe I want to paddle your behind. But I'll leave that to your parents."

"I don't get paddled," Marnie informed Jack. "Gina doesn't believe in paddling." Marnie's thin shoulders slumped a little. "But she's gonna be real *disappointed* in me. I'm not lookin' forward to that." She shook her tangled little head. "Gina believes in *good works*. You know what I mean? She believes in making beds for old people and washing the cars of people who can't do it themselves. She believes when a person's real sorry she did something, then a person ought to do a lot of good works to show she's not going to do that again. In fact, Uncle Jack, it'd probably be easier on me if you *did* arrest me."

"I'll think about it," Jack promised. "Now come on with me." He caught Lucas's eye. "We'll be in the truck."

Marnie heaved a heartfelt sigh and trudged out behind Jack, leaving Lucas standing there, looking at the son he'd secretly feared he might never see again—and wondering where to begin.

Mark regarded Lucas doubtfully. "You gonna start yelling at me, Dad?"

Lucas's eyes were suddenly grainy and hot. He rubbed them with the heels of his hands. Not far away sat a dingy easy chair with the stuffing erupting from it in several places. Lucas strode over to the chair and dropped into it, stirring up a cloud of greasy-smelling dust.

"Well," Mark prompted, "*are* you?"

"Am I what?"

"Gonna start yelling at me?"

Lucas gave a small, humorless chuckle. "I yelled at you on the phone the other night. And you disappeared. I think maybe I'll have to come up with something better to do than yell."

Mark shifted on the couch. "I didn't know what—" His voice broke over the tears that were trying to push through. He gulped, then tried again. "I didn't know what...to do. You're just so busy all the time, Dad. And then you promised we could come here before your book tour. I really wanted that. Just to come here for a while. But then you broke your promise.''

Lucas felt as if there were a band around his chest, tightening, cutting off his air. "I know. I...screwed up.''

Mark swallowed again. "What...what did you say?''

"I said I screwed up. I lost track of what's important. And I'm sorry.''

"You're *sorry?*'' Mark took in a breath that turned into a sob.

"Yeah.'' Lucas couldn't stay still. He stood. "I'm sorry. Please forgive me, son.''

Mark stared at him, through the sunshine and the shadows and the swirling motes of dust. "Oh, Dad...'' he whispered.

And then he shot off the couch and projected himself straight at Lucas. Lucas grunted at the impact, and then gathered him close, thinking how good he felt, all bones and sharp angles and the dusty puppy-dog smell of a healthy, rather dirty boy.

"Oh, Dad. I'm sorry, too.'' Mark was crying openly now, his words tumbling over each other between sobs. "I feel awful, I do. But I didn't know what else to do, to get you to listen to me.''

"I know, I know....''

"You wouldn't listen. And then you wouldn't bring me here. And I ran to Aunt Heather. And she just called you. So I ran again. I just ran off, across town, in the dark, across the river at a shallow place. And I wandered in the woods. It was scary, Dad.''

"I know, I know....''

"And I hid in this pipe. It was so dark and it was wet in there, and I kept hearing noises. Finally I fell asleep.

"In the morning, I woke up, and I started walking. I just wandered around like some crazy person for a while. And

I realized I'd lost my Swiss army knife. That was bad. That I would lose that. Marnie said they found it, though."

"Yes. Yes, they did."

"Good. I went to Marnie that next night. I waited late, as late as I could stand it and I threw rocks at her window. She climbed down that big tree by the side of the house and she was great. She's the best friend a guy could have, Dad. She tried to tell me about her dad, that she has lots of problems with him, but that she never runs away. She stays and works it out. But I wouldn't listen. I told her if she didn't want to help me, fine. And I started to walk away. I knew the whole time that she wasn't going to let me leave.

"And she didn't. She helped me. She brought me here that night. And she brought me food and blankets and candles and even some books, her and Kenny. And every hour that went by, Dad, all I kept thinking was how I wanted to go back to you. But somehow, going back just kept getting harder to do."

"I know," Lucas said as he hugged Mark close against him. "I understand. I do."

Mark sobbed again. "Oh, Dad..."

Lucas clutched his son tighter still and went on murmuring reassurances, while inside himself he vowed he would not waste this second chance with Mark. Things would be changing in their lives. His work was going to come second to the most important thing: his son.

When Lucas and Mark emerged from the old house, Jack had already radioed ahead to say that Mark had been found.

Heather stood by the four-by-four, waiting. At the sight of Mark, she let out a joyful, silly shout and started running. Mark saw her and ran, too. They met in the middle of the weed-tangled yard, grabbed on to each other and spun around in a circle beneath the bright morning sky.

When they finally let loose of each other, Heather saw that Mark's nose was running and his eyes were red. She gave him one of the tissues she always kept in a back pocket.

"Good to have you back," she said.

He blew his nose. "Good to be back."

Heather glanced up, and caught sight of Lucas, still standing in the shadows of her grandfather's porch. He started down the steps, the movement slow and fluid. Heather waited, staring, not even knowing she was holding her breath, until he was fully in the sun.

She saw his eyes at last, so dark, and yet burning with heat and light. And memories of the forbidden night before assailed her.

She thought of the way his lips had felt on her skin, so warm in the hollow of her neck, of the trail of ebony hair down his solar plexus, and of the smell of him, that was dark and sweet and foreign. Captivating in its very alienness.

Mark tugged on her hand. "Come on. Deputy Roper is ready to go."

Heather made herself breathe. "Yes. Of course."

"We'll ride in back, with Marnie." He glanced at his father, who now stood beside them, but was looking at Heather. "Is that okay, Dad?"

"All right," Lucas said. "That's fine."

Jack drove Marnie home first, leaving her in the able hands of her stepmother. Regina hugged the girl fiercely and then listened while Jack explained what her stepdaughter had been up to. When she'd heard it all, Regina promised Jack that Marnie would think twice before ever doing anything like that again.

Marnie shook her head. "See what I mean, Uncle Jack? I prob'ly woulda been better off in jail."

Jack drove the rest of them to the sheriff's station next, where he filled out the final report on Mark's disappearance. While they were there, Mark talked to a lady from child protective services, who filled out another report that said Mark and his father seemed perfectly capable of resolving their family problems by themselves.

After all the paperwork was taken care of, Jack drove them back to Heather's house, where the reporters were already gathering.

"Good luck getting through that," Jack said, when he pulled up on the street and they saw the crowd they were going to have to plow through to get to the gate.

Lucas spoke then. "Thanks."

"Hey, it's my job—and you and Mark are family to Sunshine. No thanks are required."

"Maybe not. But I offered a reward, did you know that?"

"I think I read about that. A million bucks, right?"

"Right."

Jack threw back his big, blond head and laughed at the roof of his four-by-four. "Well, hell. What do you know?"

"The money's yours, Jack."

Jack grunted. "Tell you what. You keep it. I've got everything a man could want already. A home, a job. And a rich wife."

Mark spoke up from the cage in the back where he was sitting with Heather, "He's not kidding, Dad. His wife's dad is rich. Richer than you, even."

Lucas chuckled. "Good for you, Jack. But the money's still yours."

"Naw. You pay back the county for the cost of the search."

"You know I will."

"And, if you're still in a giving mood after you've handled *that* bill, then give some to the volunteer fire department and maybe a little to the community church."

Lucas studied Jack for a long moment. "You're serious, aren't you?"

Jack nodded. "Serious as a forest fire."

"Okay, then. If that's how you want it."

The two men shook hands.

Then Heather, Mark and Lucas climbed out of the four-by-four and elbowed their way through the crowd of reporters to the front gate.

Inside, Lucas thanked Tawny and gave her two hundred-dollar bills. Blushing and stammering with pleasure and gratitude, Tawny left her post by the phone for the last time.

After that, Mark headed straight for the shower. Heather went to call Lily, who yelled for a minute and then congratulated her on Mark's safe return.

"But this place is a zoo," Lily complained. "I need you now. Sooner. I needed you at six-thirty, when you were supposed to have been here."

"It's been a crazy time, Lil."

"I know. Get over here."

"I'll be there as soon as I can. Cross my heart."

"A half hour, then. No more."

Heather agreed she could make it by then.

When she turned from hanging up the phone, Lucas was standing there. The sight of him surprised her a little and she gave a startled, "Oh!"

He smiled. Heather thought he looked ten years younger than he had last night. The deep furrows in his face and the drawn, haunted look had disappeared.

A miracle had happened. Mark was back. Heather's endless prayers had been answered. The world was as it should be once again.

Lucas kidded her, "Lily's on the warpath, right? She wants you at work pronto, or else."

Heather let out a put-upon groan. "She granted me a half hour."

"Such a generous soul."

"There's no one else like her."

"Ain't that the truth."

They were smiling together over the meaningless banter. And then his gaze moved.

It found her mouth.

At the same moment, he took a step toward her, only one. But the movement was catlike. Predatory.

And last night came back to her again. Full force. All of it. From the moment she had entered this very room and found him sitting in the dark, until that final sigh when she had dropped at last into a brief, sweet oblivion born of satisfied exhaustion.

"Don't..." she whispered, the word too weak to make much sound.

But he didn't listen. He took another step.

The counter was at her back. She pressed herself against it, while down inside her, hot flowers of need were budding, blooming, opening wide.

"Oh, don't..."

He stopped, not more than a foot away. His eyes burned her. "Candace will be here in an hour or two. When she sees Mark's all right, she'll hug him and kiss him and tell him how much he's grown. She'll make him promise never,

ever to run away again. Then she'll take him out for ice cream—at your precious Lily's, since it's the only game in town—and she'll leave before nightfall. Mark and I will be leaving, too. Unless..."

She stared up at him, hungry for him, bewildered at these words he was saying. "But I don't—"

He repeated, "Unless."

"I...what?"

"Mark and I will leave right after Candace does, unless you give me a reason to stay on."

What reason? she almost asked. But she held it back. She knew exactly what he wanted from her. And, right at that moment, she wanted nothing so much as to give him what he wanted.

She yearned to throw herself into his arms, to sigh, *Yes, Lucas. Stay with me. Make love to me. All through this night. And the next night. And the night after that...*

But how could she say such an impossible thing? Nothing good could come of it. She was a small-town girl who waited tables to make ends meet, a woman who wanted the most basic things: a man to stand beside her and children to raise.

Lucas was an international celebrity. His name was a household word. He moved in the kinds of circles Heather read about in the dog-eared magazines at Santino's Barber, Beauty and Variety while she was waiting to get her monthly cut and blow-dry.

What was between them now was purely physical. Consuming. Delicious. And as fleeting as the tiny bloodred wild roses that bloomed on the trail up to Sweetbriar Summit in the early days of June.

It would not last. They had so little in common. And he had told her two nights before that he was not the marrying kind.

And beyond that, in the deepest part of her heart, there remained Jason Lee, and the promise she'd made him, when they weren't much older than Marnie and Mark.

"*Aw, Heather. I can't picture a world without you and me together. Do you know what I mean?*"

"*Yes, Jason Lee. I know exactly. I do.*"

"*So then, are you saying that we'll always be together, you and me?*"

"*Yes, Jason Lee. You know we will. For always and forever. Until the end of time....*"

Heather knew that Jason Lee's dying changed the meaning of forever. She knew it in her mind. But her heart hadn't quite caught on yet.

"All right," Lucas muttered, though Heather hadn't said a word.

She drew herself up and made herself regard him levelly. "All right, what?"

"I see your answer in your eyes. Mark and I will be out of here before you get home from work this afternoon."

Chapter Nine

Heather said a fond goodbye to Mark before she left for work. The boy came into the living room, grabbed her and hugged her tight.

"I'll miss you, Aunt Heather."

"And I'll miss you."

He gazed up at her, smiling. Heather smiled back, thinking that he seemed subdued and honestly contrite about all the trouble he'd caused.

But also, beneath the regret, there was a quiet contentment. He'd gone about it all wrong, but in the end he'd found what he so desperately needed: his father.

As Lucas had predicted, Mark appeared at Lily's with his mother in the early afternoon. Candace, who was tall and model slim with ash blond hair, bought her son a huge banana split and watched, wearing an expression of bemused wonderment, as he ate every bit of it. She thanked

Heather profusely for all she'd done. Heather replied that she'd been glad to help, then pointed out that she'd readied the spare room upstairs so that Candace could spend the night. But Candace said she had to get back to Phoenix right away.

Mark showed Heather his Swiss army knife before he left. "Deputy Jack gave it back to me. I'll be more careful of it from now on."

"See that you are."

He threw his arms around her in a final hug, causing all the regulars at the café to burst into spontaneous applause.

At a little after five, Lily told Heather she could call it quits for the day. Heather walked home, where the first thing she noticed was that Lucas's big car no longer waited beneath the dappled shade of the locust tree in front of the house. No reporters milled on the sidewalk either, jostling each other in their eagerness to hear any tiny tidbit Heather might be willing to toss them concerning the Shadowmaster and his son. Heather trudged up her front walk unobstructed, let herself in the door and confronted an empty house.

It was awful, that emptiness. It was lonely and sad and completely forlorn. It was the emptiness she'd learned to live with—until the past few tumultuous days.

Now, somehow, she was going to have to learn to live with it all over again.

In the kitchen, Heather saw that Lucas had left her the answering machine, which was blinking as usual. On the table, between the salt and pepper shakers, a white envelope had been propped up, bearing her name.

Heather played the few messages first. They were for Lucas, from three different reporters. None of them seemed that important, so she cleared the machine and forgot about them.

Next, she sat at the table and confronted the envelope. Her heart thudded painfully in her chest. If he had dared to leave her money, she didn't know what she would do. She was born a Jones, after all. And a Jones had pride, if nothing else.

She ripped the thing open with stiff, awkward fingers.

A check fell out, along with a note in Lucas's bold, slanting scrawl.

This is to cover the phone bill—and nothing else. Believe me, if I was going to try to pay you off, it would have been a hell of a lot more money than this. So be smart. Don't send it back. And don't tear it up. Cash it. If you don't, you'll have to deal with me.

And I meant what I said that last night. You did keep me sane while Mark was gone.

My brother was a lucky man.

Lucas

Like the fool that she knew she was, Heather ran the pad of her forefinger over his name, as if it might still hold a little of him in the dry scratch of ink. She was smiling, though tears burned her throat.

He'd understood her exactly. He'd known she couldn't have borne it if he'd tried to give her money. So he hadn't; he'd only taken care of the phone bill as he'd always said he would. She was ridiculously glad.

After a while, Heather got up and put the check in her purse to deposit the next time she went to the bank. She tossed the note in a wastebasket in the living room, then went to have a bath. When she was through with the bath, she put on clean clothes and made dinner, then watched some TV. She went to bed at nine.

But at midnight, she crept from her bed and tiptoed downstairs to the dark living room. She rescued the crumpled note from the wastebasket, smoothed it out and took it back upstairs, where she folded it carefully and tucked it inside the purple velvet jewelry case that had once been her mother's.

Then she climbed back into bed, curled up on her side and managed, eventually, to drop off to sleep.

In the weeks that followed, the nights were the worst. Heather would lie staring at the ceiling, longing for sleep and instead reliving the few forbidden hours she and Lucas had shared—experiencing all over again the drugging heat of his lips against her mouth, recalling the precise taste and texture of his skin, remembering the way his hands had felt on her breasts.

Days were more manageable. She kept them full of activity so she had no time for loneliness or regrets.

Whenever there was a community project to help out with, Heather was there. She threw herself into the final preparations for the community church's Fourth of July picnic in Sweetbriar Park. She baked pies for the Pioneer Daughters' bake sale and manned one of the tables for the Volunteer Fire Department's annual rummage sale. And every day after work, she'd put on old jeans and a tattered shirt and head back to Main Street, where the Mercantile Grill and the Hole in the Wall Tavern, burned out nine months before, were under reconstruction.

Her uncle Patrick was overseeing the job. They'd raised the walls of the Hole in the Wall. The Mercantile Grill, which was made of brick and thus had merely been gutted rather than burned to the ground, now boasted a new roof.

Heather knew how to handle a hammer, so she often pitched in, nailing down floorboards or even helping to fetch and carry if that was all that was needed that day.

She felt better, she kept telling herself. The vivid carnal memories haunted her a little less frequently. Every day dawned just a little brighter, she was sure of it. She was managing it, getting over this new siege of loneliness—getting over her single night with Lucas Drury. She reminded herself constantly that she would forget all about him soon.

Until the third week in July, when she could no longer deny the fact that her period hadn't come.

Heather went two weeks past her due date before she let herself even think that she might be carrying Lucas's child. By then, her breasts felt swollen and tender. And she'd developed a sensitive, queasy stomach.

On her day off, she drove to Grass Valley and bought a test, which she took the minute she got home again.

It was positive.

Heather couldn't believe it, even with all the physical signs. The whole time she'd been married to Jason Lee, they had never used anything. They'd wanted a houseful of babies. But in four years of marriage, she'd only managed to get pregnant that one time. She'd assumed she wasn't very fertile. And that night with Lucas had been during her safe time. Or so she had thought.

No. That was a lie. She hadn't thought at all, not really. There had been Lucas's need. And her need. And the awful, aching necessity to find oblivion from the possibility that Mark might be gone forever.

She had behaved like an irresponsible fool. And now she was pregnant, with absolutely no idea what she was going to do.

It was too much. One catastrophe too many.

Heather couldn't cope. She went numb. She moved through the next few weeks in a daze.

And people noticed. How could they help it? Heather just wasn't her usual sunshiny self. She rarely smiled and her skin seemed to lose its luster.

She did her job by rote, saved only because she'd worked at Lily's so long that half the time she could just *look* at her customers and know what they were going to order.

And if she didn't know, it didn't matter. She gave them what she thought they *ought* to order—and if they complained, she didn't hear them anyway. She was lost in her numbness.

"What in the world is wrong with you, dear?" Nellie Anderson sniffed on a Friday afternoon three weeks after Heather had taken the pregnancy test. "I asked for extra mayo. I always ask for extra mayo. But lately, you just never bring it. My goodness, are you ill?"

"No, Mrs. Anderson. I'm fine. And your mustard is coming right up."

Then later, Rocky Collins started in on her. "Sunshine, what is it?" he complained in that sad voice of his that was always slurred by lunchtime from one too many shots of the tequila he loved. "You ain't smilin'. What's the world comin' to if Sunshine ain't got a smile?"

"It's nothing, Rocky. I'm fine."

"Aw, no you ain't."

And Tim Brown had to toss his two cents in. "Yeah, come off it, Sunshine, give us a smile."

"Yeah, what's up with you, anyway?" Roger McCleb, who made up in brawn what he lacked in brains, demanded. "You look like somethin' the cat dug up in the yard and drug in the house and left on the rug. Somethin' still wigglin' just a little, but not much. As good as dead, is what I'm sayin', covered in blood and dirt, with its guts spillin' out. Somethin' that's just lyin' there, barely breathin', starin' with eyes that can't see anymore." Roger wrapped a beefy hand around his own massive throat and imitated the final gasps of the pitiful creature he'd just described.

Rocky turned to gaze at Roger through unfocused eyes. "God, Roger. That's really disgusting."

And Roger lifted his beer and saluted them all with it. "Thank you very much." He drank, then put his beer down hard on the counter and flexed one of his biceps slowly and meaningfully. "So this is a warnin', Sunshine. You start smilin', or else . . ."

"Aw, leave 'er alone," Rocky whined.

"Yeah, back off, Roger," Tim Brown commanded. Then he braced his hands on the counter and craned toward Heather, squinting. "You sure you're all right?"

"I told you, I'm just fine," she said, while inside all she felt was numbness—and the vague longing for her Uncle Patrick to hurry up and get the Hole in the Wall into operation again, so that Rocky, Tim and Roger could go back to hanging out at the bar where they belonged.

About then, Rocky slid off his stool and tottered to the men's room. Heather suspected he planned to enjoy another nip from the flask he kept in his hip pocket while he was back there. Lily's didn't serve hard liquor, and tequila was all Rocky would drink. He'd already paid several visits to the men's room today. Heather knew that she should probably try to get him to eat something when he returned this time.

For years, everyone had counted on her to take care of things like that. To cajole drunks into eating a decent meal. To insist that single men remember their vegetables and children drink their milk.

But Heather just wasn't up to cajoling and insisting lately. It was about all she could do to show up at work on time and deal with getting out the food people actually asked for.

A half an hour later, Eden came in with baby Sally. Sally reached out her arms and Heather took her for a moment.

Heather managed a smile for the plump little darling. And when Sally grinned back and stuck her fingers into Heather's mouth, Heather chuckled.

"Come to dinner," Eden said. "Tonight. Six sharp."

"Oh, Eden…" Sally started squirming. Heather passed her back to her mother. "I don't think so."

"Why not?"

"Well, I've got a million things to do."

"Like what?"

"Well, I—"

"Save the excuses. Be there."

"I—"

"Not another word."

"You're not lookin' good, Sunshine," Jared said. "To tell the truth, we're all a little worried about you."

"I'm all right, Dad, really. Would you pass the bread, please?"

Her father handed her the basket with the rolls in it, then he picked up the gravy boat and shoved it under her nose. "Put some gravy on those potatoes."

Heather shook her head and tried not to breathe in the rich, savory smell. Lately, gravies and sauces made her faintly nauseated. "No, thanks."

"You love gravy."

"Jared," Eden murmured with a tiny shake of her head.

Jared grumbled something unintelligible under his breath, but he did retract the gravy boat.

Heather took a bite of bread and a sip of water. Her father looked at her, grunted in disapproval at her minuscule appetite, and spooned a second helping of mashed potatoes onto his own plate.

"Heather, how about driving down to Grass Valley with me tomorrow?" Eden suggested. "You *are* still off on Saturdays, aren't you?"

"Yes, I'm off," Heather said, watching Sally, in her high chair, eating potatoes with her own baby-size spoon.

Sally shoveled in a bite so big that only a third of it actually made it to her mouth. The rest plopped to the tray in front of her. She looked down. "Uh-oh," she said and dropped her spoon to grab at the fallen hunk of white goo with her hand. She brought the glob quickly to her mouth and shoved it in, smearing half of it across her chin in the process.

"You little barbarian," Eden chided. She wiped Sally's chin, then took her pudgy hand and wrapped it around the spoon. "Use the spoon."

Good-naturedly, Sally did as she was told—until the next bite got away from her.

"Well, what do you say?" Eden asked as she serenely handed her daughter the spoon once again.

Heather took a small bite of her own potatoes and tried to remember what Eden was talking about. "About what?"

Patiently Eden reminded her, "Driving to Grass Valley with me tomorrow. I want to start picking out some things for the bar and restaurant. We'll have lunch, of course. And then Sally needs new p.j.'s. And I thought I'd stop in on the way home for groceries. You know, the usual. We'll shop till we drop."

Heather smiled at Eden to show she appreciated the offer, but she said, "I don't think so. Like I told you today, I've just got a million things to do around the house."

Jared, who was in the process of forking up a second helping of rare roast beef, dropped the beef in disgust. The serving fork clattered against the rim of the platter. "Damn it, Heather. What the hell is the matter with you?"

"Nothing. I—"

"Don't you tell me *nothing*. I know what nothing is— and this ain't it."

"Dad, I—"

"Jared, please—"

"Shut up, Eden," Jared said to his wife. Then he glowered at Heather. "And *you* stop interrupting your elders."

Both women fell silent, except for a pair of resigned sighs. Even baby Sally stopped beating her spoon on her tray and stared at her father with wide, wondering eyes.

Jared blustered on, "Whatever this is, it's got to be stopped. Lately you're lookin' as skinny as a plucked sparrow. And your eyes aren't more than two black holes in your head. You drag around like a dead woman. Everyone in town says so. Now, I know you lost your man last winter. But you were getting through that. This has come on more recently. And I'm not sitting by and watching you fade away to nothing. There's something seriously wrong with you. So I've made an appointment for you Monday with Will Bacon over at the clinic."

Heather gaped at her father, amazed. Jared Jones wasn't a big talker as a rule, and he'd just delivered what practically amounted to a speech.

Jared cleared his throat. "Well. You hear me, Sunshine?"

Heather said nothing. No way was she paying a visit to Will Bacon on Monday. If she did that, Will would find out about the baby. And no one was going to know about her pregnancy until she was good and ready to tell them.

"I said, did you hear me, Sunshine?"

"Yes. I heard you."

"Good. So it's settled, then."

Heather squared her shoulders. "No, Dad. That's not true. It's not settled at all."

Jared did a double take, then barked, "What did you say?"

"I said no." Heather stood. Defying Jared Jones was something best attempted on one's feet. "I won't see Will Bacon."

"I'm your father. You'll do as you're told."

Heather couldn't believe her ears. *"I'll do as I'm told?* What is this? I'm a grown woman, Dad. I've been married and I've buried a husband. You haven't run my life in years. And you're not starting in again now."

"The hell I'm not." Jared shoved back his chair and rose to confront her eye to eye. *"Someone* has to look out for you."

She stood her ground. "I can look out for myself."

Jared let out a loud grunt of disgust, then he balled his napkin and threw it down beside his plate. "You can look out for yourself?" he mocked. "Just look at you. Skinny as a rail, walking around half dead. It can't go on. You'll see Will Bacon."

"I will not."

"Jared," Eden ventured gingerly, "I really don't think laying down ultimatums is the way to settle this problem."

Jared turned to his wife. "Didn't I tell you a minute ago to let me handle this?"

"Actually," Eden said, correcting him too sweetly, " 'shut up' was what you said."

Jared coughed. "I did?"

"Yes."

"Well, whatever I said, what I meant was I'll handle it." He turned on Heather once more. "You'll see Will Bacon if I have to drag you there by the hair."

"No, I will not."

"You will!"

"I will not!"

From her high chair, Sally let out a little cry of distress. Heather and Jared looked at her guiltily, snapped their mouths shut in unison and dropped to their chairs.

Jared carefully picked up his napkin and smoothed it over his knees again. "You're going," he said quietly.

Heather said nothing. She'd do what she had to do when the time came. She bent to grab her own napkin, which had dropped to the floor unheeded when she stood.

Sally made a few questioning, cooing sounds.

"There, honey," Eden murmured. "It's okay now."

Heather folded her hands in her lap and breathed deeply. Her stomach didn't feel too great right at that moment. Pregnancy and shouting matches, evidently, weren't a good combination.

Jared's appetite, however, remained undiminished. He reached over and forked up the slab of roast beef that he'd dropped a few minutes before. Bloody juices dripped from it. Jared plunked the juicy beef on his plate in the middle of a half-congealed puddle of gravy and potatoes. Then he ladled more gravy on top of it all, cut off a big hunk and shoved it into his mouth.

Heather, frozen watching all this in appalled fascination, felt her stomach rise and roll. She knew with stunning certainty that she was about to throw up.

"Heather, are you all right?" Eden asked.

Heather didn't waste time answering. She shot to her feet and ran for the bathroom.

"What the—?" her father began.

"Heather?" her stepmother cried in concern.

But Heather hardly heard them. Every fiber of her being was concentrated on making it to the commode before the contents of her stomach came out her mouth.

She did make it, barely. She shoved the door shut behind her and dropped to the floor, yanking the seat up and out of the way in the nick of time.

She retched, repeatedly. And then she slumped there, in that ignominious position, hugging the cool, white porcelain and waiting to see if there would be more.

Shortly, there *was* more. She submitted to it, riding it out, until she was heaving up nothing.

She heard the door open. She moaned.

"Oh, honey," her stepmother said, crooning.

Heather breathed deeply and moaned again. She heard water running, and then Eden was sitting on the floor beside her, rubbing a cool, moist cloth over her forehead.

"Is it stopping?"

"Yes. I think so."

"Oh, honey," Eden murmured again. And they both waited, Eden stroking the soothing, cool cloth on Heather's forehead and temples, Heather breathing deeply, a little more sure as each second passed that it just might be over—for now, anyway.

"Well?" Eden asked.

Heather nodded. "Yes. I think it's okay. Yes." She moaned. "My mouth tastes so awful. Like something died in there."

"We can take care of that." Eden laid the wet cloth over the rim of the tub. Then she pulled open the door of the cabinet beneath the sink and produced a new toothbrush and a tube of toothpaste. She quickly unwrapped the brush, squirted a line of toothpaste on in, and handed it to Heather.

Heather dragged herself upright, leaned over the sink and brushed the foul taste away. She felt a little better, once she'd rinsed her mouth and wiped it dry.

"Come back down here." Eden, who was still sitting on the floor, held up her arms. "Come on." Heather sank beside her again. Eden gathered her in and cradled her gently, rocking her a little, smoothing her clammy hair back with a tender hand and murmuring soft, wordless, soothing things.

Heather went limp. It felt so good to be held. Lately, the world had seemed such a dangerous, hard-edged place. But now she was surrounded by loving arms. Safe. For the moment, at least.

After a time, Eden asked gently, "How far along are you?"

Heather dragged in a shuddering breath. She should probably lie, she knew it. Deny she was pregnant. Keep her secret, at least for now, when she didn't know how she was going to handle it all yet. But she felt so tired of holding everything in. She needed someone to talk to. Someone she could trust. And she knew Eden was that someone, if anyone was.

After a quick glance at the door to see that it was firmly shut, Heather cuddled close to Eden again and confessed, "About two months." And then she laughed against Eden's soft bosom. "It's so pitiful. I thought I wasn't very fertile, you know? We, um, didn't use anything. It was only one night. And it was my safe time. But I guess no time is really safe, is it?"

Eden went on gently rocking her. "No. No, it's not."

"Oh, Eden. I just don't know what to do. A baby. It was what I longed for. But not exactly this way."

"It's all right. We'll work it out," Eden reassured her. "Have you decided what you want to do?"

"Only that I'm going to keep it. Someway. Somehow."

"Is Lucas Drury the man?"

Heather went still.

Eden chuckled, a sisterly sound, full of love, acceptance and complete understanding. "Hey. Come on. He stayed alone with you during those awful three days when Mark ran away. And that was two months ago, so the timing's perfect, right?"

Heather burrowed closer to Eden. "Mmm."

"Is that a yes?"

"Okay," Heather breathed. "Yes, it was Lucas." Lord, how it hurt just to say his name. "But promise me you won't tell Dad."

Eden didn't hesitate. "Of course not, if that's how you want it."

"It is."

"All right then." She smoothed Heather's hair some more. "Have you told Lucas?"

Heather groaned. "Oh, no. I haven't. I couldn't...."

"Then it's damn sure time *somebody* did."

Both women gasped at the sound of the cold, raspy voice.

Heather sat bolt upright; Eden gave a little cry as she craned her head around.

Jared stood in the doorway, his hand on the knob, his chest thrust out and his booted feet planted wide apart. Heather cursed her own thoughtlessness in not checking to see that the door was locked as well as shut. When he wanted to, Jared Jones could move with all the stealth of a stalking cougar.

"Jared." Eden's voice was weighted with dread. "How long have you been standing there?"

"Long enough to know what's wrong with my little girl—not to mention who the hell's to blame for it."

Both women stared at him, then shared a grim glance. Jared had that look. That ready-for-a-fight look.

It was a look he used to get a lot, back in the days before Eden. But since he'd found love, everyone had thought the street fighter inside him was tamed.

Apparently not.

Heather tried to make her voice sound threatening. "You stay out of this, Dad. It's not your business. It's my problem and I'll handle it myself."

"The hell you say. I'm leaving for Monterey. Right away."

"No!" Heather cried out.

"Jared, please—" Eden began.

But Jared wasn't listening. "I want his address, Heather."

She scoffed. "Forget it. No way."

He glowered at her for a moment, then shrugged. "Fine. I know who else has got it. Marnie. I'll get it out of her." He started to turn.

Heather scrambled to her feet and launched herself at him, managing to snare his arm. "Please, Dad. Don't."

"Let go of me, Heather."

She looked up at her father, pleading with her eyes. But she knew she was wasting her time. Her pleas would do no good.

The best she was going to be able to do was put a condition or two on his going. Because he *would* go. She could only mitigate the disaster he was determined to create.

She agreed, "All right. I'll give you Lucas's address."

"Smart girl."

"Under one condition."

"No conditions."

"Hear me out."

Eden stuck up for Heather. "Yes, Jared. At least listen to what she has to say."

Jared looked at his wife, then nodded briefly at his daughter. "Say it. I don't have all night."

"Take me with you," Heather said.

Jared considered, then told her, "No. If it gets too ugly, it won't be good for you—in your delicate condition, I mean. You already threw up once tonight from yelling too much. You take it easy. I'll handle this. Now let go of my arm."

Heather held on, furious at his idiotic, macho pigheadedness, but knowing her fury would do her no good. She tamped it down, her mind racing a thousand miles a minute to come up with another compromise. She had it. "Then take Grandpa Oggie—and I'll give you the address."

Jared's brows drew together. "What for? Why your grandpa?"

Because if anyone can keep you two from killing each other, it's Grandpa, she thought. But all she said was, "Take him. Please."

Jared considered again and this time he nodded. "Hell. All right. Call the old coot right now."

Eden stood. "I have a better idea. I'll go over to Delilah's and get him. You two wait here."

Jared leveled his suspicious gaze on one woman and then the other. But then at last he grunted, "All right. Go get him."

Eden returned with Oggie twenty minutes later. Jared and Heather were waiting outside for them.

"Good to see you're all finally learnin' who to come to in a crisis," Oggie announced, when Eden stopped the pickup truck in front of the cabin.

"Yeah, right," Jared muttered.

"Now what the hell's the problem?" Oggie inquired.

Jared had baby Sally in his arms. He held her out to Eden as she emerged from the truck. "Didn't you tell him?"

Eden took the child. "I said it was an emergency, that's all. It's Heather's business, after all, Jared."

"What's Heather's business?" Oggie leaned out the passenger window to shout the question so that everyone could hear him. "What is going on?"

"Heather's got herself pregnant and Lucas Drury's to blame," Jared said with his usual tact and finesse.

"Oh, Dad," Heather groaned. She wanted to cry. She wanted to hit her father on the head with a large, blunt object. Unfortunately there wasn't one handy.

Oggie let out a low whistle. "Well, what do you know? That is deep. That is moving."

Heather wondered if her grandfather might be losing it just a little. "What are you talking about, Grandpa?"

"Life. Its mysteries, its wonders."

"This isn't a wonder, Dad," Jared muttered. "It's a baby on the way with no husband in the house."

But Oggie's rheumy eyes were misty. "No. It's another of life's wonders. More than forty years ago, I stole my beloved Bathsheba—God rest her sainted soul—from that dirty weasel, Rory. And now we've come full circle. Rory's son will marry our Sunshine. The ugliness of the past will be put forever to rest."

Jared let out one of his disbelieving grunts. "You haven't got the picture, here, Dad. He hasn't said he'll marry her yet."

"He doesn't even *know* yet," Eden said. "Be fair."

"Fine." Jared shot back the word. "So we'll see to it that he *does* know. And if he doesn't make things right, then whatever happened forty years ago is nothin' to the ugliness I'll be showing you tonight."

Oggie shook his grizzled head. "Always with the negative. We'll see, we'll see."

"Fine. We're outta here." Jared turned to Heather, who'd been standing there slightly stupefied, telling herself that this couldn't really be happening to her. "Sunshine, give me the address."

Heather bestirred herself. "I don't have it with me." She turned for her own car. "Follow me to my house and I'll give it to you there."

At Heather's, Jared and Oggie waited outside. Heather ran up the steps, let herself in the house and rushed to the phone to call Eden.

"Eden, listen. I'm going with them. If Dad won't take me, then I'll follow in my own car. Will you do me a mammoth favor?"

"Anything. Ask."

"Call Lucas for me. I know I ought to do it myself, but I don't have the heart to. Besides, Dad's got the engine running outside, so I don't have the time, either."

"Certainly I'll call him."

"Tell him—oh, I don't know. Tell him that Jared Jones is coming to his house to bust his face in. Maybe he'll get smart and clear out of there. But I doubt it. He's as bullheaded as Dad."

"Don't worry. I'll handle it. Somehow."

"Oh, thank you." She gave Eden the Monterey number. "Tell him we're on the way and say that... Oh, I suppose you'd better tell him about the baby. The mood Dad's in, it won't be a secret for long anyway. Okay?"

"Count on me."

"I do, you know I do."

Heather thanked Eden again, then hung up, stuck her address book into her back pocket and headed out the door.

Chapter Ten

At two in the morning, Jared pulled up to the wrought-iron gate that barred the entrance to Lucas's estate.

"What the hell's this?" Jared growled under his breath.

"It's a gate, Dad," Heather told him.

Jared shot her a surly look. "I don't need any smart-mouth remarks from you."

"Now, now, you two." Oggie chuckled. "Let's not get testy."

Just then, a speaker in the brick wall not far away from the truck crackled to life. "Yes. What is it?" The voice was a woman's voice, very clipped and impatient sounding.

"It's trouble, is what it is," Jared announced. "Open the gate."

"Give me your name, please."

"Jones. Jared Jones. Here to have a little talk with Lucas Drury."

There was a pause, then the voice said, "Yes. All right. Follow the driveway. Go left when it forks, or you'll end up at the stables."

Before them the gate slowly swung back.

Oggie chuckled some more. "Yessiree. Rory's boy did all right by himself, and that's a fact."

"Rory's boy is a dead man," Jared muttered, and drove through the gate, which closed slowly and smoothly behind them. Ahead, the driveway twisted away into darkness.

Heather glanced back and watched the gate disappear as they rounded the first bend in the road. They climbed a gentle incline, winding gradually upward through a forest of high, tangled eucalyptus trees, turning left, as they'd been instructed, when the road forked. After that, the forest of eucalyptus faded away on either side. Now the only trees were twisted Monterey cypress, reaching out their gnarled limbs to the night. Close-growing brush clung to the rocky hillside and Heather could smell the salty wetness of the ocean through Jared's open window. Overhead, the stars seemed few and far between in the black, moonless sky.

They saw the house well before they reached it. It was a sprawling Spanish-style villa, so well lit, even in the middle of the night, that they could make out the fanned designs of the panes beneath the window arches, the diamondlike pattern that embellished the iron railings, and the splashes of vermillion made by climbing roses in bloom. The tires of the pickup crunched on a bed of white pebbles as Jared swung around a huge stone fountain and pulled up twenty feet from the pillars and arches that framed the gargantuan front door.

In the bleak silence after Jared turned off the engine, Heather stared up at the mansion where Lucas lived, dread like a cold block of ice in her stomach. Two powerful urges warred within her. She longed to lay her head down on the dashboard and sob out her shame and frustration—and to shove her father out of the way, jump from the truck and run back down the twisting driveway in the dark.

Anything, *anything* to escape the mortifying, potentially violent scene that lay ahead.

"Er, maybe you oughtta wait in the truck for a few minutes, Sunshine," Jared suggested. "This could be ugly, I'm afraid."

Heather sent him a grim look. "Thanks for thinking of my feelings, Dad. But it's a little late, you know."

"What's gotta be has gotta be," her father said sagely.

"You're enjoying this," Heather accused.

Her father didn't even bother to argue. "A man does what he has to do."

"You don't *have* to do this."

On the other side of Heather, Oggie started chortling again. "Face the facts, girl." He patted her hand with his gnarled old claw. "Your dad's a hooligan at heart, family man or not."

Heather turned on her grandfather. "Thanks, Grandpa," she said with as much sarcasm as she could muster. "I made Dad bring you along to keep trouble from happening, not to stand by and philosophize about it."

"There'll be no trouble," Oggie said. "Wait and see."

"Enough talk," Jared growled. "You coming or not?"

"I'm coming," Heather replied through clenched teeth.

A pained looked crossed her father's craggy face. It was obvious to Heather that, while Jared had no qualms about humiliating her, he wished she wouldn't insist on watching him do it. "You sure?"

"I'm positive."

"Fine. Then don't dawdle." Jared jerked the keys from the ignition, pushed open his door and stepped down, where he suddenly grew chivalrous and held the door open for her.

She didn't move.

He commanded, "Stop foolin' around."

On the other side of Heather, her grandfather had already hauled his old bones to the ground and was waiting by the truck patiently, leaning on his cane.

"You comin', Heather Jane?" her father asked again.

In a totally meaningless gesture of defiance, Heather turned her back on him and slid out on Oggie's side. When her tennis shoes touched the ground, she realized that what she'd thought were pebbles were actually thousands upon thousands of tiny, translucent white shells. She thought it strange and decadent that anyone would choose to pave their driveway with shells.

They went up the tiled tiers of steps and under the wide, triple-arched portico. They rang the bell and the door was drawn back instantly by a thin, aloof-looking woman in her fifties who reminded Heather of upright, unimpeachable Nellie Anderson.

"We're here to see Lucas Drury," Jared announced.

The woman granted them a single, sweeping, thoroughly disapproving glance. "Of course. He's waiting in the atrium. This way."

They left the huge entry hall from which a curving staircase spiraled upward and went down another hall, then turned left and went down another after that. Heather's palms were clammy and it hurt to draw breath. Behind her, her grandfather's cane tapped hollowly on the antique tiles of the floor.

At last, the hall opened up to a two-story, skylit room.

"Holy guacamole," Oggie muttered as he and his son and granddaughter halted in a tight little knot on the edge of the room.

Heather agreed with him. The room was spectacular. It could have graced the palace of some Moorish conqueror. The tiles underfoot shone with a rich patina of age. And there were more tiles, painted with elaborate, flowing designs, that continued halfway up the pure white walls. An arch on the wall opposite them was framed in an intricate plaster relief. Through the arch and an iron gate so splendidly worked that it resembled black lace, a swimming pool could be seen, gleaming and shimmering in the play of strategically placed artificial light, looking both eerie and magical at once.

Overhead, below the five diamond-shaped skylights, an iron chandelier sent out twining arms on which black candle sconces perched, each one tipped in golden light. The rug was off-white, woven in squares. The couches were upholstered in a sky blue fabric. Thick, textured brocades covered most of the chairs.

The majority of the tables and the wood-backed chairs on the edges of the room were fashioned of rich, reddish mahogany. But two chairs stood out from the rest. They were of ebony, with sweeping curved arms, their back-rests carved in an intricate pattern of twining leaves and vines. The pair of black chairs faced each other, one toward the arch with the swimming pool glimmering behind it, one toward the entrance to the hall where Heather, Jared and Oggie stood.

Lucas sat in the chair that faced the hall. He wore black, as he had that first morning, when he came to Heather's house to claim his son. Soft black, Heather thought rather dazedly. Loose black slacks and a shirt that looked like brushed silk. Black shoes that could as well have been slippers. No socks. He sat slouched in the chair, with his feet crossed at the ankles in front of him, his hands folded over his belt. His eyes, as usual, gave nothing away. He regarded Heather, her father and grandfather with a thoroughly infuriating half smile on his chiseled face.

He waved a long-fingered hand. "Thank you, Hilda. Sorry to interrupt your sleep."

The thin, aloof woman nodded and left them. For a moment after that, they all just stared at each other. Heather thought about nightmares. Surely this was one. To be standing here in this Moorish prince's palace at two in the morning, wearing old jeans and a frayed shirt, flanked by her hell-raiser of a father and her wily old grandpa, facing down the dark-haired stranger with whom she'd spent one unforgettable night.

"Drury." Jared broke the silence at last, growling the single word like a pit bull about to pounce.

"Welcome," Lucas said, and rose lazily to his feet.

"This isn't a social call." Jared sneered, stepping forward, putting Heather behind him.

"But we wouldn't mind a little toot, if you got one handy," Oggie said, feinting forward on Heather's other side, leaving her in the rear. "It was a damn long drive out here, and I'm so dry my eyeballs have calcified."

Jared turned on his father. "Knock it off, Dad. You don't need a drink."

"Take it where you can get it, I always say." He grinned at Lucas. "Black Jack, if you're pourin', son."

Still wearing that infuriating half smile, Lucas strode to the wet bar between a pair of stone columns and quickly poured out three fingers of amber liquid from a crystal decanter. Oggie stumped over and took the glass. He raised it high. "Here's to... the next generation."

Heather wished she could sink through the floor. She hated her father, she loathed her dear old grandpa and she wanted to murder Lucas Drury.

He knows, she thought. *He has to know. Eden promised to call him, and Eden always keeps her word.*

Which meant he was stringing all of them along, playing out this absurd farce for everything it was worth.

Her father said, "You want to know why we're here, Lucas Drury?"

Lucas just looked at him, one eyebrow raised in a parody of interest.

Heather jumped forward and grabbed her father's arm. "Let me handle this, Dad."

Jared frowned down at her. "Sunshine, you're out of line."

"What? It's *my* problem. You're the one who's out of line."

Oggie knocked back the rest of his drink and poured another. "She's right, Jared. It *is* her problem. If she's up to it, we should let her handle it."

"I don't need any advice from you, old man."

"Sure, you do," Oggie argued good-naturedly. He lifted his glass. "Always have, always will." He took a big swallow, groaned, sighed and then pulled a cigar from his pocket, which he lovingly began to unwrap.

"How about if you tell me exactly what the problem is," Lucas suggested quietly.

Heather shot him a furious glance. *You know very well what the problem is,* she thought darkly. *And if I had a gun, you'd have a hole in your heart.*

"Heather's knocked up," Jared said.

Heather let go of his arm. "I hate you, Dad," she told him softly.

"Well, it's the truth, isn't it?"

Heather turned away. She looked back down the hall through which they'd come, wishing she were out in the pickup. Or drowned in the ocean. Or lost in the eucalyptus forest on the outskirts of Lucas's estate. Anywhere, *anywhere* but here.

Jared spoke to Lucas. "And we know you're the father."

"I see," Lucas said.

Heather couldn't see his face. She refused to turn and look at him. But his voice had been calm. Now she *knew* that he'd known all along.

"So, you got anything to say for yourself," Jared asked, "before I rearrange your face for you?"

"Yes," Lucas said. "I think Heather and I should be married right away."

Chapter Eleven

Oggie threw back his grizzled head and crowed at the diamond-shaped skylights overhead. "See? What'd I tell you? I said he'd do the right thing!" He picked up the decanter of whiskey again. "This calls for a toast."

"Not so fast, Dad," Jared cautioned. He eyed Lucas warily. "This is no bunk? You'll marry my little girl? You'll take care of her?"

"Yes, I'll marry her."

"When?"

"Immediately. We can leave for Reno right away."

"Well," Jared said, and ran his hand through his graying hair. "Well, what the hell." He turned to Heather, his eyes alight with relief and self-satisfaction. "See there, Sunshine? It's all gonna be all right. I said I'd handle this situation and I have. In spades."

Heather stared at her father, her love for him and her fury at him rising and rolling inside her like angry clouds before a thunderstorm. "Yes, Dad. You really did. You handled it. There's no arguing about that."

Her father actually smiled. "Well, what's a father for, anyway?"

Heather wondered the same thing at the moment, but she didn't say so. Instead she told him, "Now, if you and Grandpa will excuse us, I'd like a few words with Lucas alone."

"Not a good idea." Oggie piped up from his station at the wet bar where he'd found a match and was lighting his cigar. "Get 'em in the car and on their way to Reno, that's my advice."

Heather whipped her head around and pinned him with a glare. "I had you brought along to keep Lucas and Dad from hurting each other. The danger of that has blown right on by. Your advice is not required."

"Whoa, Sunshine." Oggie gestured grandly with his glass of whiskey, causing a good deal of it to slosh over the rim. "I know it ain't been your day. But don't take it out on your poor old grandpa."

Heather gave him a look that should have seared him to a cinder right where he stood. "Then stay out of it."

Oggie contrived to appear chastened. "All right, all right."

Lucas stepped in. "Heather's got a point. She and I do need a few minutes. Why don't you two wait here? Make yourselves comfortable and we'll be right back."

"Okay," Jared said, as if the decision was his to make. "But don't take forever. Dad's right. You two need to get on the road."

"Heather," Lucas said. It was the first time he'd spoken directly to her since she'd entered the room. He and her menfolk had locked up her future—all without asking her once what she thought of the way she was going to be spending the rest of her life. "Come this way." He turned and strode off through a different hall than the one Heather, Oggie and Jared had used.

Though she was the one who'd asked to be alone with him, now it was actually in the offing, she wasn't so sure it was a good idea. But then again, what else could she do? Reluctant but determined, she fell in step behind him.

Lucas entered the second door on the right. He stood waiting for her to precede him, then shut the door behind them both. Heather moved deep into the room, which was like a small living room, with a glass coffee table, two wing chairs and a couch upholstered in a rich brocade of differing shades of green. Through an interior doorway, she could see the corner of a bed with a quilted coverlet, also in swirling shades of green. The walls boasted beautifully framed Japanese prints featuring exotic birds of brilliant plumage twittering away in golden forests of bamboo.

She turned to face him. "Whose rooms are these?"

He was leaning against the closed door, regarding her rather bemusedly. "No one's. It's a guest suite." He gestured at a wing chair. "Have a seat."

"I'll stand."

"Suit yourself."

"I will." She folded her arms beneath her breasts. "Did Eden call you?"

"Yes."

"Did she tell you about—" she had to swallow before she could go on "—the baby?"

"She did."

"I thought so."

He made a *tsking* sound with his tongue, a sound that irritated her no end. "Why did that sound like an accusation?"

"Why do you think? Because it was. You knew what this was all about the whole time, but you had to... string it out, let my father and my grandfather make complete fools of themselves—"

His expression grew more serious. "I let them say what they came to say. And I don't think they were fools."

She looked at him sideways. "Oh, right. Of course you say that now."

"Only because it's the truth. They love you and they want you to get what you deserve."

She let out a low groan at that remark. "Right. Meaning what I deserve is you."

For some reason, he seemed to find that amusing. He chuckled dryly. "What you deserve is a husband, anyway. Someone to take care of you—and the baby."

"Why are you defending them? My father's acted like some crazed wild man in a bad B movie. And up till now it's seemed to me like you couldn't stand my grandfather."

"As I said, I think your father did what he thought was best for you. And as far as your grandfather goes, you're right. I never have thought much of him. But lately...well, let's put it this way—I could get used to him."

Though she was thoroughly exasperated with both Oggie and Jared, hearing Lucas say kind words about them pleased her. She almost allowed herself to give him a smile. But that would have shown weakness, and she was already at enough of a disadvantage in this situation. She schooled her expression into a disapproving frown and kept her mind on the real issue here.

"I don't know why it hasn't occurred to any of you that I am perfectly capable of taking care of myself and the baby as well."

His gaze swept her up and down, intimate and probing. All unwanted, she yearned—and remembered. "You look thin."

"I . . ."

His eyes were so dark. "Maybe you've missed me?"

Her body felt strange. Shimmery. Prickly and very much alive—And she was losing sight of the issue again.

She pulled her shoulders back. "I'm *fine*. Finding out I was pregnant has been pretty hard for me to take, that's all. I have morning sickness, which is to be expected. I'm eating less and I've lost a little weight. A lot of pregnant women lose weight at first. It's perfectly normal."

He studied her some more, while she gritted her teeth and tried to ignore her fluttery heartbeat and the slowly spreading warmth in her belly. When he spoke, he sounded matter-of-fact. "Well, it will probably help if you rest more. Now that you won't be working at Lily's, you'll have more time to—"

She threw up a hand. "Wait a minute. Who says I won't be working at Lily's? I have no intention of quitting work for several months yet."

He remained the soul of reason. "Well, you'll have to quit. You'll be living here. And besides, it's totally unnecessary now for you to hold down some menial job in order to make ends meet."

Where did he come by all that arrogance? she wondered. Had he worked for years to attain it, or did it just come naturally? Though he lived in a castle and wrote books for a living, sometimes he was so much like her father, it scared her. Heather loved her father deeply, but she'd always known she'd never be foolish enough to fall for a man like him. And yet, here she was, on the verge of being married off to one.

"What's going through that mind of yours?"

"Nothing. Except that I like working."

He lifted a shoulder. The flowing fabric of his shirt clung to the sculpted muscles underneath. "Fine. After the baby comes, you can look around for something else to occupy your time. But for now, what's the point? You'll be married to me and money won't be a problem."

Heather dragged in a fortifying breath. It was time he understood that her father and grandfather didn't make her decisions for her. "But that's just it. I'm not *going* to marry you."

For a moment, his face went blank. And then his cruel, sensual mouth lifted at the corners again. "Oh, yes you are. That's already decided."

"Not by me. You and my father and my grandpa think you can railroad me into this—though the good Lord knows why *you* would want to, Lucas. You said yourself you're not a marrying man."

He jumped to his own defense. "Things were different when I said that. Now there's a child involved."

"Right. And there was a child involved when you married Candace, too. Exactly how long did *that* marriage last?"

He didn't reply, only insisted, "This isn't the same as when I married Candace."

"It is from where I'm standing. From here, it looks so much the same, it's scary."

He was quiet, watching her. "What do you want?" he asked softly at last. "Do you want me on my knees? Will that satisfy you?" He moved toward her with that sleek, pantherlike grace that stole her breath and set off alarms all over her body.

She put out a hand. "No. Don't."

"Coward," he said, undeterred, still striding forward. "Come on, be straight."

"I don't—"

"You do." He took her outstretched, warding-off hand by the fingers.

She gasped at the contact, she shivered—and she burned. All the nights since he'd left her came back to her, all the tossing and turning alone in her bed. Mere memory of the things he had done to her had been enough to banish sleep for weeks. And now here he was, touching her, looking at her, promising things with his eyes that should have shocked her, but didn't. Not in the least.

Instead she hungered. And she yearned.

Something had happened to her. It had started that first night, after Mark disappeared, when she'd put her hand against Lucas's cheek. A new woman had been awakened inside her. She was changed, she could no longer deny it. The simple, small-town girl who had married her high school sweetheart and settled down when she was nineteen to lead a quiet, contented life didn't exist anymore.

She could never go back to the person she had been. With the touch of her hand on this man's cheek, she had changed the very direction of her life.

Heather's blood sang in her veins, the tune as old as time, the words so simple.

More. Again. Please. Again....

He lifted her hand to his lips. "I *have* missed you, Heather. I've...remembered. Have you?" She felt his breath across her knuckles, the velvet touch of his mouth, then the searing, but feather-light scrape of his teeth.

She strove for control.

"Lucas, you can't—"

"Yes, I can."

"No, you have to listen. We shouldn't. My father, my grandpa—"

"They won't bother us. They're not fools."

"Maybe not. I don't know. I only know that this isn't what I—"

"I did what you said you wanted. I stayed away from you. But that wasn't really what you wanted, was it?"

"I—"

"Was it?"

The answer came. "No."

"You did miss me."

"I—"

"Say it."

"I... missed you."

"And you want me." He lifted her chin. "Come on. It's not so hard to say. Three little words. I want you."

She tried to shake her head, but found herself nodding instead. "Oh, Lucas..."

"Yes?"

The words came. "I want you...."

That did it. He reached for her.

And she was lost. Gone. Sucked under by the hungry tides of her own desire. She swayed toward him, grasping the soft collar of his shirt just to stay on her feet.

He wrapped both hard arms around her, hauling her up against the lean length of him. His mouth opened over hers. And, oh, he tasted wonderful.

She moaned. His tongue came out and met with hers, burning, consuming, toying with her as it set her afire.

Lost, lost, she thought, and didn't care. Such sweetness could kill, but what a glorious death.

So much better than the gray world she'd been living in recently. She'd been dying for need of him and hadn't even known it. Until now. Until his body was pressed to hers and his mouth was claiming hers and she felt wonderful. She felt reborn. She felt fully, marvelously alive for the first time in two months.

His mouth went roving. His lips blazed a trail of fire along her jaw and down her neck, where he sucked the little pulse there as if he could connect himself to her heartbeat, as if the blood in her body might pass between them, back and forth, a shared river of warm red.

"Say you'll marry me," he breathed hoarsely against her throat. "Say you will. Say it now." His mouth seared up over her jaw again and hovered a breath's distance from hers. "You want me. You missed me. Admit it. You'll marry me."

"Lucas..."

"Just say it. Just say yes."

She grasped his shoulders, her fingers digging in. And somehow, she found the strength to push back from him a little.

He looked down at her, his eyes stormy and hot. "Heather..."

"No. Wait. Listen to me."

"I don't want to listen. It's been too damn long. We'll be married by this time tomorrow. Husband and wife."

"No."

"Don't tell me no. I won't take no."

"Listen. I mean it. Listen to me. We need some time. *I* need some time. Our lives are so different. I don't see how we can make a marriage work."

"We can. We will."

"We have to talk right now, Lucas. Talk. Not...make love."

Somehow that seemed to get through to him. He closed his eyes and took a long breath. Then he very carefully set her away from him. He turned, to the arched window on the wall to his right and pulled the shutter back to look out at the night. "Okay. Talk. Say what you want to say."

His back was to her, but she accepted that. She knew he was listening, just as she knew he was still getting his body under control. Also, it was easier to put her thoughts in order when he wasn't looking right down into her soul with those dark, knowing eyes of his.

She begged him, "Give me two weeks."

He didn't turn. He asked of the night beyond the window, "What do you mean, two weeks?"

"Two weeks for us to...get to know each other better. And during that time, you and Mark will be guests in my house."

"Two weeks," he repeated.

"Yes. Two weeks in North Magdalene."

"And then what?"

"Then we'll decide whether a marriage between us has a prayer of working out."

"I don't need two weeks. I've already decided. I'll marry you right now."

Heather wished—oh, she wished—that she could give him what he wanted. But all they had in common, as far as she could see, was mutual desire and a baby on the way. There had to be more. There had to be love and respect and shared goals to strive for.

She'd had those things once. She'd have them again, or nothing at all.

"I said," he repeated, "I want to marry you right now."

Yes. All right. Whatever you say, a voice deep inside her cried. She tuned it out and answered, "Then, in two weeks, *I'll* decide if I think it can work."

"And if you decide that it *can't?*"

Heather had no idea how to answer that one. "Let's worry about that if it happens."

He continued staring at the darkness beyond the glass, then his shoulders lifted with a sigh. "I'm working on a book now, Heather. I can't spare two weeks away from my office.''

She was ready for that excuse. ''Bring that laptop computer of yours. Bring everything you need. The spare room upstairs is huge. You can set it up any way you want it.''

He looked at her then. ''If you think you have to have two weeks to come to a decision, why not spend it here?''

She gave him a wobbly smile. ''I love North Magdalene, Lucas. I've always thought I'd never leave there. Maybe in two weeks, you'll come to like it a little, too.''

''Don't count on it.''

She kept on smiling. ''I won't. Just keep an open mind, all right?''

''Absolutely.''

''Does that mean I get my two weeks?''

''Do I have a choice?''

''Let's just say you're going to have a heck of a time marrying me if I won't sign the license or say 'I do.' ''

He actually chuckled then. ''You're amazing, you know? A sweet, old-fashioned girl on the outside. Tough as nails underneath.''

''I have to be tough, Lucas. I was born a Jones.''

''I told you not to let her get him alone,'' Oggie grumbled when Heather and Lucas had rejoined the two men in the atrium and outlined their plans.

''What about the wedding?'' Jared insisted. ''Half an hour ago you two were on your way to Reno.''

''We decided we needed more time,'' Heather explained.

Oggie harrumphed and blew a smelly cloud of smoke toward the skylights. ''That's bull.'' He pointed his cigar at Lucas. ''Look at that man. That man knows what he wants and more time ain't it. So watch yourself with this *we* stuff, Sunshine."

Jared broke in. "I keep asking and nobody's answering. What about the *wedding?* When's that gonna be?"

"I don't know yet, Dad."

Jared gaped at her, then tried the kind of tone patient adults use on difficult children. "But, honey, he said he'd marry you right now."

"I know. But *I* won't marry *him* right now. We need time to get to know each other better."

Jared looked from Heather to Lucas and back again, then he said grimly, "You're pregnant. By him. It looks to me like you already know each other better than you should."

"Give it up, Jared," Lucas said wearily. "She's made up her mind. And she's already made it crystal clear that it's her way or no way."

"But she can't—"

"Think again. What are we going to do, put tape on her mouth and have someone else say the vows for her? Forge her name on the marriage license?"

Jared looked at his daughter, considering. "It's a thought."

"Forget it. She wants two weeks, she's got two weeks. Now, I've got plenty of spare rooms, so let's all get some sleep. We'll leave for North Magdalene tomorrow."

The tap on the outer door of his bedroom suite came much later than Lucas had expected it. He rose from his bed, where he'd stretched out fully dressed except for his shoes, and padded on bare feet through the living area to the hall door.

Oggie and Jared were waiting on the other side. He gestured them in. "What took you so long?"

With a little groaning and grunting, Oggie lowered himself into an easy chair. "This house is bigger than the Winchester Mystery house. You got any idea what it's like stumblin' around in one hallway after another, lookin' for someone's room in this joint?"

"Well, all right. But you found it anyway."

"Yeah. And you were smart to put Heather in that other wing. No way she's got even a clue that we're having this little talk."

"Good."

"And now we don't have her to worry about, we can get down to brass tacks here."

"Fine with me."

Jared spoke up then. "We don't like it. Her puttin' you off."

"Neither do I."

Oggie said, "Too much can happen to mess things up when you wait. It's better if you get married, and then work out the problems later."

"I agree."

"So I've decided you'd better get her into bed."

Jared let out a strangled sound at that.

Oggie cast his son a sympathetic look. "I know, son. She's your little girl and you don't like to hear what this man's gonna do with her. But you gotta be real about this. It ain't nothin' he ain't done before."

Jared turned away.

Oggie narrowed his beady black eyes on Lucas once again. "Sunshine is an old-fashioned girl. She's not in the habit of sleepin' with men she's not married to. So if you can get her in bed again right away, and pop the question right afterward, your odds are damn good she'll give in and say yes."

Lucas was silent. He thought Oggie was right, though he had no intention of carrying this subject any further than Oggie had already taken it.

Oggie coughed and cut his eyes away. "Well. We'll leave the question of *how* you get a yes out of her up to you. But we'll count on you to do it. By, say, tomorrow night, when you're all settled in at her house in the bedroom next to hers."

Lucas took that in, thinking about the way she'd held him off only an hour before. "You have a lot of faith in my powers of persuasion."

Oggie shrugged. "There's her doubts. And there's the way the electricity in the air makes my hair stand on end when I'm in the same room with you two. Her doubts ain't got a chance, if you keep after her."

"Fine. I get your point."

"All right. So it's settled, then. By Monday morning, the day after tomorrow—"

"I know when Monday is."

"Good. By Monday, you'll be on your way to Reno. And by Monday night, you and Sunshine will have the same last name."

Chapter Twelve

In spite of the late night she'd had, Heather woke early. She glanced toward the window where a patch of sky could be seen above the shutters. She saw gray. Fog had crept up on the huge house in the final hours before dawn.

Her stomach heaved. Dressed in the underwear she'd slept in, Heather leapt from the bed and sprinted for the bathroom of the suite. She made it to the pink marble commode just in time. She was sick, but not as badly as the night before. Probably because there wasn't much of anything in there to lose.

When it was over, she was surprised to discover that she didn't feel half bad—and she was starved. She found a new toothbrush in a drawer, brushed her teeth, washed her face and combed her hair. Then she put on her T-shirt and jeans and poked her head out of the suite's living room. She saw a maid in a pink polyester uniform pulling linens out of a closet not far away.

"Excuse me. Do you know where everybody is?"

The maid pointed the way to the breakfast room, where Heather found Lucas, Oggie and Jared gathered at a damask-covered buffet table. Lucas turned to look at her when she entered the room, though her sneakers couldn't have made that much noise on the tile floor.

"Good morning."

Her skin tingled. Her cheeks felt warm. "Good morning."

"Come on. Help yourself."

"I will, thanks. I'm starved." Heather joined the men as they helped themselves to eggs and croissants from silver chafing dishes.

While they served themselves, they discussed what they were going to tell Mark about the visit to North Magdalene. Lucas, Jared and Oggie were all for telling the boy that wedding bells would be ringing soon.

But Heather vetoed that idea.

"That decision won't be made for two weeks. There is no reason to turn his whole life upside-down quite yet."

Heather intercepted the covert look that passed between her father and her grandpa. She didn't like it. She knew it meant they must still be trying to come up with a way to force her into marriage immediately. And she knew her grandpa's wily ways.

Well, let them do their worst. She wasn't going to change her mind. She and Lucas needed the time she'd insisted on, and she was determined to see that they got it.

Lucas chose a slice of smoked salmon. "Mark would love it if we were married. You know that damn well."

Heather took a single croissant and turned her head to look at him. A little arrow of liquid fire shot right down to the core of her when their eyes connected.

Somehow, she managed to speak firmly anyway. "Fine, then. We won't get his hopes up. We'll let him believe it's a vacation, like the one you promised him last spring."

"He should know what's going on," Jared insisted.

Heather turned to her father, who stood on her other side. "Please. I know what you're up to here. If we tell Mark now, I've as good as made my decision. And I *haven't* made my decision. So give it up, all of you."

"*Psst*. Put a lid on it." Oggie gestured over his shoulder.

They all turned in unison to see Mark, still in his pajamas, standing in the entrance to the hall. He stared, eyes wide and mouth agape, from Oggie to Jared to Heather and back to Oggie again.

"Oh, wow. Aunt Heather. And Jared and Oggie Jones." The boy breathed the men's names as if two superheroes had come to call.

Heather set down her plate and held out her arms. Mark ran to her.

After the hugs and the greetings had been exchanged, Lucas explained about their impromptu vacation, starting that very day, in North Magdalene. Mark ate three helpings of sausage and eggs, wearing an ear-to-ear grin the whole time.

Oggie and Jared left soon after breakfast. Heather stayed while Lucas and Mark packed their bags and Lucas made arrangements to have the equipment he needed delivered to Heather's house the next day.

Though fog had made the morning gray and dark, the last wisps of it had blown off by the time they left the estate. Heather sat in the front passenger seat of Lucas's car, wearing dark glasses against the bright glare of the sun and watching the craggy terrain of the peninsula give way to the farmlands around Salinas.

Lucas didn't talk much. He drove the car and answered when spoken to. From the back seat, Mark kept up a steady stream of happy chatter. Heather talked to the boy and dozed off once or twice and tried to ignore the way her body seemed electrified, stunningly alive—and connected by hot, invisible wires to the silent man a couple of feet away in the driver's seat.

They cut through the Diablo Mountain Range at Pacheco Pass and soon, on either side of them, the massive fields and orchards of the central valley were rolling by. At last they switched to Highway 80 in Sacramento, on their way to Roseville and Auburn and the climb into the Sierra foothills.

At a little after six, they pulled up in front of Heather's house. Once they'd carried all the luggage inside, she showed Lucas and Mark to their respective rooms. She left them to get settled in while she enjoyed a quick shower and made a simple dinner.

Mark cleaned his plate in record time and then begged to be allowed to visit Marnie. Lucas gave his permission, cautioning Mark to be back by nine.

When Mark was gone, Heather imagined she and Lucas would talk a little, share a little of their feelings about the two weeks of mutual discovery that they were embarking on. She suggested they go out on the front porch and enjoy the evening from the comfort of the padded wicker settee that waited in front of the living room windows.

But Lucas had other plans. During the drive from Monterey, he'd had a few thoughts about the chapter he was working on. He wanted to get them down while they were fresh.

Heather said that of course she understood. She cleaned up the dishes after he disappeared upstairs, then she read for a while. Mark came in right at nine, had his bath and went to his father's room, emerging half an hour later and trundling off to bed.

Heather decided to call it a night herself shortly after Mark turned in. Her room was the first one at the top of the stairs. But for some reason, she found herself standing in front of Lucas's room farther down, staring at the sliver of light gleaming under the door.

She lifted her hand to rap lightly and call his name gently. But at the last second, her nerve deserted her. If he'd wanted to see her, he would have come downstairs earlier, or at least left the door open as a signal that he wouldn't mind company. She let out a sad sigh and started to turn for her own room.

Right then, the door swung open. She gasped in surprise and whirled back around to meet Lucas's eyes.

"Afraid to knock?" He had his glasses in his hand and he was actually smiling. Maybe he'd been hoping she would seek him out after all.

Still, she felt awkward. "I didn't...that is, I..." Something totally mundane came into her mind and she decided to use it as an excuse for coming to his door. "You'll have to use Mark's bathroom downstairs. The only other one is in my room."

His eyes gleamed at her. He knew very well she hadn't come to his door in order to explain which facilities to use. "I did grow up in this house, remember? I know where the bathrooms are."

"Oh. Well, of course you do. How silly. I..."

"Heather?"

"Um, yes?"

He stepped back a little. "Come in."

She bit her inner lip. She'd been thinking all night that she wanted them to have some time alone together—but not in his bedroom, for heaven's sake. Though her body hummed and pulsed at the mere thought of him, she had no intention of making love with him again. Not until they knew each other better on an emotional level.

Thus it seemed very dangerous to step beyond the threshold of the room where he slept.

Still, the room itself didn't look dangerous. Not at all. The furniture was furniture she dusted whenever she got around to it: a four-poster with pineapple finials and a white chenille spread. A bow-front bureau with a lace runner on top. A sea chest and a dark, looming armoire. In the corner was a spindly little desk with a cane-seat chair. Lucas's laptop sat open on the desk.

"Come in," he said again. "Come on."

She stepped over the threshold and he closed the door behind her.

He noticed she was looking at the makeshift work area he'd set up. "My own desk will be here tomorrow. And my home computer."

"Oh," she said. "Great." She could see that there were words typed on the glowing screen of the laptop. Curiosity seized her. "Could I ... I mean, would it bother you, if I looked at what you wrote?"

He seemed unconcerned. "No. Go ahead." He pulled back the cane-seat chair for her. She approached cautiously and sat, scooting the chair closer to the desk in order to be able to read more comfortably.

Lucas leaned over her and set his glasses on the desk beside the laptop, distracting her with his warmth and his scent. He was close enough that she could have pressed her lips to his strong, olive-skinned neck.

"Look," he said.

She made herself stop staring at his neck and turned her attention to the little computer.

Lucas punched two buttons that made the screen read Chapter Two. "That's the start of this section." He pointed out the arrow key that would allow her to reveal more lines of text on the screen. "Think you can handle it?"

"Oh. Yes. Certainly."

Blessedly he stepped away then. She drew in a relieved breath and began reading. Immediately she recognized the main character as one from an earlier book of his. She read quickly, punching the arrow key in sharp little taps, eager to get to the next line.

It ended too soon. There were only about ten pages. She turned to him when she'd read the last line, clapping her hands in unabashed delight. "Oh, that's great. I always loved him."

"Who?"

"The reluctant murderer, from *Shadowdance*."

Lucas had taken a seat on the sea chest. Now he leaned toward her a little. "You read *Shadowdance?*"

"Oh, of course. I've read all your books, Lucas. And not just since we've..." She felt herself blushing and willed the redness away. "I mean, not just since the time we spent together in June. I've always read them. As each one came out. Over the years. They're grisly and gory and scary and romantic. I can't put them down." She lowered her voice to make it teasingly confidential. "Neither can Linda Lou Beardsly, to tell you the truth."

He wasn't buying. "Oh, come on. *The* Linda Lou Beardsly, Nellie Anderson's best pal?"

"The very same. She hates herself for reading them. But she can't stop. Just like me." It occurred to her she'd put her foot in it, so she hastened to amend, "Oh, what am I saying? Of course I don't mean I hate myself for reading your books. I don't at all. It was the other part, about not being able to *stop* reading them, that's what I meant."

"Heather," Lucas said. "It's okay. I understand."

"Oh, good. I'm so glad, because I..."

All of a sudden, he rose from the sea chest.

She found herself looking up at him. "Because I..."

He closed the distance to her chair. Her eyes tracked each movement. She felt like a rabbit, frozen in an open field, watching the steady, stalking approach of a hungry mountain lion.

He stood looking down at her. "Because you what?"

She grasped the spindly back of the chair as if it could save her from the inappropriate thoughts that were racing through her mind. "I just wouldn't want you to think that I hated myself for..."

"Reading my books?"

"Yes. Because I don't. Not at all."

"I'm so relieved." His voice was like honey, pouring over her warm and slow. "Stand up."

"I...what?"

"Stand up."

She considered his command, fully aware that it wasn't something she *had* to do. She could simply tell him no and that would be that.

But the thing was, she *wanted* to stand up. Those invisible electric wires she'd felt on the drive from Monterey were crackling between them again. And the barrier of the chair was...interfering with them. The wires seemed to pop and snap in complaint, demanding that she stand up and step free of the chair. That she face him with nothing but an inch of air between them and give all the hot, wondrous currents a straight line from him to her and back again.

"Heather."

She stood, and slid around so that the chair was behind her.

"Better. Now kiss me."

She reminded herself that she had no intention of making love with him right now. "I don't think—"

"Right. Don't think."

"No, really, I—"

"Don't argue. Just kiss me." He held out his hands, to the sides, palms up. "I won't do anything. I'll keep my hands to myself. You do everything. That's how it'll be. For now."

"But Lucas." She got out the words, though all she wanted was to rise on tiptoe and press her lips to his. "It's not what we're supposed to be doing, kissing. We're supposed to be getting to know each other. Getting to understand..." The words trailed off. She'd completely forgotten what they were supposed to be getting to understand. "I..." She ran a hand back through her hair. "Um..."

"May I point out something?"

"I..."

"When two people want to touch as badly as you and I do, it becomes... artificial to hold back."

She gulped. "It does?"

He nodded. "In fact, holding back is getting in the way, for me."

"Getting in the way of what?"

"Of getting to know you better."

She really hadn't thought of it that way. "It is?"

He nodded again. "All I can think of when I'm with you is that place on your neck that I love to suck...."

Heather realized she wasn't breathing and forced herself to draw air into her lungs. She knew exactly the place he meant, on the right side, at the pulse. Right now, that place was throbbing. She had to restrain herself from rubbing it with her hand.

"Wait," he said, "that's not entirely true."

"It isn't?"

"No."

"You don't want to...?"

"...kiss that place on your neck? Yes, I do."

"Then what?"

"There's more."

"There is?"

"Mmm-hmm. There's the soft skin behind your knees."

Her knees started quivering. The skin in back of them felt like it was shimmering, itching, yearning...

"I want to lick you there."

"You do?"

He nodded. "And that's not all."

"It isn't?"

"Uh-uh. There's also the sweet, slick taste of your tongue and the feel of your—"

"Lucas, I..."

"You've got your two weeks." His voice was rougher, now. Nubby velvet rubbing at all of her most sensitive places, crazy-making. "Let's make the most of them. I want you and you want me. Here. And now."

He was so compelling. And what he said did make sense, now that she thought about it. Maybe—

But then she remembered Mark.

He seemed to read her mind. "Mark is downstairs, sound asleep. He's not going to bother us. And he isn't going to know what we do in the night."

"If we—"

He snared her hand then, and laid it on the hard ridge at the front of his black slacks. The casual intimacy of the gesture stunned her—and sent all her nerves singing, sent her blood roaring in her veins.

"This is part of what we'll be to each other, when you marry me," he said. "Part of getting to know each other. A major part. Now kiss me, Heather. Kiss me now."

All her good intentions of waiting until things were more settled between them seemed to have flown out the window. She couldn't help herself. Her hand relaxed, cupped him.

"Yes," he whispered, his voice all honey again.

She put her hands on his shoulders, rose on tiptoe and touched his lips with her own.

Chapter Thirteen

Heather's lips met his. Soft, hesitant, so very vulnerable.

Lucas resisted the urge to wrap his arms around her and pull her close, though he wanted nothing so much at that moment as to feel the pliant length of her against him, to crush her breasts against his chest.

She mewed; a tiny, needful sound. Like a kitten begging to be stroked. But he didn't stroke her. Not yet. There would be time for that. There would be the whole night.

He concentrated on kissing her, keeping his hands to his sides, letting her lead the way as he'd told her he would.

And lead the way she did. Splendidly. Her mouth nuzzled his. He parted his lips. She took his tongue into her own mouth.

He held back a groan as she broke the kiss. She began to caress him. Her slender hands brushed his shoulders, molded the shape of his chest. She went to work on the buttons of his shirt, bending her head to her task. The buttons fell open. She put her hands, so warm and soft, on his bare chest, then rubbed them, flat palmed, against his small nipples.

He did groan then, but it was a small sound, quickly quelled. He let the shirt drop down his arms and tossed it behind him, onto the sea chest.

"Oh, Lucas..."

He savored the sweetly ragged tone of her voice. She splayed her hands on his chest again and kissed him, at his breastbone, her lips opening in the mat of hair there, her tongue sliding out. He closed his eyes and tipped his head back, giving himself up to her. And then he looked down at her once again.

"Now, take off *your* shirt." His own voice sounded ragged, too, harsh with the effort to control his desire.

She looked up at him. Her greenish eyes with their gold lights seemed glazed, tender and a little afraid.

"Do it." He softened the command with a whispered, "Please."

She took her short-sleeve knit shirt by the hem and raised it over her head, dropping it behind her on the desk chair. Her gold-shot red-brown hair tumbled around her bare shoulders, crackling with electricity. He wanted to shove his fingers in it, to know once more its silky feel against his hands.

And he would. Oh, he would.

Her bra was plain, white and functional—as he'd known it would be. He stared at it for a moment, wondering why the sight of it increased his already considerable excitement. Because it spoke so clearly of her basic innocence, he supposed.

"Take off the bra."

She swayed a little, then steadied herself, lifting her chin and reaching behind her to undo the back clasp. The bra fell away to join the shirt on the chair.

Naked from the waist up, she seemed to regret her own boldness. She tried to cross her arms over herself.

"Uh-uh," he said. "I want to see you."

She took in a long breath and forced her arms to her sides.

Her breasts were full and round—maybe fuller than he remembered them. Because of the baby, he supposed. And now that he could see them, he found they were as pale as fine porcelain, the nipples a tempting dusky pink. He wanted to touch them, to kiss them.

But he wanted to see all of her, here, in the light, even more. It was of the utmost importance. The other time had been in the shadows. But not anymore.

"The rest." His tone was hoarse, rougher than he intended.

She obeyed, unsnapping her jeans, shimmying them down. They gathered at her ankles, stopped by her shoes. Her panties were like her bra—plain and functional. They were made of white cotton, waist-high and cut low on the thighs. Before he could really look at them, she knelt. He looked down at the sweet bumps of her spine as she untied her tennis shoes, slipped them off and got rid of her socks as well. She stood again then, an easy, graceful movement and kicked her jeans away. His breath stuck.

This was the essence of her allure. The wide, innocent, hungry eyes. The tumbling hair, the fine bones and the ripe breasts. And plain, white panties. The most purely responsive woman he'd ever known—and in his younger years, he'd known more than a few—and she wore the underwear of a Catholic schoolgirl.

He made himself breathe again. "The panties," he said.

She hooked her thumbs in them. And then she gave a slow smile that managed to be both innocent and seductive at once.

He almost lost it right there. "What?" he demanded.

"These are all I have left, Lucas." She looked down at the panties. "And you've still got everything on but your shirt."

"So?"

"It doesn't seem fair."

He made himself play along. "Well, then what do you want me to do?"

She slid her hands under the elastic of the panties, considering. He sincerely hoped he would not explode.

"Take off the rest of your clothes," she instructed.

He did, quickly. She watched, her eyes still as wide and innocent as ever. But when he got to his briefs, he stopped.

"We're even," he said.

"Yes." She looked wary. "So?"

"You first."

"No. At the same time."

He couldn't believe her. That other night, he'd been the leader. She'd responded to his every whim and caress, but he had run the show.

This was different. He'd meant to let her take the lead a little, but she was actually *playing* with him. He was enchanted.

He put his thumbs under the elastic waistband of his briefs. She matched him, thumbs under the elastic of her plain, white underwear.

"On a count of three?" she dared to inquire.

He nodded.

"One, two, three!" She yanked, bent and jumped out of the panties.

He didn't move.

She straightened, the panties in her hand, and saw that he still wore his. "You cheated!" she accused.

He looked at her. "Come here."

"Oh, Lucas." The panties fell to the floor.

"Come on. Come here."

Now she was biting her lip a little, grown shy suddenly. But she closed the short distance between them. He took her hands, put them at his waist, guided her thumbs beneath the elastic waistband.

"Make us even," he said.

And she did. She peeled the briefs slowly down and away, brushing him twice with her fingers and making him gasp.

When the briefs were gone, he said, "Touch me."

Her warm, hesitant hand encircled him. He closed his eyes, thought of the percentage he was paying his agent, of the speech he was supposed to be giving to a book club in Washington, D.C. three weeks from then that he hadn't got around to writing yet. But concentrating on business did no good.

She was driving him crazy. He really was going to lose it.

He gave in and reached for her, pulling her close. Her body met his and both of them moaned.

He kissed her, letting his hands roam, down the delicious bumps of her spine, over the sweet pair of dimples at the top of her hips. He cupped her buttocks, pulled her up and in, rubbing himself against her.

She was sighing and whimpering a little, her hands clutching his shoulders. The bed wasn't far. Four steps and they were there. He guided her down, his hungry mouth already roving.

He took her breast, closing his mouth over one tender nipple and drawing it in, laving it with his tongue. She writhed and moaned. He took the other breast. She arched her back and held him close.

He cupped her breasts in his hands, while his mouth traveled down, over her ribs, to her soft, still-flat belly, and then lower still.

"Oh. Oh, Lucas..." She sighed. "Oh, you shouldn't..."

"Shh. You're beautiful, Heather. So beautiful. Everywhere."

She moaned some more, and then she stiffened and cried out. He drank in her completion, drawing it out, making it last and last, until she was clutching him, begging him, contradicting herself in broken phrases.

"Lucas. Please. Don't. Stop. Never stop...."

He rose above her then, and she eagerly reached for him. He buried himself to the hilt in her. Her long, slim thighs locked around him.

He rolled, quickly, or he would have finished it then. From the top position, she looked down at him, sweetly dazed, her breasts flushed, her eyes half-closed. He took her legs and folded them on either side of his thighs. She caught on immediately, and began to ride him.

She set the rhythm—slow, then fast, then slow again. He knew she was building once more. He encouraged her, bringing his hand between them and finding the little bud of need. She threw her head back, rocked frantically—and shattered for the second time.

She fell against him, her hair spilling over his neck and shoulders, her sweet breath fanning his chest. He stroked her hair, combed through it with his fingers, and kissed the top of her head.

After a while, she moaned again, a questioning little sound. She could feel him, and knew he hadn't finished when she did.

"Lucas?"

He lifted himself, pressing higher up into her.

She cried out, so soft and sensitive now, in the aftermath of fulfillment. He knew he could bring her, quickly, to the brink again.

But he didn't. He dropped back to the bed and lay still. They had all night. And he meant to make it last. He meant to bring her to a point where she wasn't sure where her own body left off and his began.

And then, when the boundaries of ecstasy had all been crossed, when she was as vulnerable as she would ever be, he would extract from her the vow he sought.

Far back in his mind, it was true, lay a small kernel of regret that it should be necessary to go about getting her agreement this way. However, it couldn't be helped.

She claimed she needed two weeks to make up her mind. But he didn't buy that. The real problem was Jason Lee. She might put him off forever, mourning for his sainted brother.

"Lucas?" She broke through his troubled thoughts.

And then, as she too often did, she surprised him. She slid to the side and was gone, making him moan at the movement and catching him off guard, so that he didn't think fast enough to hold her there.

"Oh, Lucas. Yes. I see what you mean."

"About what?" He was throbbing, aching, missing the soft warmth of her. He rolled his head a little, shutting his eyes and gritting his teeth.

"About being beautiful. Because you're beautiful, too."

And then her hand closed around him.

"Heather...." He was lost, out of control. Completely at her mercy in the space of mere seconds.

And then her mouth was there, moist, awkward and wonderful, taking him in. He managed to reach down and bury his hands in her hair.

At last, vanquished, he threw his head back and let her do what she would with him. There was no point in fighting it. She had taken control.

His own finish came at him like a zephyr. It hit and exploded, shattering him into a million bursting shards of light and sensation. He let it have him.

When it was done, she cuddled up beside him and kissed him on the neck. He drew her close, savoring the sleek, satiny feel of her.

"Lucas?"

"Hmm?"

"It's getting late."

"So?"

"Maybe I should go to my room now."

He held her a little tighter. "No, you shouldn't."

"But..."

"Shh. Rest a little. Get your strength back."

"And then what?"

"And then we'll start all over again."

Deep in the night, he commanded, "Marry me."

She didn't reply.

He tried again. "Marry me."

"Lucas, we agreed..."

"Marry me."

"I can't. We need..."

"What? What do we need?" He put his hand on her.

She cried out, her body lifting in immediate response to his caress. But she would not give up those two weeks of hers.

Some time later, when she lay slumbering beside him, Lucas had yet to get the answer he sought.

He'd put aside what scruples he possessed tonight, certain that it was the only way to get her to say she would marry him.

And it hadn't worked. She'd held out.

He considered the coming morning. Perhaps he could give it one more try then.

Yes, he thought, when she wakes beside me. When she's blushing with sweet shame over the things we did tonight. I'll put on the pressure again in the morning. And she'll come around.

But then he let out a small grunt of self-disgust. Who did he think he was kidding? She'd held out against him up till now. He didn't see how waking up next to him in the morning was going to make any difference at all.

Someone was knocking on the door.

Heather opened her eyes just as Lucas opened his. They stared at each other.

Then the knock came again. "Dad? Dad, can I come in?"

Lucas shot to a sitting position, while Heather yanked the sheet over her head.

"Dad?"

"Er, not now, Mark."

Heather heard the knob turn. She peeked over the edge of the sheet in horror as Mark stuck his head in the doorway. "But, Dad. I told you last night. I have to..." Mark gulped and stared. "Aunt Heather?" he blurted in complete disbelief.

Heather wanted to die, right then and there. "Mark, I..."

Her voice trailed off as Mark's shocked expression underwent a startling change. All at once, his face was suffused with a joyful inner light.

"Oh," he said in awe and wonder. "I know. I know what this means."

"You . . . you do?" Heather stammered.

"What?" Lucas got out.

"That you're getting married." Mark punched a fist high in a victory salute. "Yes!" Then he clapped his hands. "I'm right, aren't I? You're getting married, I know it. I can see." Hooting in glee, Mark did a little triumphant dance, holding both hands high and prancing in a circle right where he stood.

Heather looked at Lucas and Lucas looked back. Then they both turned their heads to force a smile for Mark.

"Yes," they said in unison. "We're getting married." And Lucas added, "Right away."

Chapter Fourteen

Over breakfast, Mark told them that he was the happiest kid in California. Since last winter, he'd had a secret dream that this might happen. And now his dream had come true.

Mark ate fast. He'd been invited to attend church with Marnie and her family. Then, after that, he and Kenny and Marnie planned to head out on a hike to an abandoned ball mill Marnie knew about northeast of town. Marnie's stepmom was making lunch for them to take.

Soon enough, the happiest kid in California was bouncing out the front door. Behind him, he left two abashed adults warily regarding each other across the remains of breakfast.

Lucas spoke first. "I'll call Regina. She can keep Mark with her tonight."

Heather glanced down at the pancakes she'd barely

touched, felt her stomach lurch a little, then looked up at Lucas again. "Why?"

"So we can drive to Reno."

Heather took a sip of apple juice. "And get married today?"

"Yes."

The apple juice seemed to settle her stomach, but Heather pushed her plate aside anyway. "No."

She watched Lucas's eyes grow stormy, though when he spoke, his voice stayed controlled. "I'll remind you that now Mark believes—"

"I know what Mark believes. And I don't plan to disappoint him."

Lucas relaxed a little. "So you will marry me?"

"Yes. Mark's walking in on us this morning kind of tipped the balance for me. I agree with him, really. I think that people who sleep together ought to be husband and wife. And then, there *is* the baby to consider." She lifted her napkin from her lap and laid it beside her plate. "Though I also think that taking the two weeks I wanted to learn about each other would have been wiser."

"We're a long way past wisdom, Heather." His voice was soft now, slightly rueful.

She thought of the night before. She'd done such shocking things. And loved them. "I guess we are."

With a small sigh, Heather picked up her plate, flatware and napkin and carried them to the counter. As she dumped her uneaten breakfast down the disposal, she couldn't help thinking that this was a strange way to agree to marry someone. It was so cut-and-dried, so bluntly matter-of-fact. And there had not even been a mention of love.

But what could she expect? She'd gone and got herself pregnant. And Lucas was only trying in his domineering, take-charge way to make the best of a tough situation.

Heather didn't like herself much at that moment. She'd once told Lucas that she would never settle for less than what she'd shared with Jason Lee. And yet, here she was. Settling. Agreeing to marry Lucas primarily because there was a baby on the way.

"What is it?" Lucas demanded from behind her at the table. "What's on your mind?"

Heather didn't turn. She looked out the window at the side porch and baldly lied. "Oh, nothing. It's just a big step, that's all."

"It's the right thing to do."

"Yes. Yes, I suppose that's true," she agreed, and told herself to be satisfied. She and Lucas couldn't keep their hands off of each other, Mark was getting his dream come true—and her baby needed its father.

For now, that would have to be enough. Certainly, with the commitment made, they'd grow closer in the other ways. She would simply have to do everything she could to make that happen.

Heather put the dish and flatware into the dishwasher. Behind her, she heard Lucas's chair scrape the floor as he stood. He came up beside her carrying his own plate and Mark's as well. Heather stepped back a little, so he could get to the sink. He rinsed the dishes and then bent to put them beside hers.

She looked down at his dark head, feeling that little contraction of heat and longing in her belly as she recalled how silky his hair had felt between her fingers last night.

He straightened and met her eyes. A slow smile lifted the corners of his mouth. He knew exactly what she was thinking about.

"I...uh..." Her voice was as befuddled as her mind.

"What?" He was still smiling.

Heather reminded herself that there was more to be decided. "I don't want to be married in Reno."

His smile faded a little. "Then where?"

"I want to be married here, in North Magdalene."

"Why?"

"I want my family around me, at least everyone who can make it. It doesn't have to be anything fancy, just my father and stepmother, my grandpa and my aunts and uncles. And I want Mark to be a part of it. This marriage will mean a lot in his life, too."

"All right. That's reasonable."

"Aunt Regina has a big backyard. I'll ask her if we can have the ceremony there."

"When?"

"Next Saturday. Less than a week. Is that soon enough for you?"

The dishwasher was still open. He bent again to close it, then straightened once more. "All right. That's fine."

Now came the tough part. Heather swallowed nervously. "And Lucas..."

"What?"

"I don't think...we should make love again. Until after the wedding." She hastened to make herself understood, the words tumbling out of her, nervous and awkward. "It's only a few days. It probably seems kind of silly to you, after everything we've done. But I would feel better. As I said, I think people who sleep together ought to be married. And with Mark in the house, well, you saw what can happen."

He was looking at her so strangely. As usual, she hadn't a clue what might be going through his mind.

"Um, well?" She tried again. "Is that all right with you?"

He nodded. "I think I can control myself."

She knew her cheeks were red. "Oh. Yes. Well. Good."

He smiled a little then, seeing her embarrassment. "So. Is that it?"

"I think so," she replied, then couldn't resist a gentle taunt. "I suppose you can call my dad now and tell him you broke me down."

Lucas glanced away. "Heather..." He actually appeared a little nonplussed.

She put up a hand. "Hey, come on. It's all right. I know my father. He wouldn't have laid off you until a date was set. And now it is. We can relax—for about five minutes, anyway, until my aunts start going crazy putting a wedding together in six days."

"You're sure it won't be too much for you? We could go to Tahoe or Vegas if you don't like Reno."

"No. I want it here. I do. And afterward, I want my other week. Here, as we agreed."

"All right. But start packing. Because when the two weeks are over, we're going back to Monterey."

Heather thought about the huge house Lucas lived in, and the isolation of it. How would she grow accustomed to living there? She wasn't sure. But she was obviously going to have to give it her best shot.

"All right. Unless I can get you to change your mind before the two weeks are up, we'll live in Monterey."

He looked relieved. "Good."

Right then the phone rang. Heather picked it up.

"Hello, Sunshine," Jared said. "Put Lucas on, will you?"

She knew what he was up to—checking to see if Lucas had convinced her to say yes yet. "What's this about, Dad?"

"Nothing important. Just put him on."

"Sure," she said, then added, as if it were only an afterthought, "Oh, guess what? We're getting married. Next Saturday."

"You are?" Her father's raspy voice was buoyant suddenly. "That's great!" And then he thought again. "But why are you waiting so long?"

"It's only six days, Dad."

"Well, sure. But I get nervous. Anything could happen between now and then."

"Nothing's going to happen, Dad."

"So you say now."

"Look. I want to get married here in town, with the family around us. Maybe at Aunt Regina's, if she'll let us use her backyard. And that will take a few days to arrange."

"Well." Jared thought about that and decided he approved. "Well, that's *damn touching*. That's okay. You get together with the women right away, you hear?"

"Yes, Dad."

"And congratulations, to you both. I'll talk to you real soon."

"Dad."

"Yeah?"

"What about Lucas?"

"What about him? Give him my congratulations."

"I thought you wanted to talk to him."

"Me? Naw. It was nothin'."

"Why did I know you were going to say that?"

That afternoon, Heather met with Eden and her aunts in the kitchen of her aunt Delilah's house. After all the hugs and kisses and best wishes had been exchanged, Regina said she'd be delighted to hold the ceremony in her backyard. Olivia, who was a trained chef, volunteered to provide the refreshments, including the cake. Eden would take care of the seating and the flowers and also be Heather's matron of honor. Aunt Delilah and Aunt Amy would help wherever help was required.

In fact, Heather was not to worry about a thing. She should concern herself with getting her blood tests, buying a special dress, spending time with Lucas and Mark and preparing for the big move to Monterey. Her family could handle all the wedding plans.

Heather was reminding them that she didn't want anything fancy when her Grandpa staggered in carrying a huge, dusty box.

"Get outta my way, all you women. I ain't steady without my cane."

He hobbled into Aunt Delilah's kitchen and dropped the big box in the middle of the room. Dust flew up from it as it hit the floor.

Delilah seemed to recognize the box; her black eyes filled with tears. "Oh, Father. How lovely."

"What *is* it?" Aunt Olivia asked.

"Open it," Oggie said. "Have a look."

The box was sealed with tape, so Delilah produced a pair of scissors.

"It's for our Sunshine," Oggie instructed proudly, backing toward a kitchen chair. He wheezed a little as he sat. "So you give those scissors to her and let her see what's inside."

Delilah passed the scissors over.

Heather went to work slitting through the tape. Soon enough, she was peeling back the flaps of the box. Inside she found a fan of dead cedar boughs and a mountain of tissue paper.

"Cedar keeps the moths away," Delilah said.

Heather lifted off the crumbling boughs and set them on the floor. Then she peeled back the tissue. Folded carefully within was a dress.

"Take it out, girl," Oggie said.

Heather lifted out a floor-length wedding gown, a marvel of white satin, with a bodice of delicate lace intricately woven with glass beads and seed pearls. The beaded lace extended to the short bell sleeves, which had satin puffs beneath. The neckline was high in front, dipping to a modest V in back. Heather fingered the beaded lace.

"It was your Grandma Bathsheba's," Oggie said. "I saved it for Delilah."

"Yes," Delilah said. "And when I married Sam two years ago, Father brought it out. But it simply didn't suit me." Delilah sighed. "One needs long arms to carry off those sleeves. And the actual fit was all wrong. Mother was long-waisted and tall." Delilah looked down at her own diminutive figure. "I'm not."

"So instead of cuttin' it up and tryin' to make it over, we just put it away again," Oggie added.

"Here." Eden scooped up the train and smoothed it out of the way. "Hold it up to yourself."

Heather did as her stepmother instructed. It really did look as if it might fit her—and the appreciative sighs from the other women made her pretty sure it would look just fine.

Delilah said, "I think, if you'd like, we can make any alterations it needs and even get it cleaned before Saturday."

Heather looked down at the dress. "It's so...white," she said.

"It's a *weddin'* dress," Oggie replied. "What the hell color should it be?"

"Well, Grandpa. I already had a wedding where I wore white."

"She means it's not traditional to wear white the second time around," Delilah told her father.

"So who gives two bits for traditional?" Oggie turned to Heather. "The question is, do you want to wear it or not?"

Heather met her grandfather's eyes. To turn down the dress would hurt him. She didn't want that.

"It means a lot to your old grandpa—" Oggie pulled out all the stops "—that you should marry Lucas Drury in the dress your grandma wore to marry me. Will you do that for me, Sunshine?"

Heather looked down at the yards of satin and pearl-embroidered lace. Oh, she'd pictured something different. Something in dusty rose, maybe, or sunny yellow.

And yes, she had to admit it to herself. She'd pictured something *less.*

There was something so...sacramental about white. And this wasn't that kind of marriage, not really.

"Sunshine," Oggie groused. "Don't take a week. The weddin' day'll be over, and you'll still be standin' here, tryin' to decide. Get to it. You gonna wear your grandma's dress or not?"

It seemed almost sinful, to wear a dress like this for anything less than a true love match.

But it was so beautiful. And it would please her grandpa so very much....

"Sunshine, I'm an old man. At this rate, I could pass on to the next life before you make up your mind."

She looked at him and forced a smile. "Okay, Grandpa. I'd be honored to wear it."

Right after the meeting with her aunts, Heather went to see her boss. Lily tossed her spatula down on the grill, threw up her hands and bellowed as if Heather had stuck her between the ribs with a carving knife.

"What are you doing to me? You're killing me. How am I gonna run a business when my head waitress ups and quits? I'll go broke, I won't make it. And do you care, does it matter one bit to you? Oh, no, *you're* getting married to a rich man. You don't have to work no more!"

Heather let Lily yell for a while, so she could get it out of her system, though she knew all the customers out in front were getting an earful.

Finally, when Lily was all shouted out, she grabbed Heather in a bear hug and whispered fiercely into her ear, "You be happy, you hear me? And don't be a stranger, either."

"I won't," Heather promised, though Monterey was six hours away.

But then, it didn't matter how far away Monterey was. She could visit. Often. Nothing would keep her from doing that.

Lily took her by the shoulders and held her at arm's length. "You sure you can't just work two more days? Monday and Tuesday, to give me a chance to find someone else?"

"Oh, Lil."

"Please?"

"You know I can't stand to watch you beg."

"Is that a yes?"

"Oh, all right. But that's absolutely all I can do."

When Heather arrived back at the house, Mark had yet to return from Marnie's. Lucas's car was parked by the front gate and the door to his room was closed. Heather assumed he must be working, so she didn't disturb him.

She had plenty to do, anyway. Even though she hoped to change Lucas's mind about the move to Monterey, she intended to play fair and assume, for the time being, that she actually would be living there. She went down into the basement for some empty boxes and a stack of old newspapers and began the long process of packing up the things in her house.

Heather started in the front room, with the books and figurines, the candy bowls and flower vases.

Once all the books and knickknacks were tucked in boxes, she moved on to the framed photographs on the mantel and on the side tables at either end of the sofa, most of which were mementos of her life with Jason Lee. She carefully wrapped the wedding picture, and some snapshots of the two of them on an uncle's boat at Bullfinch Bar Reservoir.

Heather paused to muse over the senior ball picture.

At the time, of course, she had felt terribly sophisticated in the sheath of plum velvet, while she'd considered Jason Lee to be nothing short of a man of the world in his rented tux with the ruffle-front shirt. But now, all she could think of was how painfully young they both looked, smiling stiffly and holding hands beneath a papier mâché arch all painted up to look like marble, with plastic flowers twined around it. Behind them, the photographer had draped midnight blue satin.

Heather smiled to herself. One reason she loved the picture was that Jason Lee's thick blond hair hung in his eyes. Heather had asked the impatient photographer to wait, so she could brush the unruly curls into place with her fingers. However, they had fallen right back over his eyes as soon as they faced the camera once more.

Lightly, through the glass, Heather touched the image of her former husband. He had been a tender, gentle boy. And a good man. And she would always love him.

But somehow, over the past couple of months, most of the pain of thinking about him had faded. There were only sweet memories of the happiness they'd shared. And sadness that his life had been so brief.

Heather's eyes filled as she stared musingly down at Jason Lee's face. A single tear got away from her, trickling down her nose to fall on the glass, in the middle of the ruffles on Jason Lee's rented tux.

Lucas, standing in the arch that led to the dining room, was close enough to watch that tear fall. He waited, barely breathing, as Heather wiped it away with the hem of her shirt. Then he turned on silent feet and went back up the stairs he'd just come down.

That evening, Lucas didn't emerge from his room until Heather called him to dinner. When the food had been cleared away, he and Mark got out Jason, Sr.'s old chess set and played, for two hours. Then Mark headed for the shower. As soon as the boy was in the bathroom, Heather suggested an evening walk, just Lucas and herself.

"I really should try to get in a couple of more hours tonight," Lucas said.

But Heather persisted, mindful of her objective that they should spend time together.

Finally Lucas relented. They told Mark where they were going and walked down to where Heather's street met the long and meandering Rambling Lane. There they turned north, and strolled past her aunt Delilah's old house, where Uncle Jack and Aunt Olivia lived now. They went on from there, almost to the point where they'd have come out on Highway 49.

Lucas seemed withdrawn, so Heather filled the silence with chatter, reporting on the meeting with her aunts and the wedding dress that had belonged to her grandmother. She told him of how Lily had shouted at her and then hugged her and then extracted a promise that she'd work for two more days.

"And in case you didn't notice that the living room is almost bare, I started packing," she announced proudly.

"Oh?" he asked. "And what did you pack?"

She shot him a look, thinking he sounded a little sarcastic and wondering what could be going through that brilliant, bewildering mind of his.

She kept her tone carefully light. "Well, not a lot, but I did break the ice." Lucas seemed to be walking faster all of a sudden. She quickened her own pace to keep up. "I took care of the books and knickknacks in the dining room and living room. And a bunch of pictures."

"Great."

"Lucas?" She pulled on his arm then, until he stopped on the side of the road beneath the drooping branches of a birch tree.

He looked down at her questioningly through the growing shadows of approaching twilight. "What is it?"

"Is . . . something wrong?"

He took just a fraction too long before he answered, "No. Nothing."

"Are you sure?"

"Yes. Now, let's get back. I really want to rough out a few more things before I knock off for the night."

Back at the house, Lucas disappeared immediately. Heather watched television with Mark for a while, then both of them called it a night.

Heather climbed the stairs and found herself hovering in front of Lucas's door as she had the night before. She waited, shuffling her feet shamelessly, hoping he would hear and come to the door without her having to knock.

But then she realized she was being ridiculous. She tapped twice. "Lucas?"

She waited and was almost going to knock again when the door opened and he was standing there, looking studious in his reading glasses. His hair was mussed, as if he'd dug his fingers through it while he was thinking.

"What is it?"

She forced a shaky smile. He made it so difficult sometimes. But she wouldn't give up. "Just stopped by to say good-night."

He was frowning, but then he seemed to relax a little. He took off his glasses. "Well, all right. Good night, Heather."

He wasn't helping her out one bit here. She sighed. "I forgot to ask. Did you get your stuff today?"

"My office equipment?" He stepped back a little. "Take a look."

She peeked around him and scanned the room, which now contained two new lamps, a large bleached-oak desk, a swivel chair and a full-size computer, complete with printer. Norma Conley's watercolors were gone from the walls and in their place were a large planning calendar and two big bulletin boards. There was also a bookcase with several reference books in it.

"Looks great," she told him.

He said nothing.

"Now you can really get some work done."

He shrugged.

She wondered what she was doing standing at the end of the landing, casting about desperately for something— anything—to say to the man she was going to marry in six days' time. She backed up a little. It was time to go.

"Well. I suppose I ought to leave you alone so you can work."

He had another of those strange looks on his face. He had so many strange looks. He was a truly unfathomable man.

"Well," she said again, and thought that she said *well* much too much when she was around him. "Good night."

She started to turn. But his hand shot out and closed around her arm. He tugged her gently and the next thing she knew she was in his arms.

"Oh!" She stared up at him, bewildered, trying not to notice how good and solid and warm he felt, trying not to think about how lovely he smelled, or the tenderly cruel shape of his mouth.

He lowered that mouth and brushed it across hers. "Good night, Heather."

Without another word, he backed away and closed the door, leaving her standing there, touching her lips with hesitant fingers, sure of only one thing: she wished that the kiss had lasted longer than it had.

By the next morning, when Heather went to work at Lily's, the news of her upcoming marriage to Lucas was all over town.

"My dear, are you sure you know what you're doing?" Nellie Anderson wanted to know when she and Linda Lou Beardsly dropped in for identical sandwiches and glasses of iceless ice tea.

"About what, Mrs. Anderson?"

"Oh, don't play coy with us. You know what. Marrying Lucas Drury. Surely you know his history."

"Of course I know all about Lucas, Mrs. Anderson. And I·know exactly what I'm doing."

"Well, we certainly hope so." Nellie and Linda Lou exchanged extremely doubtful glances, but then Nellie relented marginally. "At least you look somewhat better today than you have recently."

"Thank you, Mrs. Anderson." Heather turned away to put their order in.

Behind her, she heard them whispering. She left them to it, thinking that there were a few things about North Magdalene she wouldn't miss one bit.

A little before the end of Heather's shift, Rocky Collins grew maudlin.

"Aw, Sunshine. How c'n you leave us? We can't live without you. You're the heart of this damn place."

"Rocky, I'm not dying. I'm just moving to Monterey."

"Tha's too far. Don' do it." He wove on his stool a little.

"That does it. I'm making you some toast." Heather turned and popped two pieces of bread into the toaster. "You need something in your stomach."

Rocky belched. "Skip the toas'. I got plenny in my stomach."

"Plenty of Cuervo Eighteen Hundred," Tim Brown muttered.

Rocky hooted with laughter. "Cuervo Eighteen Hundred. Don't I wish. You know I can't afford the best stuff. I ain't no millionaire. And I mean it, Sunshine, skip the toas'."

"I'll put grape jelly on it, just like you like it."

"Aw, c'mon. Yer makin' me cry. Who's gonna butter my toast for me? Who's gonna put the jelly right out to the corners? Who's gonna do that, huh, if you're gone?"

"Rocky, cut it out. I'm serious. Or I'm going to have to ask you to go on home."

Rocky wailed, then grabbed Heather's hand. "Sunshine, I'm beggin' you. Don' do it."

"Aw, get wise, Rocky," Roger McCleb advised just as Heather managed to pull her hand free of Rocky's sweaty grip. "Sunshine's a waitress and that guy is a gazzillionaire. She'd be a fool *not* to marry him. This is her big chance."

"Sunshine wouldn't marry someone jus' 'cause he was rich," Rocky whined. "Would ya, Sunshine?"

Just then the toast popped up. Heather spread the butter and jelly on it and set it in front of him.

"Well, would ya?" Rocky asked.

Heather sighed and answered wearily, "No, Rocky, I would never marry a man just because he was rich."

Right then, Rocky's face turned an unhealthier color than usual. Sweat broke out on his forehead. He fell all over himself agreeing with her. "Aw, naw, Sunshine. Now, I know that. You got a heart of pure gold, and that's the God's truth." He looked down at his toast and let out a strangled sound that Heather assumed was meant to indicate delight. "And look at this toas'. Just the way I like it. Yessiree." He glanced up again, but only long enough to cast a frantic, furtive look beyond Heather's shoulder. Then he bent his head over his plate and started shoving the toast into his mouth as if he was starved.

Heather looked over her shoulder in the direction of Rocky's glance, toward the door to the street. Lucas was standing there.

She also noticed that everyone in the place seemed to have stopped breathing. Even Nellie Anderson had nothing to say.

Heather looked at the clock. Almost quitting time. As soon as she was done for the day, she and Lucas were going over to the clinic for their blood tests.

She cast a quick prayer toward heaven that Lucas hadn't heard her last remark to Rocky. The idea was for him to get to like it in North Magdalene. That was unlikely to happen if he learned that most folks in town considered him a dangerous character with nothing going for him but his bank account.

She beamed him a thousand-watt smile. "Be ready in a sec."

"What was that all about?" Lucas demanded when they were settled into the plush leather seats of his car for the drive to the medical clinic a few miles outside of town.

"Um, what?" she asked, feeling both idiotic and dishonest at the same time.

"That crack you made about not marrying a man for his money."

"Oh," she said, "it wasn't anything, really. Just a remark."

"I know it was a remark, Heather. But what made you say it?"

"Well, I . . ." She resigned herself to being honest. "It's not a big deal. I'm just getting a little flack, that's all."

"For what?"

"For, um, marrying you."

He took a moment to digest that news, then asked, "Flack from who?"

"My customers."

He let out a patient breath of air. "Which customers are we talking about here, specifically?"

Most of them, she thought. But she said, "Well, all that happened was that Roger McCleb said that I'm marrying you for your money. And Rocky said I wouldn't do a thing like that, but then he looked at me and asked, 'Would you?' And I said no, I wouldn't. And that was when you came in."

Lucas looked at her some more, as if awaiting a punch line. Then he asked, "That was all?"

"I said it wasn't a big deal."

"Rocky. That's Rocky Collins, right?"

"Right."

"As I remember, he was always a big drinker."

"He still is."

"His face turned green when he saw me."

"It was already green. Like you said, he drinks too much."

"You're missing the point, Heather. I'm saying he looked scared to death of me."

Heather opened her purse for no reason, looked in it and shut it again, wishing with all her heart that this conversation would just die a natural death.

"Heather, I said he looked scared of me."

"Yes, I suppose. Maybe he was. Just a little."

"Why would he be scared of me?"

She tried to think of a gentle way to say it. "Well, because nobody knows what you might do."

"I see. Because I've done such awful things in my life, is that it?"

"Well, yes. They don't know the real you."

"The real me?"

"Right. All they know about you is, um ..." She realized she was getting into deeper trouble with every word she said and so she let the sentence fade away unfinished.

Lucas revived it. "... that I stabbed my father when I was seven, never got along with anyone while I was growing up and then, in my twenties, almost went to prison for assault and battery?"

What could she say? "Well, yes. More or less, that's about it."

"More *or* less? Which one?"

She slanted him a pained glance. "Well, you left out the books you write."

"They don't approve of my books?"

"Well, some of them don't. But I told you that. Remember how I said Linda Lou Beardsly—"

"—hates herself, but won't stop reading them."

"Right."

There was silence. Heather hoped Lucas wasn't offended. She really did want him to discover the goodness at the heart of most people in North Magdalene—and she *didn't* want him going after Roger or Rocky.

She decided she ought to point this out, "But not Roger or Rocky."

"Not Roger or Rocky what?"

"They don't have problems with your books. Roger and Rocky couldn't care less about your books. I don't think either of them has read a book on purpose since they got out of high school."

Lucas started up the car at last. But then, instead of driving away, he draped an arm over the steering wheel and turned to face her again. "Look. Do you want me to have a little talk with those two or something?"

Heather stifled a groan. "No. Please. Just let it be. They mean well, they really do."

"Right." Lucas shook his head, then muttered under his breath, "I can't wait to get out of this place." He pulled the car away from the curb.

Heather sank deeper into the luxurious seat and tried to pretend she hadn't heard his last remark. But then, as she pondered the conversation, Heather couldn't help wondering if maybe what she'd said in the restaurant had hit a nerve with him. Lucas *was* a wealthy man. And he was marrying her because of the baby, not because he loved her or longed to share his life with her. Maybe he resented the idea that she'd now have a wife's claim on all he owned.

When they'd pulled into the small lot of the clinic and Lucas had parked the car, she turned to him. "Lucas, I really wouldn't marry a man because he was rich, you know?"

"I know that," he said without hesitation.

Those words warmed her. She ventured more. "In fact, if you want, we can put together a prenuptial agreement. That would be fine with me."

"Oh, really?" He looked distant and impossible to reach again. "And what would this agreement say?"

"That everything you have stays yours, that's all."

"And what about you? What about what *you* have?"

She hadn't thought about that.

"Well?" Lucas prompted.

Heather was confused. "I don't know. I wasn't really thinking about what *I* have."

"Maybe you should."

"Well, all right." He just looked at her, so she assumed he was waiting for her to continue. Gamely she did. "I'm nowhere near being rich, but I have several thousand in savings, mostly the profits from the sale of the house Jason Lee and I were buying before Norma died and left us *her* house. And then there's the insurance. Jason Lee was a big believer in insurance." She smiled a little, thinking of him. "So I get money every month from that. And there's a little from the county and then the Conley house itself." She smiled wider. "Well, I guess I've got more than I realized, now that I think about it."

"Good. So you're not marrying me for my money. You know it and I know it. Let's cut the prenuptial agreement talk and do what we came here to do." He leaned on his door and pushed it open.

Heather grabbed his arm. "Lucas. Don't."

"Don't what?"

"Don't just . . . walk out on a person like that."

"We're here to get blood tests, aren't we?"

"Well, of course we are. But—"

"But what?"

"But we were *talking*."

"About how you don't need my money. I know. And I thought it was settled. You don't need my money and I don't need yours. And neither of us really wants any prenuptial agreement."

"Yes, that's right. That's how I feel."

"Good. Then was there something more you wanted to say?"

"Well, no. I just, um . . ."

"What?"

"Are you . . . mad at me for some reason?"

"No."

"But you act like you are."

"Well, I'm not. Now let's go."

She stared at him for a moment more, wondering if she would ever come to understand him, and beginning to fear his heart and mind would forever be closed to her. Then she shrugged and let go of his arm. "All right. Let's go."

He left the car. She got out, too, and followed him into the building.

Chapter Fifteen

That night was the same as the previous one. Lucas spent some time with Mark, but seemed preoccupied and distant whenever Heather tried to start a conversation with him. He was shut up in his room when she went to bed. And she was feeling just discouraged and irritated enough with him that she didn't go to his door again. She could get by just fine, she decided sourly, without her nightly pat on the head.

But she woke the next morning ready to try again. She was, after all, born a Jones. And a Jones never gave up.

When she arrived home that afternoon, Lucas was upstairs. She left him alone and did some more packing. But then, after dinner, when Mark went to Marnie's to watch a rented video, Heather insisted Lucas spend the evening with her.

He agreed, though rather grudgingly. They took another evening walk, then sat on the couch, where she told him about her last day at work. Lily had actually baked a cake and Tamara had cried and hugged her and asked if she could have Heather's lucky tip jar.

"What's that?" Lucas asked.

"The jar I put my tips in. It's lucky, everyone says so. A lot of quarters have gone through that jar."

"Maybe it's lucky because of you."

They were sitting on either end of the couch. Heather had kicked off her shoes and folded her feet under her. "Because I'm such a great waitress, you mean?"

"No. Because you're great, period."

That was nice to hear. "Lucas, I think that was a compliment."

"I think you could be right. Stretch out your feet. Come on."

She did, and he rubbed them. His hands were warm and strong, easing the aches away, and she cautioned herself not to think too much about how good those hands had felt on other parts of her body three nights before.

"Lucas?"

"Yeah?"

"Would you just . . . talk to me?"

"What about?"

"Yourself."

His hands stilled, cradling her right ankle. "What about me?"

"What you think. And feel."

"Such as?"

"Well, are you okay? About marrying me, I mean? Do you feel that I'm *trapping* you, or something?"

He actually chuckled. "Think back, Heather. I was the one pushing for marriage, not you."

She laughed, too. "You've got a point. But there's something wrong. Something—"

''What?''

She studied him, feeling very far out of her depth. ''You didn't let me finish.''

''All right, then. Finish.''

''Well, it seems like there's something bothering you, that's all.''

''No. There's not.''

''You're sure?''

''Positive.''

She pulled her feet free, but only so she could slide closer to him. ''Well. Great instincts I've got, huh?''

He put his arm around her and kissed her on the nose. She reveled in the hardness of his lean chest against her own softness and wondered shamelessly how she was going to last without his lovemaking for that night and three more nights to follow.

How could this be happening to her? She'd gone twenty-three years without his lovemaking and managed just fine. And yet here she was wondering how she would make it through the next four nights.

''Don't worry about your instincts,'' he whispered in her ear. ''You have other things going for you.''

She shivered a little. ''Like what?''

''I could show you.''

Oh, she shouldn't, she knew it, yet her lips were saying, ''Yes. All right. Please do.''

He kissed her, his mouth covering hers in a caress both tender and consuming. She pressed herself eagerly against him. It was a long kiss and would have been longer had there not been the sound of sneakered feet bounding up onto the porch.

They pulled apart, both breathing a little too hard, and turned to smile at Mark when he came in the door.

* * *

Heather floated through the rest of the evening in a state of dreamy arousal, smiling to herself at the thought of how Lucas's lips felt against her own, telling herself it wasn't *that* long until Saturday. She could wait. Somehow.

But then later, when she lay in her bed unable to sleep, she couldn't help suspecting that he'd done it again— avoided the subject of what was really on his mind.

The next day they drove to the government center in Nevada City and got the marriage license. Then they went out to lunch at a nice restaurant. Heather had a lovely time. Lucas was attentive and charming. They talked about his books and she told him just what she thought of each one. He told her that he and Mark lived a very private life in Monterey, that the only time he really got out was for the required publicity tours whenever one of his books was released.

"Are you trying to reassure me that I'll get along all right in your world?" she asked.

"I'm just telling you that there isn't any big social scene for you to get used to."

She thought about that. "Maybe I wouldn't mind a big social scene. I'm a pretty social person, after all."

"If you want to get out, we can do that."

"Maybe we could just . . . stay in North Magdalene and live? If you want a bigger house, we could even build one."

They'd just left the restaurant. He stopped in the middle of Commercial Street and turned to her. "Are you ever going to give that up?"

She gave a little shrug. "Probably not. I love my hometown."

"I gathered. But we're living in Monterey." He started walking again.

She had to hurry to catch up with him. "Don't be grumpy." She took his arm and beamed up at him.

He granted her a grudging smile. "Then knock it off."

"Okay. For now."

Heather was so encouraged by their afternoon together, that she didn't even hesitate to seek him out in his room again as soon as Mark was in bed. When he opened the door to her, she caught a quick glance of his computer before he blocked it with his body. The screen was dark.

"You're not working," she accused teasingly.

"Yes, I am. I'm thinking."

"About what?"

"About my work."

"Let me come in."

"That could be dangerous."

"I'll take my chances."

He stood back and she entered the room. She heard the door close and turned to find him leaning against it, his arms crossed over his chest, watching her. He wore loose black slacks and a crew-neck black shirt and his feet were bare. They were very well-formed feet, actually, lightly dusted with dark hair.

"What are you up to, Heather?"

She tore her gaze away from his toes and made herself confront those unreadable eyes. "I thought... we could talk."

"We talked all day."

"Well, I know but..."

"But what?"

"I just, well, it's only two days until the wedding. And I don't feel as if we really know each other yet."

He straightened from the door and came toward her, his bare feet silent on the hardwood floor. Oh, he was wonderful to watch when he moved. So fluid—and yet so direct.

All she wanted as she watched him approach was to know his touch again. She felt a little ashamed of herself, really. He'd been right; her coming in here was dangerous if they planned to keep their hands off each other until Saturday night.

So what was she doing in here? And why hadn't she protested when he closed the door?

He stopped in front of her. She could feel the warmth of him, smell his special scent. "What is it you think we should know about each other that we don't already know?"

Her throat felt tight. She coughed a little to loosen it. "Well, everything. What we think. What we feel. The... secrets of our hearts."

He regarded her quizzically for a moment, then agreed, "Okay. Start talking. Tell me what you think. And what you feel. And all your secrets. I can't wait to hear."

He was taunting her. A moment ago, she'd felt like his equal. Now she felt about two inches tall.

"Oh, Lucas." She looked away.

He captured her chin and brought her head back around, so she had to look at him. "Not so easy, is it?"

His hand felt so warm against her skin. Oh, what was the matter with her? All she could think of was the way he felt. She had to put her desire aside for right now. She had to concentrate on getting through to him, on getting to *know* him in a deeper, more honest way than she knew him now.

She attempted once more to explain her unease. "I don't know, I just..."

"You just what?"

"There's just something..."

He lifted his hand and brushed her hair back over her shoulder. Then he idly caressed the side of her neck with the back of his fingers. "Give it up, Heather."

"Give what up?" Her voice was dreamy. His fingers had magic in them. Just the lightest breath of a stroke on the side of her neck, and her whole body was on fire.

"You can't know everything about me. Not in a few days—probably not in a lifetime. And I can't know all there is to know about you. Just relax. Let it be. We'll be married. I'll take care of you." His hand strayed. He took her earlobe between his thumb and forefinger and worried it, gently, maddeningly.

"Lucas..."

"You should go. Or stay." He cupped the back of her neck, his fingers under her hair, pressing on her skin.

Her breath got stuck in her chest. "I...we agreed..."

"Then you should go."

"But I..."

"Then you should stay." He pulled her closer, so their bodies almost touched.

She swayed a little, and had to hold onto his shoulders to steady herself. "Oh, Lucas. I have no backbone."

He chuckled. His fingers moved downward, tracing the bumps of her spine through her blouse. "Yes, you do. I can feel it. Right here." He reached the small of her back and stopped there, his hand warm and possessive against the curve of her hip.

"This time...I would have to go, before morning. Just in case Mark—"

"Yes." His hand slid lower still, then back up to clasp her waist. "That would be best."

"You knew, didn't you, when I asked you to wait until the wedding, that I wouldn't last? That's why you gave me that strange look."

He stepped back a fraction. Her heart thudded, heavy and needful beneath her breast, as his fingers began working at the buttons of her blouse. "I wasn't thinking about whether *you* could last, actually," he muttered low and rather hoarsely.

The buttons fell away. With a forefinger, he guided the blouse to the back of her shoulders and then off to the floor. He used both hands to unhook her denim skirt and soon it fell around her sandaled feet.

And then he reached for her, scooped her up against his chest and carried her to the bed.

It was hours later, after she'd returned to her own room, that she realized he'd evaded her once more. And she had helped him do it.

She lay between the cool sheets of her bed, her body limp and sated, her mind and heart unsatisfied.

Heather moaned and wondered what was happening to her. Lucas was like a drug in her system. She wanted more and more of him. And yet, he wouldn't let her get truly close.

He wouldn't show his heart to her.

She turned over, pulled up the sheet, then kicked it off again.

When at last sleep came, Heather dreamed she was swimming at the special, secret swimming hole that only she and Jason Lee used to visit. It was night and the moon was full, the stars so thick they seemed to run together. The expanse of beach was silvery in the moonlight.

Naked, Heather lay in the sand, staring up at the moon, waiting for Jason Lee. But he didn't come.

Finally, with a sigh, she rose and went to the water. She waded in. The water was warm, much warmer than she ever remembered it being. Like heated liquid silk all around her. She dived deep, opening her eyes and discovering, after a moment, that she could breathe in the water. She swam for a long time, under the surface, breathing the water, soothed by its silky feel.

At last, she grew weary of swimming. She poked her head above the water. And Jason Lee was sitting there, as naked as she was, on the bank, at the place where she'd gone in.

She knew it was him, though his body seemed leaner and taller and the moon was behind him so that she couldn't make out his face. It had to be him. No one else knew this secret place.

Heather rose from the water and he stood at the same time. They walked toward each other and met in the shallows. And that was when she saw who it really was, when she understood that she really hadn't been waiting for Jason Lee after all.

She'd been waiting for Lucas. And now he was here.

"Let's talk about what's in *your* heart," Lucas whispered.

"My heart?" She looked down at the water that lapped around their calves, then back up at him.

"You love *me*," he said.

She said nothing. It was only the truth.

Chapter Sixteen

Heather woke the next morning with the dream vivid in her mind. For a moment she lay there, staring at her bedside radio alarm clock, which she hadn't bothered to set since she didn't have to go to work. It was eight thirty-five—and her stomach was acting up on her as usual.

Heather threw back the covers, jumped from the bed and stumbled to the bathroom where she bent over the commode. But after a minute, she discovered she didn't need to throw up after all.

When she was sure her stomach could be trusted, she looked in the mirror over the sink.

She didn't look that much different than she had yesterday. Yet she was irrevocably changed.

She loved Lucas.

That was it; that was her secret. The one she'd been keeping from everyone. Including herself.

He was exactly the kind of man she'd never meant to love. Too much like her father, and all the other Jones men. And yet it had happened. She loved him.

Which made no sense. She hardly knew him. He would not let himself be known.

But when she closed her eyes and tried to conjure Jason Lee's face in her mind, it would not come. All she could see were black-lashed ebony eyes, a hawklike nose and that cruel, sensuous slash of a mouth.

All she could see was Lucas.

"Aunt Heather, you okay?" Mark asked her around a mouthful of Super Wheat Crunchies at breakfast.

"Of course. Why do you ask?"

"Well, you closed your eyes there for a moment and I thought you were gonna fall off your chair."

"No. It's just . . . I'm just . . . It's the wedding. I have a lot of things on my mind."

"Yeah." Mark dipped up another huge spoonful of cereal. "It's gonna be a serious event, no doubt about it." Mark stuck the cereal into his mouth and started crunching it. He was going to stand up for his father as best man, and was quite proud of himself.

"I know I'm young, Dad," Mark had said when Lucas asked him. "But I won't let you down."

And Mark was right about the wedding being an event. Somehow, the ceremony that Heather had envisioned as an intimate, casual gathering of the closest members of the family, was growing into a bigger deal as each day passed. Part of the reason was that the family was pretty large in itself. Grandpa Oggie had fathered five children, after all. And each of those children had a wife or a husband and most of them had kids. And then there was dear, departed Grandma Bathsheba's side of the family, the Rileys, who happened to be related in some distant way to just about everyone who'd ever lived in the area in the past hundred years. And beyond the Rileys, there was Heather's own deceased mother's side of the family, the Willises. Most of them no longer lived nearby, but Aunt Delilah had called a few of them. And some said they'd come.

And on top of all the family, there were the friends— friends who were so much *like* family that it seemed it would be a crime to leave them out. Eden's and Aunt Regina's phones were ringing night and day with people calling up to say they wouldn't miss the wedding for all the gold in the mother lode.

Aunt Regina had finally decided to put up a notice at the post office inviting everyone who wanted to be there. The immediate members of the family would arrive early and for everyone else, it would be first come, first served.

This morning at eleven Heather was scheduled to try on her grandmother's wedding dress for—she sincerely hoped—the last time. And tomorrow there was even going to be a rehearsal in Aunt Regina's backyard, after which Aunt Delilah was putting on a big feast at her house. Then on the morning of the wedding, Aunt Amy was having everyone over to her house for a family breakfast.

"Morning," Lucas said as he entered the kitchen. "What's up with the two of you?"

"Aunt Heather looks like she's gonna heave, but other than that, nothing much," Mark said.

Lucas turned his dark gaze her way, his brow furrowing in concern. "Heather?"

Heather's air seemed to be cut off. Her heart was bouncing around in her chest. She loved him. *Loved* him....

"Heather? Are you all right?"

From some impossible place within her, she came upon her own voice. "Oh. Yes. Fine. Just fine." She shot to her feet. "Sit down. I'll pour you some coffee." She pulled out the chair he usually sat in.

Mark and Lucas exchanged baffled glances, then Lucas turned to Heather again. "You look strange," he insisted.

"Well, I'm not. Just sit down."

Shaking his head, Lucas took the chair.

Mark finished chewing his last bite of cereal and announced, "Listen. I'm going to Marnie's. But we'll be back over here in an hour or two, okay? We want to work on the tree fort." He and Marnie had spent the last couple of hours of the previous afternoon rebuilding the old fort in the walnut tree out back. Clearly, more repairs were in the offing.

"That's fine," Heather heard herself say. Mark left. Heather realized she was still staring dreamily at Lucas, who was staring back at her, his expression caught midway between puzzlement and concern.

"Are you *sure* you're okay?"

"Me? Absolutely. Top-notch."

"Are you upset about last night?"

"Last night? Why would I be upset about that?"

"We broke our agreement that we wouldn't make love until after the wedding."

"Our agreement?"

He lifted a brow at her. "Heather. You do remember the agreement we had. It was your idea, after all."

"Yes. Of course, I remember."

"Then are you upset because we didn't keep it?"

"Um. No. I suppose I should be. But I'm not."

"Then what is going on with you?"

"Nothing. I told you. Everything's fine. Really. I'll get that coffee for you." She went to the counter, got a cup from the cabinet and poured his coffee, then returned to give him the cup. When she set it in front of him, a little sloshed on the table.

Lucas snared her wrist before she could pull it away. He looked up at her. She melted inside.

"You're shaking," he said.

"No, I'm not." His grip was so warm. She loved it when he touched her. She loved just the feel of his skin against her own.

"Heather . . ."

"If you let go of my wrist, I'll make you some breakfast."

He released her and she moved away from him quickly. It was too much right then, being next to him. She fled to the cupboards, where she took down a mixing bowl, then banged things around for a few minutes in search of the frying pan.

"Have you seen a doctor yet?" he asked from behind her.

"A doctor?"

"About the baby."

"Scrambled all right?"

"Fine. Have you?"

She set the frying pan on the stove and moved to the refrigerator to get the eggs. "That's today, as a matter of fact. In Grass Valley, at one. Of course, I'll have to find another doctor, if and when we move to Monterey. But it seemed like a good idea, to make sure everything is going along fine."

"Good," he said. "I'll drive you there."

Heather's heart slammed against her rib cage. He would drive her there! She couldn't wait. Yet how would she bear the drive in the car all that way alone with him, knowing she loved him? It made everything different, that she loved him.

And she was going to have to tell him. Maybe she'd do it then. This afternoon. On the trip to Grass Valley to see the obstetrician.

Just thinking about telling him made her forget about the carton of eggs in her hands. It slipped free. "Oops." She had to execute a tricky little dip to catch it before it hit the floor. "Hah!" she exclaimed triumphantly, then felt like an idiot. She held up the carton and grinned sheepishly. "Caught them."

Lucas stared at her. "What is the matter with you?"

She opened her mouth to say, *I love you, with all my heart.* But then closed it at the last minute, and turned to open the carton of eggs. "Nothing's the matter. Three eggs about right?" She waited, the first egg poised at the side of the bowl, for his answer.

Finally he gave it. "Yes. Good. Three."

Carefully she cracked the eggs into the bowl.

"Are you getting nervous about the wedding?" he asked.

"Yes. A little." She sprinkled some spices on the eggs, then pulled a wire whisk from a drawer and whipped them to a froth.

A few minutes later, she set the food in front of him.

"This looks perfect. Thanks."

Heather had to restrain herself from dropping to her knees before him and swearing she'd cook anything he wanted, any way he wanted it, for as long as they both should live.

Heather went to Eden's house to try on the dress, which her stepmother had picked up, cleaned and altered, at eight that very morning. If it didn't fit, Heather would take it back for one more set of alterations when she went to Grass Valley that afternoon.

But it did fit—as if it had been made for her. Eden burst into tears when Heather stood before her in the yards of satin and lace. "Oh, Heather. It's beautiful. Beautiful."

Heather turned to look in the mirror that hung on Eden's bedroom wall and found that she was crying, too. She swiped at the tears with the heel of her hand.

Eden, her tears trickling unashamed down her cheeks, came up behind Heather and peered over her shoulder. "Have you seen the pictures of Oggie and your grandmother on their wedding day?"

Heather sniffled and nodded. "Yes, I've seen them. Grandpa has them in an old album."

"You look so much like her," Eden said.

"Like Grandma Bathsheba?"

"Mmm-hmm."

Heather sniffled some more. "You think so?"

"Yes. There's no doubt about it. The resemblance is…stunning." Eden grabbed a tissue from the box on the nearby vanity table and wiped her eyes. Then she sighed and dropped out of Heather's line of sight as she sat at the brass-backed vanity chair. Heather turned around so that she could see her. Their gazes caught and held.

"This marriage is about more than a baby on the way, isn't it?" Eden asked softly. "You love him, don't you?"

Heather looked down. She fiddled with a seed pearl on the bodice of the dress.

"Don't pull on the beadwork," Eden chided. "And answer me. Do you love Lucas Drury?"

Heather left the pearl alone. She lifted her head and looked at her stepmother again. Then she sniffled one more time. "Yes."

"I knew it." Eden yanked out another tissue and held it out to Heather. "I'm so glad."

Heather took the tissue and blew her nose. "I'd like to sit down, but I'm afraid I'll wrinkle the dress. Can you undo the hooks for me?" She showed Eden her back, sweeping her hair to the side.

Eden rose and began unhooking the dress. Neither woman spoke until Eden had helped Heather out of the gown and laid it carefully across the bed.

After smoothing out all the wrinkles, Eden turned and looked at her stepdaughter again. "All right, so you love him and you're marrying him. But you're not happy. Tell me what's wrong."

Heather stepped out of the three-layered, tulle-bordered slip and reached for her jeans. "Nothing. And everything."

"Doesn't he love you, too?"

Heather pulled on the jeans and buttoned them up. "No."

"Are you sure?"

Heather pulled her T-shirt over her head, flipped her hair out from under the neckline and then tucked in the shirt. "Who can be sure about anything when it comes to Lucas?"

"Does he know that you love him?"

"Uh-uh."

"You must tell him."

"I know." Heather sat in the vanity chair and picked up her socks, then dropped them again and hung her head. "But I can't. You don't know what he's like. *I* don't know what he's like. He won't let me in. He's . . . an impossible kind of man."

Eden smiled. "So's your father. But we worked it out. You tell Lucas how you feel, that's all. And let him take it from there."

Easier said than done, Heather thought of Eden's advice later, when she and Lucas were on their way to Grass Valley. Somehow, she just couldn't get those three little words out of her mouth.

So they drove in silence.

At the doctor's office, Heather filled out a lot of forms. She was given another pregnancy test. Then she received a complete physical.

An hour later, after the doctor had told her she was pregnant and doing just fine, she and Lucas headed back home.

"Well?" Lucas asked when they were out in the car again.

Heather shrugged. "I'm pregnant. And there are no problems so far, according to the doctor."

"Did you tell him you get nauseated a lot?"

She cast him a glance. "It's called morning sickness, Lucas."

"Don't be sarcastic."

"Sorry. But really. He says there's nothing wrong."

"Did you tell him about the incident this morning?"

"What incident?"

"How you couldn't keep your train of thought, you dropped things and your hands shook."

Heather had to look away to avoid bursting into hysterical laughter. Lucas had seen the signs of her love for him—and he was certain she must be seriously ill.

"Well, did you?"

"Yes," she fibbed.

"And?"

"He, um, said it was nothing to worry about—as long as it doesn't keep up."

"Well. All right, then." He started the car, backed it up and turned it around to leave the parking lot.

Through the entire drive, Heather kept trying to think of a way to tell him of her love. But when they pulled up in front of her house, she was still thinking. And nothing had been said.

They went inside. Lucas went back to work. Heather took a little nap, then did some packing later. From the backyard, she could hear Mark and Marnie, hammering away at the tree house and laughing together like the best buddies they were.

Marnie stayed for dinner and then to play chess with Mark afterward. Heather enjoyed having the kids there— and it made it easier for her to let the whole evening go by without trying to tell Lucas her feelings.

But once Mark was in bed, Heather knew what she had to do. She went to Lucas's room. When he let her in, she was the one to close the door.

"Lucas," she said, leaning back on the door as much for support as to keep him from escaping before she made her declaration. "We have to talk."

His lips slowly turned up at the corners in a smile that was incredibly sensual—and totally unknowable. He came toward her, took her face in his hands and kissed her.

And then he took her to bed.

Afterward, dazed and physically sated, she found herself in her own room once more. She had told him nothing; he hadn't allowed her to.

The next day was Friday, the last day before the wedding. At breakfast, before Mark came to the table, Heather did manage to speak to Lucas privately for a moment. She asked for some time alone with him before the wedding. Some time for a talk, when they would not be interrupted.

He promised they would talk that night, after the rehearsal dinner.

"*Talk,*" she insisted, "not . . . make love."

He gave her a hooded look. "You don't enjoy making love?"

She couldn't decide whether she wanted to strangle him—or kiss him. "Of course I do," she whispered shyly. "But there's really something I, um, want to say to you."

Mark appeared from the hall right then, still in his pajamas. He yawned and stretched. "What's for breakfast?"

"French toast," Heather said.

"Yum."

She turned to Lucas again before she rose to fix Mark's food. "Tonight, then. No matter what."

Lucas seemed to be looking out the window.

"Lucas, did you hear me? I said tonight."

He gave her a distant smile. "Of course."

After that, the day flew by. Lucas worked all morning; Heather packed. Then after lunch there was the rehearsal at Regina's. And then the big family dinner at Delilah and Sam's.

They arrived back home at a little after nine. Mark stayed up for another hour after that. And then, at last, Heather and Lucas were alone.

They sat on the couch in the living room. And Heather leaned close to him.

"Lucas, I—"

She was cut off by the sound of men's voices in the yard. Men's voices singing.

Roll me over, in the clover.
Roll me over, lay me down
And do it again . . .

"Oh, no," Heather moaned.

Lucas looked bewildered. "What is *that?*"

Before she could answer, her grandfather burst in the door, followed closely by her father and her uncles.

"Drury, you're comin' with us," Oggie announced. "Get 'im, boys." He snapped his fingers and his sons and son-in-law moved toward Lucas.

"Oh, please. You can't be serious," Heather cried.

"Don't be whinin', girl," Oggie said. "It's Lucas's last night of freedom. He's gonna spend it with the men."

"Getting drunk and getting into trouble." Heather shook her head. "I don't think so."

But her uncles and her father had already slid past her. They surrounded Lucas, who stood by the couch.

"I hope you'll come with us peaceablelike," Uncle Patrick said in a fair imitation of the sheriff in a bad melodrama.

Lucas put up his hands. "I surrender, boys." He looked perfectly content to be spirited away.

Heather saw her last chance for a quiet talk slipping from her grasp. "Lucas, you promised."

He had the nerve to shrug. "Heather. Come on. What can I do here? These guys are serious."

"You're damn straight," Oggie said. He snapped his fingers again.

The men grabbed Lucas and, between them, lifted him high in the air. They carried him out, ducking in unison to clear the door.

Oggie followed behind them, barking instructions. Heather took up the rear.

"When you get back, Lucas!" she shouted as they strode off down the front walk. "No matter how late it is!"

Lucas only waved from his prone position on the shoulders of her male relatives.

Muttering to herself, Heather climbed the stairs. She put on her pajamas, found a book to read and went to Lucas's room. After propping the pillows against the headboard, she climbed into the bed and turned on the reading light. She didn't care how late her blasted menfolk kept him out. They were going to talk when he got home. She was not going to marry Lucas until he knew the truth she held in her heart.

At a quarter to four, Lucas quietly let himself in the front door. He took off his shoes, almost falling over sideways in the process because he'd consumed a large amount of beer.

They'd taken him to Jared's place, where Eden and the baby were nowhere to be found. Oggie had produced several kegs of beer and the men had laughed and talked. It had all been pretty harmless really, except for all that beer. The toasts had been never ending.

Lucas had enjoyed himself. In fact, he was discovering that he could get used to his in-laws-to-be without much effort. They were good people, expansive and true at heart.

With his shoes in his hand, Lucas tiptoed up the stairs and slowly pushed open his bedroom door.

Heather was there in his bed as he'd suspected she might be. She'd fallen asleep sitting up. An open book lay across her lap, right where it had fallen when she couldn't keep her eyes open any longer.

Lucas hovered near the door, not daring to approach her. She might wake. And want to talk. She was getting insistent enough about talking that he doubted he could use lovemaking to sidetrack her again.

But this was it. The day of the wedding. By three this afternoon, she'd be solidly committed to him in the most binding way that man and the law could devise. More and more each day, he doubted whether that would be enough. But it was all he could do.

If he could just hold out against any of the soul-baring she kept demanding, maybe...

Standing there in the doorway, Lucas shook his head.

Hell. It did no good to think too deeply about it. He was a man in a trap. And it was a trap of his own devising.

Carefully he backed away from the room. He found a blanket in the hall closet and went downstairs. There, he stretched out on the couch to see if he could catch an hour or two of sleep.

Heather woke to daylight, alone in Lucas's room. She sat there among the pillows, rubbing her stiff neck and coming to grips with the fact that she'd been given the slip once more.

The leather-covered travel clock on the bed stand said it was past eight.

They were due at Aunt Amy's for breakfast at nine. And after that, she had to get over to Santino's Barber, Beauty and Variety Store on Main Street, so that Alma could fix her hair.

Time had run out on her. There would be no more opportunities for intimate talks. Today at two she would say "I do" to a man who wouldn't let her near, a man to whom, for some unfathomable reason, she seemed to have given her heart.

She could guess without much effort where he was right now: downstairs, on the couch. Maybe, if she hurried, she could get down there and catch him while he was still asleep. She could shake him awake and announce, "Lucas, I love you. Now hurry up, we're due for breakfast at nine."

Heather groaned, grabbed one of the pillows from behind her head and threw it at the door across the room. Then she got out of bed, traipsed into her own room and stood under the shower for a good twenty minutes.

When she was done, she blew her hair dry, anchored it off her face with two combs and left the makeup for later, so it would be fresh for the big event. She put on a butter yellow sundress and a pair of thin-soled yellow sandals. Then, at 8:50, she went down the stairs.

Lucas and Mark were waiting in the living room, all dressed and ready to head for Aunt Amy's. Heather studied Lucas's face, noting that the only evidence of his night out with the boys was a slight puffiness around the eyes. His shirt and slacks weren't the ones he'd been wearing last night, which meant he must have sneaked up to his own room to change after she returned to *her* room. It was amazing, she thought bleakly, just how far the man would go to avoid a private conversation with her.

"It's about time," Mark said. "I wanted to come up and get you, but Dad said to wait, you'd be down."

Lucas lifted an eyebrow at her. "All ready?"

She was angry and disappointed with him. And she loved him so much it caused an ache beneath her breastbone. "I'm as ready as I'll ever be. Let's go."

At Aunt Amy's there were ham and eggs, muffins and potatoes, coffee and milk—and three kinds of juice. And Uncle Brendan served Bloody Marys, the oldest cure in the world for too much of a good thing the night before.

Grandpa Oggie, still going strong after staying up all night, gave a long, impassioned speech about how the bad blood between the Drurys and the Joneses was now a thing of the past.

"For now at last," he concluded in his usual extravagant style, "Drury blood and Jones blood will flow as one in the coming together of our Sunshine and Rory's boy, Lucas." Oggie raised his Bloody Mary high. "So let's drink to that, all of us. To a better world, where old hatreds are but a memory and true love rules the day!"

Everybody clapped and hooted in agreement, then drank long and deep. Heather forced down a sip of tomato juice and wished the interminable breakfast would come to an end. She adored her old grandpa, but sometimes he had a way of saying just what she couldn't bear to hear.

True love, she thought in weary bitterness, is the last thing ruling the day around here.

She knew Lucas, who sat next to her, was watching her. She made herself turn to him and she made herself smile.

He looked back at her, one of those deep, incomprehensible looks of his.

She was marrying a stranger. A stranger who owned her heart.

Four hours later, Heather stood at a window in an upstairs bedroom at her aunt Regina's house, wearing her grandmother's wedding gown and peering between lace curtains at the crowd in the backyard below.

"Standing room only," Eden said from behind her.

Heather turned. "Yes." She forced a smile. "There's barely room to move down there."

Eden reached out a careful hand and smoothed a stray hair into place beneath Heather's headpiece. "There. Beautiful." She bent closer. "Did you tell him?"

Heather took in a steadying breath. Her emotions, which had been touch and go all day, were hanging by a thread at that moment. "No," she whispered in reply.

Eden fiddled with Heather's veil, smoothing out a few wrinkles. "It's all right. You will. Tonight. On your wedding night. That will be the perfect time."

"I don't know, Eden. I just don't know."

Eden touched her arm. "Listen. Believe me. Love finds a way."

Heather had no reply for her stepmother. She honestly felt there was nothing to say. "Eden, if you don't mind, I'd like a few minutes alone."

"Of course. I'll be back up to collect you. When it's time."

As soon as the door closed behind Eden, Heather turned to the window again to study the scene below.

The window was closed, but even through the glass, Heather could hear the buzz of a hundred voices. All the family was assembled. And so many friends, too. Heather saw Lily talking to Rocky, who had a drink in his hand, as usual. Even Nellie Anderson and Linda Lou Beardsly were there, huddled together, whispering secrets that wouldn't be secrets for long.

And there was music. In a corner of the big yard, Aunt Regina sat at her piano, which the men had rolled outside for the occasion. Regina's slim fingers flew over the keys, conjuring a melody both haunting and sweet.

Not far from the piano stood an arbor of roses, which Heather's aunts had set up at the edge of the lawn near the redwood fence. It was under that arbor that Heather and Lucas were to exchange their vows just minutes from now. Reverend Johnson, now standing stiffly near the arbor waiting for the proceedings to get under way, would perform the ceremony.

Heather scanned the yard for Lucas and found him over by the refreshment table not far from the kitchen door. She couldn't get over how handsome he looked, with his hair shining as black as a crow's wing in the afternoon sun, wearing a tux that probably cost more than she could make at Lily's in a year. He was talking to Grandpa Oggie, the dark head and the grizzled one bent close together. As she watched, her grandpa threw back his head and guffawed at some remark Lucas had made.

By the look of things, Lucas was getting along just fine with her relatives. She supposed she should be pleased to see that.

But it was hard to be pleased. There was just too much unsaid between herself and Lucas. There were too many mysteries. This should have been the happiest day of her life—and yet she felt nothing but bitterness and the burning of angry tears at the back of her throat.

Lucas simply would not talk to her. He would not let her close, except to make love with her. And there was no reason for her to believe that it would be any different once they'd exchanged marriage vows.

Her future stretched before her, grim and lonely. She'd be married to a man who kept her at a distance, miles away from her home and the people she loved. Mark—and eventually the baby—would bring some solace. But could they make up for a loveless marriage to a man who held himself aloof from her?

The answer came, plain and simple: no.

She'd had a happy, caring marriage. And settling for less now, no matter if she was pregnant or not, just wasn't something she could do, after all.

Admitting to herself that she loved Lucas had changed everything. It put everything into perspective somehow. She was a woman with a heart full of love to give. And the man she married had to be capable of loving her right back. That was why she had to tell him, had to see his face when she told him. She had to know if there was even a chance he might someday love her in return.

But what could she do? How could she get through to Lucas, get close to Lucas? He was such a stubborn man, and nearly impossible to reach.

Look at poor Mark. The boy had finally resorted to disappearing for three whole days to get the man to pay attention....

The knock came at the door. It was Eden. "Ready? It's time."

"Yes. All right."

Eden entered the room and helped to lift Heather's veil and smooth it in place.

"There." Eden smiled.

Heather smiled back at her through a cloud of white tulle and a mist of unshed tears. Eden went to the dresser and collected two bouquets: a small spray of sweet peas and daisies for herself and a beribboned creation of white roses, yellow freesias and baby's breath for Heather.

Down in the yard, Aunt Regina began playing "As Time Goes By," the song they'd agreed would precede the wedding march. Both women turned, listening. Eden handed Heather her bouquet.

"Let's go," Eden said, and went ahead out the door.

Heather followed behind, moving slowly, mindful of her long skirt and the short train that brushed the floor behind her. Down the stairs she went, through the hall to the dining room and then through the dining room into the kitchen where the back door stood open onto the yard.

It was a sunny day, but mild for August. Perfect weather, people had been telling Heather since morning, for an outdoor wedding. To Heather, standing in the cool dimness of her aunt Regina's kitchen, the world beyond the threshold seemed preternaturally bright. The crowd of people appeared to glow with the sunlight reflecting off white shirts and summer cottons.

The guests stood in two groups, leaving a swatch of lawn leading up to the arbor for an aisle. At the arbor, Lucas and Mark, who was dressed in a tux just like his father's, waited a little to the side. Reverend Johnson held pride of place front and center.

Heather's father was standing by the kitchen door. Eden, Heather's only attendant, had already stepped just beyond the door to wait for the wedding march.

Heather approached her father and took his outstretched arm.

The wedding march began. Eden started slowly down the aisle. When she reached the arbor and took her place on the opposite side from Lucas and Mark, Heather and her father stepped out into the light.

A collective sigh rose from the guests at the sight of the bride in her grandmother's wedding gown.

Heather knew everyone was looking at her, but she stared straight ahead as she covered the distance between the kitchen door and the arbor. In no time, she was there. Her father stepped back. Heather felt, rather than saw, Lucas take his place.

Reverend Johnson coughed officiously. And then he opened his black bible and began, "Dearly beloved—"

And that was it. It was all Heather could bear.

"No!" The word erupted from the depths of her.

There was a silence the likes of which Heather had never known. Then, from the crowd, there seemed to come the sound of one long, indrawn breath.

Heather whirled to face them all, as behind her she heard Reverend Johnson start to sputter. "Miz Conley, I don't believe this is—"

"Quiet, Reverend," she muttered over her shoulder, then faced front again. She lifted her veil, quickly, to get it out of her way, almost ripping it in the process.

She looked out on a sea of stunned, wide-eyed faces. She didn't dare glance to the side yet, where Lucas was standing.

"I can't," she heard her own voice say. "I won't. And that is that."

"Miz Conley. Miz Conley, *please*..." Poor Reverend Johnson sounded distressed. But then, she knew he'd always loathed officiating at ceremonies involving the Joneses. Things never went as planned. "Miz Conley, we must—"

"No!" Heather whirled on the Reverend. "Do you hear me, no!" The Reverend shrank back.

Heather sucked in a breath and forced herself to turn to Lucas. "I can't, Lucas." Her voice was tortured, torn from her. She scanned the unknowable face she'd come to love in spite of herself. "Not like this. Not this way. Oh, Lucas. I just can't!"

She tossed her bouquet back over her shoulder, not caring in the least if anyone caught it. And then, as swift as the wind, Heather lifted her heavy skirts, kicked off her satin shoes and sprinted back up the grass aisle the way she had come, through the back door of her aunt Regina's house, into the kitchen, the dining room, the living room—and right out the front door.

Chapter Seventeen

Heather was halfway to the woods that began at the end of the street, yards of satin hiked up around her knees, her veil flying behind her, before pandemonium broke loose in her aunt's backyard.

The guests, who'd stood stunned as Heather fled, finally could no longer hold that collective breath they'd sucked in.

They let it out, then they started to whisper, and then mutter. And within seconds, Tim Brown shouted out loud, "She's gone!"

"She's run away!" Nellie Anderson exclaimed.

"Who woulda dreamed it?" Rocky Collins cried. "Sunshine ran out on her wedding to the Shadowmaster!"

Oggie, not far from the arbor, turned to bark at Lucas. "You better hightail it after her..." But then his gravelly voice trailed off.

"Yeah, Dad, hurry, she's getting away! You've got to—" Mark stopped in midsentence and looked all around. "Dad?"

Oggie put his arm around the boy. "We might as well save our breath, son. Looks to me like your dad is one step ahead of us."

Out on the street, Heather made the cover of the woods. But she didn't slow down. She continued to run, though branches tore her veil, pebbles cut her stockings to shreds and she tripped more than once on the trailing hem of her gown. It didn't matter. Nothing mattered, but to escape her aunt Regina's backyard and all the stunned faces and Lucas, her dark love, who would not share his secret heart or allow her to share hers.

Escape, get away, the words pounded in her blood as she ran on, tears streaming down her face, her breath coming into her lungs in great, gulping pants, until she was so exhausted she could run no more.

Finally she tripped on a tree root, and went sprawling on the ground. And since she was there, she just stayed there, her face in the dirt, sobbing, sucking in air frantically, until her heart slowed a little, she caught her breath and she got the tears under control.

After that, she pushed herself to a sitting position and wiped her nose with the back of her hand. Right then, her pearl headpiece slid down over one eye. She realized she had sat up on her veil.

With a small, *"Oomph,"* she managed to lift up enough to yank the veil out from under herself. Then, with the veil freed, she dropped to the ground again and shoved the headpiece, more or less, back into place.

At last, with her vision unobstructed, Heather looked around her, trying to decide where she was.

About two miles into the woods east of town, she judged. From a cedar tree nearby, a squirrel berated her, hanging on upside down, tipping its gray head from side to side. Heather looked down at her grandmother's beautiful dress, which was now wrinkled and torn at bodice and hem, not to mention liberally streaked with red dirt.

"Yes, I know," she said to the squirrel, "I'm a mess. You don't have to rub it in." The headpiece threatened to slide over her eye again. She took a moment to find a hairpin in her tumbled coiffure and anchor the thing a little more firmly to the crown of her head.

Then, with a great deal of grunting and groaning due to her trailing skirts, Heather struggled to her feet. The squirrel grew agitated as she stood. It squealed at her a few more times, slid around on the tree trunk until it was headed up instead of down, and scampered skyward, quickly disappearing into the thick branches above.

Gamely, Heather saluted the animal. Then she gathered up her tattered skirts and started walking—or perhaps limping was more the word for it now—farther along the trail she'd come down.

Soon enough, as she knew she would, she came to another trail that branched off to the right. She limped down that trail for a good half hour, then turned right again at a trail that she knew would take her to the highway just south of town.

When she reached the highway, she hid behind a clump of sapling oaks until she was sure there was no traffic coming either way. Then she bolted across, holding her torn skirts high. Once she was on the other side she used the sun as her guide and went north again.

An hour and a half after she'd run away from her wedding, her feet aching and her ruined dress now stained beneath the arms with sweat, Heather reached the old house where her grandpa had raised his family, the house where Mark had hidden from his father two months before. After all, she reasoned wearily, if it was good enough for Mark to hide from Lucas, it was certainly good enough for her.

The front door was locked when she tried it, so she trudged through the dry weeds to the back. The back door was locked, too. But it had glass panes in the top and two of them were broken. It was easy to reach in and turn the bolt.

Inside the house was cool and dusty. The cracked linoleum floor of the kitchen was marginally soothing to her hot, scratched feet. Heather shuffled through the kitchen, feeling just about as miserable as she'd ever felt in her life.

When she reached the living room, Heather let her dress fall around her ankles, where it sent a thousand dust balls flying. Then, with a tired little groan, she set about removing her headpiece and veil.

Her head, at least, felt lighter, once it was off. She laid it across an old easy chair in a corner.

Then she padded over to the ancient couch, held her train to the side and sank to a sitting position, stirring up enough dust to burn her eyes and make her cough. When the coughing fit passed, she leaned her head back on the couch and closed her eyes.

In the moments of stillness that followed, Heather remembered the baby. She put her hands on her stomach, her head still rested back and her eyes still closed.

No problem there, she thought, smiling to herself in spite of the awfulness of her situation. She felt a little queasy, as usual. But the baby, she knew in her heart, was just fine. It was a strong baby, she knew that, too. She would not lose it as she had the other one.

Heather sighed. She had no idea what she was going to do next. So she kept her eyes closed and just drifted for a while, trying not to think, trying only to make her mind a blank.

And then she heard something. A rustling so slight it was barely a sound. She lifted her head.

Lucas was there, standing in the shadows of the tiny hall between the kitchen and the front door. Dust, disturbed by his entry, swirled around him.

Heather felt no surprise to see him. There was only the yearning that she always felt now. She longed to reach out her tired arms to him.

But what good would it do? He truly was the Shadowmaster in more than just name. It was the way he lived. He kept his heart hidden.

Slowly, not speaking, he emerged from the hall. He came to stand looking down at her. His fine tux and silk shirt were every bit as wrinkled and ripped as her wedding gown, though he seemed to have managed to stay on his feet—at least, he wasn't smeared with red dirt as she was.

Heather stared up the lean length of him and had to swallow before she could speak. "You followed me."

One of those faraway smiles curved his mouth. "Did you think I wouldn't?"

She fiddled with her satin skirt. "I don't know what I thought. I guess I . . . *didn't* think."

He gave a sigh that sounded as weary as she felt. Then he moved down the couch a little, far enough to get past the ruined splendor of her train, and sat. He leaned back, then forward. Then he raked his hair with both hands. Finally he was still, his elbows on his spread knees, staring down at the buckled floor between his scuffed Italian shoes.

Heather gathered her courage and tried to explain. "I just...couldn't go through with it. You're just..."

Lucas turned to look at her and she thought she saw anger in his eyes. "What? I'm just what?"

"You won't...open up to me. You keep yourself *apart* from me. You won't even really talk to me. You're just not—"

He rose then, so swiftly that she gasped. He stood over her again and his eyes were as hard as black stones. "I know. I get it. You don't have to say one more damn word. I'm not Jason Lee. I know it. And I never will be."

She gaped at him. "But I...I don't want you to be Jason Lee."

He let out a disbelieving snort and whirled away from her.

She staggered upright, took a step, then faltered, wanting to approach him, but afraid to. "Lucas, please. I—"

He spun back, pointed a finger at her. "Do you want me to talk to you? Now that it's all over, do you want it all out in the open? Do you want to know all my...secrets? Is that what you want?"

Heather stepped back, but came up against the couch. She almost collapsed into it, but managed to steady herself. "Yes. Yes, I do."

"All right, then. I'll tell you. I'll tell you everything."

Now she did sit, barely managing to reach behind her and scoop her train to the side. She watched him, waiting, hardly daring to move a muscle lest he back out on her now.

But he didn't back out.

"I loved my little brother," Lucas said. "But I hated him, too." He rubbed his eyes with the pads of his fingers.

She couldn't help prompting, "But why?"

He dropped his hands and regarded her bleakly. "Life was so damn easy for him. Without half trying, Jason Lee had everything. He never left his hometown and he spent his working life on a county road crew. But he had a father and a mother who loved him, a place where he belonged—and you."

She didn't understand. "What do you mean?"

He looked away, as if what he had to tell her was too hard to say while staring into her eyes. "I mean, I know what you are. The kind of woman you are. I knew it the day you married my brother. It was like there was a light all around you. And when you smiled at him... Damn. I knew that even though I lived the life that the whole world envied, Jason Lee was the guy who had everything. And deep inside myself, I hated him for it."

Heather's chest felt tight. She had to draw in a long, slow breath before she could speak. "But, Lucas, you're saying you—"

"I fell in love with you. On the day you married my brother. And sometimes, over the past few years, I used to imagine what it might be like, if you were mine. And then, after Jason Lee died, more than once I fantasized about coming back to town for a visit, maybe dropping in on you and seeing how you were doing.

"In fact, I was thinking about dropping in on you when I told Mark we could come here in June. And then those extra stops on my book tour came up. And I didn't want to let Mark come alone, because then, if I got up the nerve to come later, he'd already have worn out his welcome."

"Oh, Lucas. Mark could never wear out his welcome with me."

He shook his head. "Whatever. The point is, I told him we weren't coming. And he ran away to get here. And then, when he ran away again, it's pretty obvious what I did."

"Is it?"

"Hell, yes. I used my son's disappearance to get a chance with you. It was a low-down, cheap trick. I know it. But I went with it. All the way."

Heather had to argue. "Oh, Lucas, you will never convince me that your suffering while Mark was gone was only an act."

"I didn't say that. I said I *used* the situation, that's all."

"No. You were as... confused by the attraction between us as I was. And really, that first night we spent together was mostly my idea."

He looked at her patiently. "Heather, one of the most effective ways to seduce a woman is to let her believe that it's her idea. I spent two nights working on you, telling you my long, sad story, letting you know I was interested. And then, on the night it happened, I was careful to put up a little resistance, to let you do the convincing. I knew exactly what I was doing."

"But then, the next day, you left. You went back to Monterey."

"Come on. I told you I'd stay if you gave me a reason. But you didn't want me to stay. You were thinking of Jason Lee. I could see it in your eyes."

Heather thought back and knew he was right.

"And anyway." Lucas went on. "I was only cutting my losses. It wasn't the end for me. Even if your father and grandfather hadn't brought you to my door and dropped you in my lap, I'd have been back around eventually to try again."

"You would?"

"Beyond a shadow of a doubt."

"Oh, Lucas." To Heather, a soft glow seemed to have suffused the dim, dusty room. She got to her feet, went to him and slipped her hand in his.

He closed his eyes, as if her touch caused him pain. "Heather..." Her name was a plea.

She mustered all her courage and asked one more time, "Do you think it might be possible that we could build a house here, live here instead of Monterey? North Magdalene is my home, Lucas. I know you have bad memories of your years here, and that the town gossips drive you crazy, but maybe, if you gave it another chance..."

"No." He pulled free of her grip.

Heather sighed. "All right. I understand."

"No. I don't think you do. I'd be willing to give this town another try, if that was really what you wanted. I can write my books anywhere. And Mark thinks this damn place is Heaven on Earth. I could live with moving back here. But having Jason Lee's memory between us—I *can't* live with that. Knowing that you'll always love him is going to drive me nuts eventually. I think I've seen it from the first, but I just didn't want to admit it."

"But, Lucas—"

He lifted a hand to silence her protests. "Look. I saw you, the other day, crying over that photograph of him. And I realized then, I think, that I wasn't going to be willing to settle for less than all of you. You were right to run away today. It just plain isn't going to work."

Heather smiled, a tender, knowing smile. "I can see what you mean, really. And it's true. I will always love Jason Lee."

Lucas made a low, pained sound. "That about says it all." He started to turn away.

Heather grabbed his arm again and turned him back to her. "I'm not finished."

"Damn it, Heather."

"Listen. I've been trying to tell you something since yesterday and you wouldn't let me. If you'd only listened, you could have saved us both a lot of misery."

He said nothing, only looked at her, waiting for her to get it over with.

She began, "As I said, I'll always love Jason Lee. I'll remember him with...great affection. He was a good man. But he's gone, Lucas. And sometimes now I can't see his face in my mind. His face is...blotted out by another face. By *your* face."

Beneath her palm, Lucas's arm went rigid. "What are you saying?"

"That I'm in love with *you*."

"Excuse me?"

"I thought I said it clearly. I'm—"

Before she could say it again, Lucas grabbed her, shoved his hands in her hair and brought her face up close to his own. "Don't say things like that. Ever. Don't say them unless you mean them."

"Oh, I mean them. I mean them with all my heart. Lucas, I...admire you."

He grunted in disbelief.

"Don't do that," she said. "Don't make light of that. I mean it. I admire you. So much. You're a wonderful man. Some men are born in goodness. And some never have a chance. That's you, Lucas. You never had a chance. But still, somehow, you fought your way to a good life, so that Mark could have the start you never did. You're the most courageous man I've ever known.

"And you did *not* take advantage of me that first night we made love. I was a full-grown woman, every bit as responsible for what happened as you were. That night was what we *both* wanted. I never blamed you for it. When you left, I missed you terribly. I tried to get over you. But I never did. The world was a gray, empty place until my dad made me track you down in Monterey. And it took me a while, it's true, to understand what I feel for you. But now I do understand. I love you. With all my heart.''

Lucas stared down at her. ''Would you say that once more?''

Her smile lit up the shadows. ''Yes, I will. If you'll only stand beside me, let me into your heart.''

''I will stand beside you,'' he vowed fervently. ''I swear it. And my heart, such as it is, is yours.''

''Then I'll say it forever. I'll say it all our lives.''

''Say it right now.''

''I love you, Lucas Drury.''

''Say it again.''

She did, slow and sweetly. Lucas pressed her close, sipped the words from her lips and gave them back in kind.

A little while later, they walked down the rickety front steps of Oggie's ramshackle house. Hand in hand, they hobbled through the center of town, Heather leaning heavily on Lucas because of her tender feet.

It was nearly five when they arrived back at Heather's aunt Regina's once more. They went directly to the backyard. Though several of the guests had departed, all the family members were still there. And so was Reverend Johnson. Oggie had refused to allow the man to leave.

At the sight of Heather and Lucas, Mark cried out and ran to them, throwing his arms around them both.

''You guys look terrible.''

''We know,'' they said in unison.

''But you look ... happy.''

''We are,'' they said, again with one voice.

''Is everything okay now?'' the boy asked.

Heather and Lucas gazed at each other, then down at Mark. They nodded.

"Er, then if you've worked out your... difficulties, do you think we could get started now?" inquired the reverend.

Aunt Regina took her seat at the piano again. The wedding march began.

Dressed in her grandmother's torn and ragged wedding gown, Sunshine once more walked up the makeshift aisle toward the Shadowmaster, who stood waiting for her in his tattered tux. This time, when she reached his side, she put her hand in his and smiled up into his eyes.

And Lucas Drury learned at last what it meant to be the guy who had everything.

* * * * *

It's our 1000th Special Edition and we're celebrating!

Join us these coming months for some wonderful stories in a special celebration of our 1000th book with some of your favorite authors!

Diana Palmer   **Nora Roberts**
Debbie Macomber   **Christine Flynn**
Phyllis Halldorson   **Lisa Jackson**
                mini-series by:

Lindsay McKenna, Marie Ferrarella, Sherryl Woods, Gina Ferris Wilkins.

And many more books by special writers.

And as a special bonus, all Silhouette Special Edition titles published during Celebration 1000! Will have **<u>double</u>** Pages & Privileges proofs of purchase!

Silhouette Special Edition...heartwarming stories packed with emotion, just for you! You'll fall in love with our next 1000 special stories!

Silhouette

SPECIAL EDITION ™®

Congratulations!

In September, enjoy a special tribute to life's
happiest moments, featuring some of your
favorite authors!

KISSES AND KIDS by Andrea Edwards (SE #981)
Pat Stuart's company wanted to reward him for a job
well done. But the surprise present they gave him
would lead to lasting love!

JOYRIDE by Patricia Coughlin (SE #982)
Catrina "Cat" Bandini had just graduated from college
and was off on the road trip of lifetime. But she was
about to get some *very* unexpected company!

A DATE WITH DR. FRANKENSTEIN
by Leanne Banks (SE #983)
Andie Reynolds was getting a new neighbor next
door. Eli Masters was handsome, smart—and, yes,
single. Would he be her dream date, or...

Be the first to congratulate the happy couples when
love comes calling in September—only from
Silhouette Special Edition.

**Congratulations! Because life can be a
celebration, and love is its ultimate prize.**

OFFICIAL RULES
FLYAWAY VACATION SWEEPSTAKES 3449
NO PURCHASE OR OBLIGATION NECESSARY

Three Harlequin Reader Service 1995 shipments will contain respectively, coupons for entry into three different prize drawings, one for a trip for two to San Francisco, another for a trip for two to Las Vegas and the third for a trip for two to Orlando, Florida. To enter any drawing using an Entry Coupon, simply complete and mail according to directions.

There is no obligation to continue using the Reader Service to enter and be eligible for any prize drawing. You may also enter any drawing by hand printing the words "Flyaway Vacation," your name and address on a 3"x5" card and the destination of the prize you wish that entry to be considered for (i.e., San Francisco trip, Las Vegas trip or Orlando trip). Send your 3"x5" entries via first-class mail (limit: one entry per envelope) to: Flyaway Vacation Sweepstakes 3449, c/o Prize Destination you wish that entry to be considered for, P.O. Box 1315, Buffalo, NY 14269-1315, USA or P.O. Box 610, Fort Erie, Ontario L2A 5X3, Canada.

To be eligible for the San Francisco trip, entries must be received by 5/30/95; for the Las Vegas trip, 7/30/95; and for the Orlando trip, 9/30/95.

Winners will be determined in random drawings conducted under the supervision of D.L. Blair, Inc., an independent judging organization whose decisions are final, from among all eligible entries received for that drawing. San Francisco trip prize includes round-trip airfare for two, 4-day/3-night weekend accommodations at a first-class hotel, and $500 in cash (trip must be taken between 7/30/95—7/30/96, approximate prize value—$3,500); Las Vegas trip includes round-trip airfare for two, 4-day/3-night weekend accommodations at a first-class hotel, and $500 in cash (trip must be taken between 9/30/95—9/30/96, approximate prize value—$3,500); Orlando trip includes round-trip airfare for two, 4-day/3-night weekend accommodations at a first-class hotel, and $500 in cash (trip must be taken between 11/30/95—11/30/96, approximate prize value—$3,500). All travelers must sign and return a Release of Liability prior to travel. Hotel accommodations and flights are subject to accommodation and schedule availability. Sweepstakes open to residents of the U.S. (except Puerto Rico) and Canada, 18 years of age or older. Employees and immediate family members of Harlequin Enterprises, Ltd., D.L. Blair, Inc., their affiliates, subsidiaries and all other agencies, entities and persons connected with the use, marketing or conduct of this sweepstakes are not eligible. Odds of winning a prize are dependent upon the number of eligible entries received for that drawing. Prize drawing and winner notification for each drawing will occur no later than 15 days after deadline for entry eligibility for that drawing. Limit: one prize to an individual, family or organization. All applicable laws and regulations apply. Sweepstakes offer void wherever prohibited by law. Any litigation within the province of Quebec respecting the conduct and awarding of the prizes in this sweepstakes must be submitted to the Regies des loteries et Courses du Quebec. In order to win a prize, residents of Canada will be required to correctly answer a time-limited arithmetical skill-testing question. Value of prizes are in U.S. currency.

Winners will be obligated to sign and return an Affidavit of Eligibility within 30 days of notification. In the event of noncompliance within this time period, prize may not be awarded. If any prize or prize notification is returned as undeliverable, that prize will not be awarded. By acceptance of a prize, winner consents to use of his/her name, photograph or other likeness for purposes of advertising, trade and promotion on behalf of Harlequin Enterprises, Ltd., without further compensation, unless prohibited by law.

For the names of prizewinners (available after 12/31/95), send a self-addressed, stamped envelope to: Flyaway Vacation Sweepstakes 3449 Winners, P.O. Box 4200, Blair, NE 68009.

RVC KAL